SNUGGLY TALES OF THE AFTERLIFE

Brian Stableford's scholarly work includes *New Atlantis: A Narrative History of Scientific Romance* (Wildside Press, 2016), *The Plurality of Imaginary Worlds: The Evolution of French roman scientifique* (Black Coat Press, 2017) and *Tales of Enchantment and Disenchantment: A History of Faerie* (Black Coat Press, 2019). He has translated more than three hundred volumes from the French, mostly in the genres of *roman scientifique, contes de fées* and Romantic and Symbolist fiction. His recent fiction includes the visionary science fiction novel *The Revelations of Time and Space* (2020) and its sequel *After the Revelation* (2021); the last in his long series of "Tales of the Genetic Revolution," *The Elusive Shadows* (2020); and the comedy fantasy *Meat on the Bone* (2021), all published by Snuggly Books.

I0591226

SNUGGLY BOOKS

SNUGGLY TALES
OF
THE AFTERLIFE

EDITED, TRANSLATED,
AND WITH AN INTRODUCTION BY
BRIAN STABLEFORD

THIS IS A SNUGGLY BOOK

ISBN: 978-1-64525-114-9

CONTENTS

INTRODUCTION

IMAGES of a hypothetical afterlife experienced by the human psyche following the death of the body are among the purest products of the human imagination: a blank canvas on which creativity can be exercised—in theory, at least—with complete freedom. The notion that such a state of being might, or must, exist is a reflection of the reluctance of consciousness to believe in its own ultimate extinction. That reluctance is undeterred by the experience of temporary cessations, partly because the most commonplace of those cessations, sleep, is routinely associated with dreaming, in which the psyche is not annihilated but merely displaced or transmogrified into an arena of experience that is vulnerable to bizarrerie, where the limits of seemingly-material possibility are flexible. The idea that the death of the body might deliver the psyche into a kind of permanent dream-state is a natural leap of the imagination, difficult for rationality to overcome because of the human mind's equally natural tendency to optimism: the fundamental disease of reason, for which it can be dangerous to seek a cure.

The most pernicious form of the disease of optimism is, of course, faith: the tendency to seize beliefs devoid of any rational basis, and to cling to them all the more fervently and insistently precisely because they have no such basis: "Faith is believing something you know damn well ain't so," as the great American philosopher Mark Twain is reputed to have put it, although it is usually quoted without the damnation, editors of his era being inclined to hypersensitive censorship. Religious faith—the most tyrannical kind—frequently deals extravagantly in images of the afterlife, which provide the heavy artillery of moral terrorism. Christianity, the great Behemoth of Hypocrisy, allotted its savior the primary rescue mission poetically known as the Harrowing of Hell, although the Church has always been far more intent on menace than cultivation, following the customary logic and practice of protection rackets.

It might seem slightly paradoxical that the most evident production of an imaginative faculty whose essential motive force is optimism would be the imagery of eternal punishment, even as one part of a couple whose imagistically-starved antithetical counterpart is paradisal bliss. It must be recognized, however, that optimism is itself merely a counterpart, a product of fear. Fundamentally, hope is not so much a valiant expectation—against the odds—of a fortunate result, but a craven desperation in the attempt to avoid uncomfortable confrontation with the certainty of ultimate doom: *angst*, as Martin Heidegger's succinct version of existentialism puts it. Weak-kneed and faint-hearted optimists sometimes make the effort to imagine Hell as simply being not-Heaven, but the vast majority of sturdy soldiers of belief, whose onward-surging optimism is fully-armed with ferocity, are more than content to imagine Heaven as simply being not-Hell. The principal effort of creative endeavor has always been to picture and symbolize the objects of fear to be avoided or escaped, not the peace and tranquility that might be theoretically conceivable if the against-the-odds escape were to be effected. The essence of fiction, and the whole of its elaboration, is menace; the remainder is usually handled, to the satisfaction of most readers, by some version of the curt and blatantly mendacious formula "they lived happily ever after."

In post-Renaissance Western literature the imagery of the afterlife has been crucially informed, if not actually formed, by the great exemplar of Dante Alighieri, the author of the *Commedia*, commonly called the *Divina Commedia* because one of the book's reviewers, Giovanni Boccaccio, gave it that compliment, which seemed so apposite that other admirers integrated it into the title. The fame of the work, and its esthetic appeal, rests almost entirely on the *Inferno*, the imagery of its Hell; the *Purgatorio* and the *Paradiso* are generally regarded as mere appendages—as, of course, they are. Afterlife fantasies constructed after the laying of that foundation-stone retained their perfect freedom to imagine anything they liked, but they could not do so without the *Commedia*—or, more particularly, the *Inferno*—being in view on their imaginative horizon, as a specter or a shadow if not as a substance, an awareness of absence when devoid of manifest presence.

Dante did not invent the Hell of eternal punishment by torture, and he took care to acknowledge his most important literary predecessor by giving Virgil to his narrative *persona* as a guide to the Inferno, but Dantean imagery became the most highly-polished magnifying lens through which that Hell could be glimpsed. Every modern writer setting out to pen an afterlife fantasy, even in the nineteenth and twentieth centuries, had to start out with the luggage of being post-Dantean—a valise of variable weight, but always ponderable, irrespective of any decision made as to whether and how to whittle down the alpenstock of expressed faith.

It goes without saying, of course, that some such whittling had to be done, even by the devout; faith is reputed to move metaphorical mountains, and thus has little difficulty moving metaphorical pens, but it cannot sharpen them for the task without being bent or blunted itself. Indeed, the whole point of setting forth to pen an afterlife fantasy is to subject the generative ideas to stress and transfiguration; the subgenre is inherently experimental, even at its most trivial, but the counterweights in the balance of judgment always contain the Dantean Inferno, whatever other imagery can be recruited or discarded. Modern literary images of the afterlife need not be Heavens, Hells or Purgatories, and many deliberately shun such Gothic imagery, but even if they are not Dantean they cannot help being not-Dantean in the context of the reader's consciousness, and hence being partly defined by that absence.

The contents of the present anthology are all products of Romanticism, in a broad sense, if only because the literary criticism of the era in which they were produced—from the early nineteenth century to the mid-twentieth—had not yet fallen prey to the eccentricity of inventing a notion of "post-Romanticism," although it did embrace the notion of a Decadent Romanticism, which evolved in France from Symbolism to Surrealism. The Romantic Movement, in France as elsewhere, initially wanted to recover and refresh the imaginative elements of Medieval Romance, refusing to regard them as psychologically and esthetically obsolete, but that process of renewal was transformative, not repetitive; it was a process of modernization, sophistication and extrapolation. Because the innovative inevitably becomes passé with the passage of time, it was inevitable that the new Romanticism would eventually become Decadent, and then Surreal, but its soul retained an essential continuity, perhaps even a certain immortality; and where could that quasi-immortality be more clearly reflected than in images of afterlives, or, at least, of not-exactly-deaths?

All of the fantasies in the present sampler attempt originality, wanting to be different from their predecessors and their contemporaries; is a sense, their whole *raison-d'être* lies in being not-Dantean, envisaging the question of what life after death might involve from a new angle, or through a new imaginative lens. Some attempt to forge a metaphysical rationale for their inventions, respectful to some degree of recent advances in natural philosophy, others are content simply to accept that no such rationale is conceivable, and that an afterlife can only be one more dream, experienced while still alive, or perhaps existentially condensed into the very moment of death—a common positivist literary motif, represented herein in more than one variant. In either case, however, the substance of the fantasy retains the same moral imperatives. The purpose of an afterlife cannot, by definition, be anything but a reappraisal of life and a reassessment of its significance, or lack of it.

In these stories, necessarily, death is not an end but a transition, not merely an existential transformation but, *ipso facto*, a shift in moral viewpoint. Seen from a hypothetical afterlife, life is bound to appear different, to lend itself to a different evaluation. In attempting to be original, therefore, the stories are inherently exploratory, essentially experimental. Some of the examples even take the trouble to list alternatives to their own vision, to place themselves deliberately within a spectrum of conceivable afterlives, classifiable into types. In the era in which they were produced, they could not help being aware not only of the Christian/Dantean schema of Heaven, Hell and Purgatory, but also of metempsychotic schemas of perpetual reincarnation, the fashionability of which was greatly enhanced in the nineteenth century by comparative studies of religion and the gradual evolution of travelers' tales into a more disciplined ethnography.

The spectrum of stories published in the era in question was widened dramatically by the literary spinoff of pseudomedical theories of Animal Magnetism, which took off in the 1780s, eventually to be absorbed into a wholesale manufacture of exotic metaphysics, sometimes labeled the "Occult Revival." Ideas of life after death played a key role in that revival, not only because of the interest promoted by neo-occultists in ideas of reincarnation derived from

Eastern religions, but because of the great popularity after 1840 of the religious movement of Spiritualism, including the quasi-scientific investigations of the phenomena produced in Spiritualist séances that gave birth to Psychical Research societies. In the same way that Dante was integrated into the conceptual back-cloth of all imaginative ventures into afterlife fantasy, so the notions of reincarnation and Spritualism were added into the conceptual weave, tacitly present even when not specifically addressed. The whole tapestry of the genre of afterlife fantasies thus became much richer as the Romanic Movement progressed, and even richer as the Movement decayed.

The present sampler, inevitably, can only offer examples of some of the many directions that the exploration in question took, only hinting at its vast complexity, but hopefully, it does offer a glimpse of the big picture and the many strands that composed it. The stories are not arranged chronologically, because they are usually distant in time from their most crucial reference points, even when they deliberately take aboard more recent developments in occult metaphysics and fashionable Spiritualism, and are thus partly detached from the moment of their composition. That is entirely appropriate to their subgenre, which attempts to wrestle imaginatively with the eternal as well as the transient—and quintessentially, to discover the eternal within the transient. There is a sense in which these stories are liberated from the precise dates of their composition, even when they reflect them clearly, and hence cannot entirely be "out of date."

These stories are not offered here as items of purely antiquarian interest, but as fragments of an ongoing collective exercise. They do not offer "answers" to questions that are, in fact, fundamentally unanswerable, but they do illustrate the fact—clearly, I hope—that just because a question is rationally unanswerable, it does not mean that there is no philosophical and psychological advantage to be gained by its contemplation. There is pleasure in that contemplation, but that pleasure is dependent on their ability to provide nourishing food for thought as well as piquant taste sensation. Some have less imaginative protein in their mix than others, but imaginative fats and carbohydrates ought not to be despised in nutritional terms, forming essential components of any nutritional diet. Afterlife fantasies, composed with intelligence and esthetic verve—all the examples assembled here have both—are life-enhancing, even, and perhaps especially, when they are infernal rather than paradisal. After all, as the French put it, *c'est la vie*.

—Brian Stableford

SNUGGLY TALES
OF
THE AFTERLIFE

IMMORTALITY

by Edmond Haraucourt

I was a little frightened to discover that my last hour was about to sound and that it was necessary to die.

I had got the most out of life, known the joys and the suffering that it permits a frail organism with our body and our soul. I had possessed everything that one can possess down here, since my imagination, making up for the insufficiencies of fortune, had given me by turns, internally, the intimate enjoyment that the real world had refused me. On my whim, I had been powerful, rich and beloved. What emperor ever imposed a more sovereign autocracy than the one it pleased me to invoke in miraculous realms? What king or sultan handled more gold or precious stones in caster coffers, or built a more sumptuous palace in which to dwell? What Don Juan embraced lovers more superb in the midst of more terrible or sweeter dramas? I had only had to close my eyes to see everything—which is to say, to merit everything and hold everything. The universe had been submissive to my desire, and, unlike those who possess material things, I had not wearied of anything, because I created them at the caprice of my changing needs, and in each one I had cherished my work—which is to say, myself; an affection that is never deceived.

I said to myself: "There are only two things in life that are worth living for: the love of art and the art of love." I had divided my human duration between the two. I had been wise enough to be a fool; I could die.

What a treasure I was about to forsake, though, in the consciousness of my thinking being! At a stroke, I was about to lose everything: not only that which exists, but all that can be conceived; no longer the essence of a human being, but that of the gods!

At least, like Horace, I thought that I was not dying entirely.

Frankly, I had reaped little glory thus far. I had just passed through half a century without raising much veritable enthusiasm, and I could not help finding that quite legitimate—certainly not by virtue of any doubt as to my vast merit, but by reason of the fact that curious minds are the last to solicit the curiosity of the crowd: the crowd that all prodigies attract except those of thought, which runs after a fossil tree, a guillotine, an acrobat or a beast, which understands them, but which finds intellect boring.

But I anticipated future justice; across the future, I saw my soul perpetuated in the memory of fraternal souls; I heard, with a hint of jealousy and rancor, some amorous beauty reading one of my amorous sonnets, and lending my words to the lips of someone absent.

"So what? What can it mean to you that, in twenty years, a woman who might give herself to you can only contemplate your bust in the foyer of a theater? She would be the first to be frightened and disgusted if you came back from your immortality to ask you for a caress . . .

"Imminent cadaver, what good is glory, if love is not its end? An end avowed or unavowed, conscious or unconscious, love is the terminus of everything, the only valid hope, and what love does not recompense is not recompensed. You have mocked Woman, but for her alone you have amassed labor in dreams, for her smile, for her kiss, and what you pretend to pursue in the beyond is merely a lie of your vanity. All glory is a decoy, if it is not proven, when night sleeps over the city, by a mouth with beautiful white teeth . . ."

These reflections had too much truth in them to soothe my death-throes, and I turned my head toward those who were weeping around my bed. Their faces gave evidence of a profound affection and a sincere grief; I was both satisfied and chagrined. The desolation of those good people pained me on their behalf and pleased me on my own. I experienced a mixture of pity and pride at seeing so much regret on my behalf, and the pity was soothing, since I rendered it in proportion to the regret devoted to my person.

My beloved was sobbing, her forehead supported on the bed, and she occasionally raised her tearful eyes toward me. She had a rare beauty thus, so beautiful and so young that I was anxious for her; I understood that she would either die of despair within a matter of months, or, too deprived of love, would replace me at the end of a year; egoism and affection struggled within me, and I did not dare to wish for either one of those misfortunes.

"Darling," I said to her, "when I am no longer here, will you love someone else?"

She straightened up, her arms extended, sublime in fear, prayer and faith, and I was severely punished for my foolish and cruel words, for she fainted; people carried her out and I died without seeing her again.

Softly, without effort and without pain, I expired, so gently that it was impossible for me to discern the precise moment when life was, and then was not; I even believe that the moment in question does not exist, for I persevered in waiting for an end when the end, it seems, had come.

Someone murmured: "The heart's no longer beating." I sensed that it was true, but I still sensed it; I retained a confused perception of the fuss that was going on around me, and almost of the causes of the sounds—and when someone approached me to close my eyelids, I had an infinitely subtle notion of the touch of a finger, which trembled over my eyes.

Increasingly, however, I was detached from any interest in things and of life, and the ephemeral, incomplete sensations did not awaken within me any need for analysis or comprehension. After my death, I lived a special life, diminishing by degrees, which would have appeared incomplete to an animal, but was a life nevertheless: that of plants that have been cut and are etiolating in vases. That vegetal persistence was succeeded by another, even less, and doubtless created by the chemical work of various elements united in my remains, which were gradually being transformed and disaggregating.

Thus, I was declining toward a more imperfect state from one minute to the next—which, by a series of ungraspable transitions, a slow progress through organic metamorphoses, was going to take me lower still—and during that play of bases and salts, acids and metals, during that alembic warmth, parts of me fled toward other bodies, disseminated to infinity, and I forgot them; while new beings appropriated them, in order to enjoy, with the debris of my self, something they called their self. Thus came, in the gradual cooling, the slumber of inert minerality.

These logical evolutions, and the minimal apperception that remained within them, permeated my defunct being, bearing nothing within them that could offend our conventions regarding the laws of eternal matter. But alongside that, outside of that, a phenomenon was produced so strange that I cannot succeed in convincing myself of it, even though it has lasted for several thousand years, and I would not dare to relate it here were it not for the hope I have of bringing to human lips the scornful smile with which they welcome every mystery or simple dream: the smile that brings joy to the greater number, and does honor to its victims.

Scarcely was I dead than I perceived that my soul was immortal, no longer in the diffuse fashion of my body, which was beginning to crumble, but immortal in all its force, with a clear and total possession of its essence.

I had difficulty comprehending it at first, so much did the revelation astound my reason, which had always affirmed the impossibility of a result without labor and an effect without cause. I was humiliated by my long error, and all the more vexed that my dialectic continued to rebel against the admission of such a hypothesis, refusing the possibility even in confrontation with the manifest fact.

In that state of mind I found myself on the threshold of a vast domain enclosed by railings and planted with magnificent trees. The gate opened before me and an old man dressed in the antique fashion came toward me with a hospitable gravity, asking to know my name. I had no difficulty replying, for we are always proud to hear our own name pronounced, as if an entire synthesis of genius and glory were magically contained in those few syllables.

"A poet, no doubt? Only poets name themselves with that simple pomposity. Please wait here."

He drew away, and came back almost immediately with a rectangular package that he was generous enough to offer to me.

"Here's your Paradise," he said, "and your Inferno. If you'd care to follow me now . . ."

My immortal soul took the bundle that was held out to it, and started walking alongside its host. I framed a thousand questions internally, of course, regarding the nature of that enigmatic gift, but I dared not ask a single one, for fear of seeming too ill-informed. The old man, doubtless accustomed to that noble attitude, smiled beneath his white beard, and, either out of compassion for my humanity or simply because he wanted to exchange a few words, asked whether I didn't want to know what my burden contained.

"It's the shade of your books," he added.

I scarcely understood any better, but I tried not to let anything show.

"They'll be useful to you in the region that awaits you, in the Garden of Letters, where those who mirror their soul in words reside. There you'll find your predecessors, those you love, and others, just as great, permanently unknown in your homeland, whom you'll revere for their misunderstood majesty. There you'll live together, in the communal exile that you have been able to merit, far from people . . ."

At these words, I felt a profound joy, and I appreciated all the serenity of a happiness forbidden in the world of nations. Is not exile the true fatherland? O Paradise, more-than-promised land, since nothing promised it in slavery! I was about to penetrate into a world that passers-by do not enter, where one speaks to one's peers, where impotence is no longer there to judge as a sovereign mistress, where one is delivered from the antagonist who makes us respect our failures, and the complimenter who makes us blush over our merits!

"I beg your pardon, amiable old man—one more word: are there at least women there?"

"A rich windfall, in a wood where they only retain their intelligence!"

"Then, truly, we shall be alone . . ."

"As in the course of life! For you're not unaware that the perpetual labor of thought is the calmest of egotisms, and that the furtive memory of emotions is engulfed therein. What use are they, profound as they are, if not to re-enter into the dream, to descend within yourself? Alone—and that will be, I tell you, your reward and your punishment; only the rare monsters who, falling in love with infinite problems, and seeking, and digging, knead errors mingled with truths; those who deign to think . . ."

"Do human beings exist who have never thought?"

"They're small in number; but less numerous still are those who link a few judgments and erect an entity. The members of the near-universal crowd, having only attained embryos of purely contingent whims, only survive death in a fashion as incomplete and as sterile as their life. Puny in ideas, they wear an appearance of soul that now procures them an appearance of prolongation, floating in limbo, as the Christians put it, among the souls of infants and beasts."

"Which is infinitely flattering for the dreamer, and which avenges them."

"Oh, they don't all get in here."

"I thought as much," I replied.

"I know. Artists are scornful of those who do not have it, and prefer those who have."

I noticed once again that the old man professed, with regard to the human species and our failings, a disdain that was slightly shocking to a son of woman; so, by virtue of a need to rebel, which is sometimes dearer to us than our ideas, I felt honor-bound to come to the defense of suspect artists of whom I had been ashamed on earth.

"They don't all get in here, you say? And how do you separate the bad from the good? Have you an esthetic tribunal, and has that tribunal the right to judge? Nature might be eternal, but not Beauty; it's the appropriation of nature to the temperament of an individual, or a race, or an epoch. Can you quote an absolute formula, then, for eternal Beauty? Great artists have devoted their lives to its embrace, but you can't name two who agreed on its definition; sages have pursued the True, and all by different paths, and we have venerated them all as sages; religions have discovered the Good, heroes have professed it to the point of martyrdom, and we have built temples, sanctified prophets, while contrary religions have, in turn, charged one another with anathemas and one cult's apostles have damned another's saints!"

"You deny the absolute! Know it, therefore, now that it is too late to repeat it to your brethren! There exists between the laws of the body and those of the soul a correlation of which humans have no suspicion, but which science will perhaps one day reveal to you. The domain of thought and that of matter arise from one unique principle, and all things are directed according to one unique method. The same harmony presides over everything, regulates everything, orders wills as well as stars and planets, and one primal law dwells in the abstract of which all the others, physical and moral, are only corollaries."

"God?"

"As you please. One of the corollaries is the law of Beauty. But what does it matter? Your human merit lies not in knowing the divine thing, but in seeking it, wanting it, cherishing it and giving its love the blood of your flesh and the effort of your soul. Your grandeur is in the worship and the will. That alone, my friend, is judged at the esthetic tribunal that you were pleased to imagine just now—which we do not have, but which resides in the sincerity of your own consciences."

"Our consciences?"

"Yes—as with animals, there are warm-blooded artists and cold-blooded artists. As with animals, the former have their personal temperature, the latter participate in the ambient temperature. The former are souls, the latter reflections; the former create, the latter assimilate. Some, at the price of a sacrificed fortune or happiness, pursue the adorable ideal, and, more often than not, repudiated by the skeptical or hateful indifference of their contemporaries, they dream, their eyes upraised to the heavens, without seeing anything around them, and seeing nothing even in the heavens at which they gaze but their own soul. The others are unconcerned with their Beauty or their Truth, but with the affirmation that it is necessary to present to people in order to please them or shock them—which comes to the same thing, since the end they are pursuing is public attention. They sacrifice their self—doubtless worthless since it cannot triumph—to the crowd, and in that bastard compromise their renown and wealth is erected. They do not produce, they produce themselves; they are full, not of talent but of their own talent; their sufficiency is made of their own insufficiency, as furtive and temporary as the moment and fashion; they are born to die, and before art they live as if they had not been born; but they are the great men on earth, while the valorous are the great men in heaven.

"So it's those praised by the vulgar to whom you close your door?"

"They have no wish to open it; having been their own judges; if they were conscious, they have opted for success rather than pure art; if unconscious, their name is impotence, and what right would they have?"

Fearing that the eloquent old man was no longer building abstruse theories, I permitted myself to interrupt, and was about to take a look at the beauty of the location when he told me that our journey was at an end.

I consoled myself effortlessly, thinking about future friends, beautiful conversations with the demigods, giants of poetry and great thinkers before whom I would be proud to humble myself, and to whom I would express my admiration in emotional terms, and who might perhaps render me some sympathy in exchange . . .

"*Adieu*," the old man said to me, "and *bon ennui!*"

✻

When he indicated the remainder of the route to me with an extended arm, I continued on my way.

There were, in turn, paths through woods, amid thick vegetation and unfamiliar flowers; walkways of opaline sand that sparkled in the light, like crushed pearls; abrupt clearings inviting dreamy repose; and shady nooks on the banks of streams, above which hung long hammocks that one might have imagined to be woven out of blonde tresses. Sometimes, a melodious aroma passed on the breeze, like the tune of a song, and sometimes unexpected music emerged from magical tree-trunks or rained down from high branches.

Above the foliage, a changing sky was radiant, and toward the distant horizons, a line of mysterious mountains slept, rose and violet.

But no one was living there; I walked for a long time.

Suddenly, I perceived, crouched at the foot of a tree, a man dressed in animal-hides, who was protecting with his hand, like a miser guarding his treasure, a large heap of gray objects resembling bones. He ran toward me brandishing a kind of club; he shouted incomprehensible syllables at me, and the same sounds were repeated perpetually in his mouth. When he reached me he put the object I had taken for a weapon in front of my face: a ewe's shoulder-blade on which symbols were engraved. Alternately, he tapped the bone and his chest with his finger, looking at me anxiously, and the syllables that he was hurling at me like a madman, with a pleading voice, were still the same. Occasionally, he darted a suspicious glance toward the tree he had just quit, as if he feared that someone might steal his wealth.

The man was suffering profoundly from my silence, and I was sorry not to be able to reply to him; I shrugged my shoulders and shook my head in a gesture of helplessness, and that gesture was doubtless terrible to him, for he extended his arms despairingly and fled toward his tree.

Then others came, who also repeated unique syllables, in the same anxious and pleading tone; they surrounded me and crowded me, jostling one another in order to speak to me; some showed me hieroglyphic cylinders or planks covered in colored streaks, others held out coarse figurines of fallen deities; one held fire in his hand. Then, I was shown wax tablets or long scrolls of papyrus; and the crowd was still growing, with monotonous cries, and the further I advanced in order to escape them, the greater their number became, and everyone who perceived me immediately ran to meet me.

Finally, amid that dolorous clamor, I discerned the language of a Greek; taking him to one side, I understood that he was telling me his name, and asking me whether that name was glorious on earth . . .

Misery! Human misery, to that extent!

They were all calling out their names and asking me whether humankind had lost their work and their memory!

Before my ignorant gaze, they stood aside, some angrily, others full of resignation. Immediately, others came to take their places, and my pity wept for them.

I saw some who did not even deign to disturb themselves as I passed by, for after a hundred centuries, they had ended up despairing.

Finally, I found myself among those who shared our language: the most ancient, having gradually, by the accumulation of days, detached themselves from our hypocrisies, solicited a terrestrial memory without any pretense. The more recent greeted me with an exaggerated benevolence and questioned me as to the present state of letters, without interrogating me about themselves. I replied to them in friendly terms. More human than they had remained, I was a better liar and concealed my thoughts; could anyone blame me for having thought that I was fulfilling a duty in concealing the unjust scorn heaped on one of them, or the diminished grandeur of another, or having hesitated to torture those shades with the ignorance or stupidity of my contemporaries?

By dint of multiplying kind words, however, I ran out of formulae, and warm as my eulogies seemed to me, I soon observed that thy remained insufficient for those in favor of whom I was inventing so much glory. Those dead men were insatiable; they hungered for nothing else. Those who, when alive, had been best able to preserve the courage of the sincerity of their dream from the vain noise of renown, no longer thought of anything now but collecting posthumous fruits, as if they had formerly worked for nothing else, as if the renunciation of present favor had only been possible for them once by virtue of their faith in the favors to come.

I had been introduced to great men, whose conversation taught me nothing beyond their books and almost diminished their greatness for me. Through their acquaintance, I was able to convince myself more exactly of an aphorism that I had once tried to establish: the vastest minds only possess, in reality, one sole idea, which haunts and dominates them, constitutes their entire personality and is perpetually reproduced in various manifestations, which they mistake for different ideas. An event in which they are involved, a sensation that touches them, a sentiment that moves them, will excite in the depths of their soul that unique wellspring of thoughts and cause it to gush; every impulse of their heart, every pronouncement of their brain is a formulation of it, the analysis of which denounces its parentage; everything emanates from that idea and everything is brought back to it; it is a trunk with a thousand branches, which generates flowers or fruit thanks to the strong trunk that assembles and fuels them.

On observing this unity of origins in an intellectual organism, I recalled the doctrines of the old man concerning the unity of the primordial law regulating the universe; every moral being appeared to me as a little world constructed in the resemblance of the great. "And if the cosmic forces are called God," I said to myself, "is it not this judgment that the holy books signify in declaring that human beings are made in God's image."

That posthumous psychology occupied the early days of my sojourn, but egotism soon claimed its rights.

A few immortals, in order to talk to me about their books, deigned to direct the conversation initially toward mine, and I discreetly expressed the desire to know their opinion of me. I therefore undertook to play for them the role that they were playing for me, but I excused myself without constraint. They, I thought, were only preoccupied with the banal impressions of the public, while I was enquiring of a chosen elect, and my case seemed honorable by comparison with theirs. Thus, I allowed several of them to extract from me the promise to confide the only copy of my works to them, and the list of my promises immediately became so long that it was necessary for me to keep an exact account of them.

The attention of that society became more welcome thereafter, and I welcomed with genuine joy the visitors whose words brought me a judgment of myself alongside a question about them. As soon as it was returned the book passed into other hands, and deteriorated somewhat, but I heard with a broad smile the friendly apologies mingled with just eulogies; was a slight tear paying too much for the compliment of so august an ancestor? And I gave no further thought to the fact that the exemplar was the only one to which my immortality had the right.

People talked about me; the officious quoted the favorable remarks made about me, and I adapted myself so well to that pomp that I could no longer envisage without a certain anxiety the prospect of a new arrival who might steal my importance.

With that dread, however, was mingled the unacknowledged desire to know what eloquence had declared over my coffin. "Adieu, dear and noble friend . . ." Oh, the beautiful speeches I could have improvised on the edge of my grave!

One day, I learned that he was there . . . the latest dead man had just been born.

Run toward him, listen to him, interrogate him? What need would I have, anyway, to ask him questions? He must be full of me . . .

But all those old ghosts barred the way and gave evidence of a truly indecent avidity. I would at least inform them of the way that a shade worthy of the name behaves! I would teach them by my example not to hurl themselves voraciously at the heads of poor deceased individuals! I waited, without moving, with an apparent impassivity—with which they were all familiar, by virtue of once having simulated it themselves.

He appeared. He was nothing but a black bard, a miserable Griot[1] whom his people and his king, ac-

---

1 Griots were a kind of ethnographic fantasy, allegedly a caste of magically talented wise men recognized by Central African tribes in the French colonial regions of Sudan and Senegambia, analogous—as the text acknowledges—to the (equally fantastic) bards of the ancient Celts.

cording to the prevailing custom with regard to poets, had immured in the hollow trunk of a baobab, and the nation had held a great feast as a sign of rejoicing.

The sorcerer could not be of interest to any civilized soul and was soon left in peace. Uncaring, he went to sit down by himself under an odorant linden tree and began to sing again, accompanying his chants with the rhythm of a drum. People went by but he was oblivious to them—and some of them envied him.

But what about a man? Is a man so rare a thing, then? Finally, someone died on the old continent, and he came from the cities of France.

"Oh," he said to me, "what a triumph, my dear friend. You're the god of fools. After the pitiful funeral rites and the obligatory necrology, a brave bureaucrat protested in a long analysis and conferred genius upon you—you know that we gladly attribute genius to dead men who, like you, only had talent. Young men became excited and gave lectures in which humanity entire was honored by your spirit; your play was produced! When sane people wanted to raise a few reservations, the old critic who had derided your poems so forcefully, and made so many bourgeois laugh with your verses, cried shame upon those who were insulting a hero in his sepulcher and the fatherland in one of its glories. He was the one who was able to march at the head of the Young, organizing their enthusiasm and enlisting them.

"The most foolish of your detractors became, with him, your most respectful disciples; and, as they had mocked you by virtue of not being able to understand you, logically, they extolled you for the same reason. An eulogy devoted to you is nowadays a qualification of intellectual delicacy and esthetic sensitivity; fundamentally, they praise you in order to be esteemed, and not for what you are; no one reads you, any more than they did before, but people buy your books. Your glory is an investment, and your statue a bid. People criticize your widow for having married her lover! Apotheosis, my dear, or fashionability, which comes to the same thing. Would you like to know a secret? It will pass."

An augury of misfortune! His prophecy was accurate. A few months, and I was dethroned—by the author of some seductive crime, or a mob, the inventor of a machine or a microbe, or a star . . . My fatherland, France, had this for its motto: *always possess a great man, and change him every spring.* It thus established a rotation of glory in conformity with its democratic aspirations, which permitted every citizen to hope for his moment of history.

I consoled myself for such a rapid fall by counting on a future rediscovery. I thought: "Truth informed by art does not act directly upon the masses; it impresses a few distinguished minds, and is plundered in turn, for their own use and by trade, by the ostentatious acrobats, vague keepers of dancing bears, who assemble the crowd and are the only ones able to please it, because of their mediocrity; they only understand half of it and only explain a quarter of it, but no one else has the voice to be heard, and the respects of vain people only return later to the ultimate origin."

We formed in the other world a group of malcontents whom the world has maltreated. When one of us became famous again he rendered his esteem to the living and left us. By way of compensation, however, the group was incessantly swelled by all the illustrious individuals fallen into desuetude, geniuses in retirement from employment who came to wax indignant in our midst and return scorn for disdain. Oh, how they legislated in vengeful adages!

"What good is effort," they cried, "and for whom? Superior beings, in the course of their lives, are submissive to rules followed by fools; they submit, being too few in number to resist, but they plant the seed on their wisdom and die; then, slowly, their solitary thought becomes wisdom for the crowd; but the crowd, in touching it, makes foolishness of it in order to assimilate it more easily; other sages suffer from it in their turn, dream, die, reform, are reformed, and so it goes on, forever . . ."

When the band of the triumphant passed by, and waved to us, we banished added:

"Patience. . . . Do you know what endures better than the most superb creations? It's conventional banality. In the whole of your soul, the representatives of posterity, guided by their instinct, will be able to discover in some poor corner one miserable phrase that formulates in a synthesis the noble stupidity of peoples: that is what they will choose of you, because it resembles them; that is what they will put in your name in anthologies, which worldly people will cite appropriately, by way of erudition, and which will follow you in the esteem of electors, until you disappear in your turn beneath a deluge of more modern ineptitudes."[1]

---

1 Edmond Haraucourt could not know, of course, that more than a century later, a search of the world wide web would repeatedly turn up one single line of his poetry, preserved in

I do not know whether these insolences are credit-worthy, but the fact is, so far as I was concerned, that the third generation displayed of me a few verses plagiarized from Boileau and a few parliamentary aphorisms; the latter got me into schools, and the baccalaureate examination became my only hope.

To show that I deserved better, I quietly put my library at everyone's disposition, but the poor books were already becoming tattered; when they were returned to me, I caressed them with loving care.

Everyone, in any case, was doing the same, and we talked in between times about art, its nature and its goal; each of us presented an authoritative definition in conformity with his own temperament, almost always contained in a chapter of his work: the supreme homage!

One said: "Art is an interpreted malady."

Another: "Talent is accumulated will."

A third: "Genius is an obsession."

And everyone: "Prettiness in art is the agreeable form of ugliness."

As befit people placed outside the struggle, who watch the foundations of their work being undermined, we easily fell into agreement in issuing recriminations against the tendency of letters.

"What remains in the sphere of publishing?" an epic poet declaimed. "Two classes: the executioners of books and the gilders of syllables. Rival classes, and both are

---

popular song, which he would probably not have regarded as his most profound thought. ("Partir c'est mourir un peu" [To depart is to die a little].)

right to cover one another with insults. The former cannot write and the latter do not deign to think! If it were
forbidden to quote the former, what would become of
the latter? Exclusive concern with form leads an author
fatally and progressively to refinements so complex that
they are confined to aberration; it is little more than a
monomania, and bears its own death within it twice
over: absence of idea, folly of form . . ."

Etc.

In that he went astray, paying no heed to the fact
that such a literature is that which suits an era in which
art is no more than a recreation.

Alas, it will soon be even less . . .

From time to time, abrupt reactions brought one of
us back into the light, and I observed that every epoch
collected, from the racial past, the poet who had had a
soul analogous to that of the new days; every civilization sympathized with its brothers of another age, and
when it was extinguished in a transformation of the
species, the elected poets returned to a second era of
forgetfulness, and others emerged for an ephemeral period, until changing humanity gave them in their turn
successors more appropriate to the tendencies of its
thought. Of all of them, successively, it was said: How
modern he is!" I understood then that immortality is
merely an intermittence.

Watching over the centuries, I looked forward to
my resurrection. One day, people of small importance
adopted me in good faith, and I was moved, without
vanity.

"Yes," I said, "to do one's work is a duty, not for the
masses, about whom it is permissible to care as little as

they care about us, but for the few, who will find joy in it, and the consolations of a stainless friendship, for the unknown brother we would have cherished, and who will cherish us, whose soul will bathe in that momentary communion, the quiet confidence of the book that listens; to persuade his soul of the duty of amity."

But then, again, buried in the distant dust of accumulated books, I was only touched by those who plagiarize, devourers of the dead, vampires of letters, who know how to rob tombs and nourish themselves on the cadaver of glory.

Meanwhile, the chronicles of the earth were becoming increasingly rare. Poetry could no longer flourish. Practical and positive life unified the minds of races. Art gave way to business; publicity called itself glory, comfort happiness and desire passion; joys having become enjoyments, money was the sole origin of everything, and the skillful heaped it up. Renown was no longer a favor stolen by intrigue but, like love, a merchandise that only the rich could buy. Some undertook, hopefully, to write books, paint canvases, sculpt marbles; then the press set the tariffs for them at which talent, genius and publicity were sold. Ambition wore away determination and need oppressed ideas; no one spent his life any more; everyone earned a living; profit was law, worship being poverty, and nothing else existed.

Sometimes, nevertheless, the world, in a spirit of dandyism, offered itself the luxury of a bad poet to pamper; sometimes, also, some demigod, who had died of starvation, would come to tell us about the sumptuous distress of our descendants.

Humanity advanced thus.

At that time, the most fortunate among us saw themselves denied in their very existence, and commentaries were published to demonstrate that they never existed.

Then, increasingly, humans detached themselves from things and, while the slowness of the ages extended in ennui, we only learned the number of years from the stories of the most recent arrivals.

Our old planet was impoverished by its artificial luxury and the soil, exhausted by over-hasty production, dried up like the human heart.

A silence fell then, and lasted so long that the heavens thought the Earth extinct; it lasted so many centuries that we watched, with amazement, other beings arrive. They were hirsute and stocky, with dark eyes, bare torsos and menacing arms. To savage rhythms, in curt and bitter words, they sang violent battle-hymns.

The Earth had, therefore, oscillating in its orbital course, inverted its poles, in order that new continents might surge from the hollows of the seas, in order that the oceans might invade the empires with their waves and foam, with forests of poisonous algae.

Everything was about to begin again.

Nothing any longer remained of our ancient passage; definitive death had erased everything and confounded the pride of great and petty alike; our time fled so far away from us that we lost the memory of it ourselves, and Dante became the contemporary of Orpheus.

Beneath the immensity of our ennui, some crouched down in the contemplation of their books, in order to find some vestige therein evocative of their abolished existence. In the restricted circle of their unique idea, those spirits turned and returned about themselves, indefinitely, and the pettiness of their human aims then became clear to their judgment, enlightened by a gleam of infinity. On the threshold of one oblivion, they became able at that moment to imagine another, which was called the oblivion of thought. And the disgust of having been was the only thing that survived of so much pride.

But life was renewed upon the globe, and that other humankind, whose newborns we had seen a little while before, undertook its own voyage through the recommencing series of centuries.

Then, weary of seeing, avid to die a second time, leaving the heap of our illusory dreams to molder under the trees, we all set off along a route far from the races that had succeeded us, toward the mysterious world of the horizon.

Thus our exile progressed, voluntarily seeking the darkness.

But when, beyond the frontiers of snow, we came to a gray land that lay beyond a colorless sky, we found a vast host sleeping on the sands: ashen faces, with lightless eyes, the shades of shades, who had once, like us, known the miseries and the vain splendor of life and thought, in the very distant past, before the first Deluge . . .

Those people, whose anterior existence we had not suspected, roused themselves from their torpor to watch us file past, and, without asking who had troubled their sleep, they lay down again in total indifference.

Beyond! In order to sleep like the elders, our renunciation demanded bleaker darkness!

Finally, in the obscure silence of an inviolable desert, we recognized our true abode; everyone lay down on the ground, desirous, since everyone had forgotten him, of forgetting himself, to bury the inanity of his dreams and his pride in the depths of a sleep that would be endless.

WHEN WE HAVE PASSED ON

by Frederic Boutet

A viscous warmth still seemed to be lingering in the great cemetery, like an equivocal vestige of the ardors of summer, in the November night. The sky was drowned, the horizon livid, the silence muffled. The last perfumes, like withered leaves, were swirling in the sultry nocturnal air. An insidious mist coiled over the ground, hanging like scarves from the branches of sculpted yews, padding the arches embroidered in the stone and the artistic lintels of narrow perpetual swellings.

The paths were tidy, the lawns green, and the trees neatly-pruned. The aspect of the ensemble, comfortable and plush, was a pleasure to behold. Only a few neglected tombs offended the gaze with their plaintive dilapidation.

A clock in a veiled bell-tower, in the pale fog and the deadened night, chimed.

"Finally, we can come out," murmured a skeleton, opening the door of a little chapel with violet stained-glass windows. With his right hand, on whose bones a signet ring glittered, he arranged his shroud elegantly over his clavicles, and with a discreet rattle he went along the aristocratic pathway where he dwelt. "I have a desire," he continued, stretching himself with an air of satisfaction at being in the world, "to go see dear Saint-Firmin. Since he lost his iliac bone at that party the week before last, he's been vexed, and one doesn't see him anywhere. My visit . . . why, what's that?"

He stopped, amazed. He was at the foot of the great outer wall, and over that wall the leg of a human clad in black trousers had just passed, next to two hands grasping the summit. The rest of the body completed the climb by means of a readjustment, with a dull rustle. A young man dressed in mourning, sitting on the top of the wall, looked down without seeing the skeleton, who had hidden himself, and then leapt down. He got up again, seemingly uninjured.

The skeleton had no hesitation in grabbing him by the collar. "What are you doing here?" he asked, severely.

The young man in mourning-dress started violently, opened his haggard eyes, tried to cry out, could not do it, and fainted.

"Why, what's got into the imbecile now?" muttered the skeleton, embarrassed. "Ah, there's water in that urn."

He sprinkled water on the young man, and slapped him vigorously with his hands.

The other came round, got to his feet, and made as if to run away, but the skeleton's fist held him in place.

"No, Monsieur," he said, dryly. "Stay there, if you please. Do you think you can introduce yourself in that fashion into private property, albeit in joint ownership. What are you doing here?"

The young man's mouth was open, but no sound came out.

"Come on, Monsieur, answer me!" ordered the skeleton, conscious of his rights and getting a little heated. "Don't oblige me to hand you over to the law! Confess! Why did you introduce yourself here by climbing over the wall? Is it to burgle our dwellings? Has the love of money brought you to this venerable enclosure to rob us? Or has some disrespectful curiosity regarding your superiors driven you to disregard peril and propriety alike? Speak up—are you a spy? That would be even more infamous! Isn't it enough that you have the liberty all day, you and your kind, to come and annoy us here, at home, and prevent us from coming out with your adipose presence? Can't the night, at least, belong to us? Can't you leave us tranquil, you living wretch? Do you have any right, you plump barbarian, to climb over walls to disturb the thin folk? Do we come to violate your homes, you lump of flesh? Come on, speak up! Answer me! Quickly—or I'll clout you over the head with this urn." And he shook the vessel.

"Mercy! Have pity on me, Monsieur!" stammered the young man in mourning, throwing himself at the severe skeleton's kneecaps. "Don't throw me out—be merciful! I didn't know! Have pity on me, a desperate unfortunate! I have a fiancée, the light of my life, an adored young woman . . . dead, Monseigneur! Dead before the wedding! And me, mad with love, intoxicated by grief, wanting to pray on her grave, far from profane eyes, to kiss the earth where she lies . . . have mercy, good skeleton, I kiss your feet! Take me to her—My God! My God!—in order that I might sob over her grave!"

And he sobbed over the bones of skeleton's feet. The latter seemed to be moved to compassion.

"Come on, come on, calm down, my poor boy," he advised. "I forgive you. Yes, I forgive you . . . for love . . . obviously . . . It's not worth the trouble, but it's serious, damn it, is love! Come on, come on, I'll take you. Come on, my friend . . . damn it!"

He coughed as if to clear his throat, doubtless to hide his emotion.

"Thank you, Monseigneur, thank you"!" sniffed the prostrate and tearful unfortunate.

"Calm down, calm down." The skeleton gently lifted him up by the arm. "I consent to take you, but I'm failing in my duty and breaking my promises, you know. It's not permissible to introduce a living person among us. In general, I ought to tell you, your society . . . well, frankly, it disgusts us . . . You lack boundaries—the flesh, you know . . . pooh! But I'm moved by your grief, and, with a little cleverness, by passing you off as a newcomer . . ."

"A newcomer?" stammered the young man. "What do you mean, worthy skeleton?"

"Why, someone recently buried, who still has his . . . his habit . . . his envelope, his shell . . . in sum, his flesh! Usually, the people who find themselves in that state, especially when they're a little advanced, scarcely show themselves. It's not good form. One waits to be proper, to be elegant, to present oneself with all one's advantages, and not leave one's relations a grotesque memory . . . However, it's admissible that one might go out on the first few nights, while one is still presentable, to make acquaintances and leave one's card. Afterwards, well, one stays at home . . . Oh, one gets bored, it's true. The hours go by slowly when one's in one's bier, and the rain, the winter evenings, also go by slowly, and come to soak or shrouds, while one hears the wind moaning in the branches . . . Oh no, it's not cheerful, damn it! And one wishes that *they*'d make haste!"

"Who's *they*?"

"*They* . . . you know . . . the ones who occupy themselves with a fellow when no one else occupies themselves with him. The little workers of the final hour, who sculpt our lines by shaping them neatly. The true undertakers, who feed on us while there's something there . . .

"One wishes that one could say to them: 'Get a move on, then,' but it's impossible. They go their modest little way without ever making haste or sleeping. One feels them tunneling through a muscle, swarm in the cavities, gnawing on a bone, and they tickle you, and one doesn't dare move for fear of disturbing them.

"In life, it makes one feel sick just thinking about them, but believe me, once one's here and once can appreciate their services, one ends up getting attached to them and one is glad to see them getting big and fat, for it's a sign that the work is making progress."

"My God!" the young man groaned. "What horror!"

"Not at all," said the skeleton. "They're the ones who get us out of the ambiguous situation is which one isn't oneself . . . when one's neither flesh nor fish, if I might put it like that . . . without which, one would never become respectable. And as I've just told you, when one understands them properly, one ends up getting fond of them . . .

"One follows their labor, one calculates the progress they've made, always nibbling without ever hurrying . . . and I repeat that one gets impatient to be finished, because, throughout that time, it's customary not to go out. Some of us don't observe that esthetic regulation, and they walk around all the time, even in their worst modifications—but we close our eyes, so to speak. Generally, they're the passionate—like, for instance, Monsieur Honorus. Do you know him?"

"No," said the young man.

"Honorus, of the great factory of Honorus, Wey & Co., the iron-founders—very plush monument, large chapel, magnificent candelabras, gilded doors, sumptuous decoration: terrible taste, but very rich. Well, Monsieur Honorus came here eight months ago, and he's outside every night. He's not pleasant to see, mind, but his behavior is scandalous. One only meets him in the young women's pathways . . ."

"What?" the young man exclaimed.

"Exactly—that astonishes you, but that's the way it is. There's an individual who can't wait to be like everyone else before resuming his debaucheries. I pity the unfortunates who . . . anyway, society always treats him a trifle coldly, for he's too attached. We long-dead folk who constitute the aristocracy, owe our status to being reserved. To be sure, we don't shun pleasure, but we observe a certain moderation . . .

"But I can see you're a little calmer now, my dear Monsieur, and my loquacity had no other purpose. We can go. Permit me, first, to introduce myself: Baron La Rose, second pathway on the left, violet stained-glass, hereditary chapel, reconstructed in 1820 . . . oh, modestly, because of the Revolution, you know . . . I'll introduce you as one of my young relatives."

"I'm Vicomte Adhémar de Léonce," sighed the young man.

"Delighted," said the Baron. "Delighted, my dear Monsieur—we are, if I'm not mistaken, related on the distaff side. Well-died people—pardon me, for you I ought to say well-born—always find one another . . . now, if you want . . ."

"To weep on her grave—oh yes, that's what I want!" And poor Adhémar sniffed again.

"Than I'll ask you . . . which person is in question?" the Baron interrogated, gently.

"Oh, forgive me—that's true!" moaned the young man. "Louise . . . Louise de Rivière. My God! When I think that she's prey to the horrors of the tomb!"

"I know," said the skeleton. "I know where she is—in the southern pathway, near the yew cross. Very honorable family, tomb in perfect taste, Vosges granite and porphyry . . . Let's go . . . but, oh, damn it! Your outfit . . . bah! That happens sometimes. One piece of advice, though! Keep your eyes half-closed. They're too bright . . ."

They went off along the main pathway.

✳

They walked slowly through the small white city, cheerful and animated beneath its beautiful veils of insulating mist. Around them, skeletons were hastening to some rendezvous of pleasure or business. Others, smoking and dreaming, were idling nonchalantly or sitting and chatting on old worn headstones, their polished skulls gleaming softly in the uncertain light, through the soft mist blurring their silhouettes. Games of baccarat, poker and bridge were in progress here and there, followed by galleries of attentive gamblers.

Amateur runners were doing laps around a large clump of bushes. On the thresholds of sumptuous monuments, decorated by evergreen plants, the masters of the houses, crowned with immortelles, draped in their finest shrouds, were welcoming the elegant groups of their guests courteously. Intimate soirées and family gatherings cheered up the most modest concessions.

In front of one mysterious vault, a few people sitting in a circle, phalanges united, were turning a slab and evoking the living. Children, watched by their mothers or nursemaids, were amusing themselves here and there. A troop of joyous companions went by, humming and rattling, while a violent altercation and domestic dispute rose up between the co-tenants of a temporary vault surrounded by a circle of idlers.

Far from all that agitation, near the cypresses and their propitious shade, on the lawns and between the clumps of bushes, amorous shadows enveloped in shrouds the color of the wall were hastening and meeting up furtively, without the slight sounds of conjunction . . . and couples, side by side and intertwined, were plunging into the protective mystery of the pathways, or closing the discreet door of some inhabited chapel or isolated cenotaph.

The young man in mourning-dress seemed impressed by so much civilization, and the obliging skeleton, in order to inform his protégé as much as to sustain the plausibility of his role as a newcomer, amicably gave him explanations while saluting friends he perceived.

"The quarter we're going through," he said, "is the chic, fashionable and rich neighborhood to which strangers come. There, on the left, is major commerce, banking and industry. The quarter we're coming to, and which I inhabit, is the aristocratic quarter, naturally stricter and more exclusive: the Faubourg Saint-Germain of our old cemetery. The inhabitants recognize one another by a dignity of manners, their finesse and their distinction. We put a high value on the delicacy of extremities, you see. That's how one discerns nobility. The Comtesse de Talk, who lives near me, is justly celebrated for the divine lightness of her small bones. She's an exquisite woman, and has the most beautiful teeth in the world, but her hand! Oh, my dear chap, that hand! It's a dream! Undulating articulations! The primness of a perforated gem! The whiteness of fresh ivory! We're intimates, and I glory in it! The dear Comtesse has told me that her sympathy for me was born in the contemplation of my foot! Yes, my dear chap."

He smiled, with a self-satisfaction full of implication. "It's true, of course, that my foot . . . well, breeding! The foot of a cavalier, you know!" And he extended an irreproachable metatarsal, finely encased, with elegant and neat phalanges.

"Yes, yes," said the young man in mourning, who did not seem to be in full possession of his faculties.

"Here, too," the skeleton continued, "status is everything. We conserve the status we possessed before, that our larva—don't take that ill; you seem to me

50

liable to make a distinguished corpse—had among the living. An aristocrat is an aristocrat forever, a rich man remains a rich man. Democracy, I beg you to believe, does not infect us unduly.

"Naturally, I'm talking about respectable folk. In the plebeian population over there"—jabbing a disgusted thumb over his shoulder-blade, he vaguely indicated the northern part of the cemetery—"it appears that they form insurrectional organizations and hold anarchic meetings, declaring that social class ceases with life, that all men die equal and a thousand other nonsensical slogans of that sort. It's of no importance, because individuals of that kind are of no account. If you could see them! They're frightful! Ignoble! One could almost prefer the living! They revel in dirt and ignominy. They haven't even found a means for each one to have his own dwelling. They live in holes, in heaps, can you believe, without observing the slightest decency, getting drunk, fighting and stealing bones from one another to complete their skeletons.

"There are old ones who are so wretched by virtue of being patched up here and there that hardly a single piece of their original carcass remains. It's no longer one skeleton, it's twenty of them; one never knows who one's talking to—every bone has a different origin. And they spend their time whining, recriminating and protesting about everything. Either that or they're making speeches standing on their little mounds, proclaiming the sovereignty of the people, declaring that we're oppressing them, that we take up too much space, that their existence is becoming impossible and that it would be better never to have died!

"In the meantime, the young women prostitute themselves in corners and the children play bowls with skulls that might perhaps have belonged to their ancestors. What profanation! It's true that those people have no ancestors! Fortunately, an extensive authority keeps them in place, otherwise there'd be everything to dread! Sometimes we go among them in disguise, in order to accompany ladies—the caprices of pretty women are the scourge of Grand Dukes, you know! But truly, it's too infamous; I shan't go again. It dishonors one to think that one is made of the same bones as such brutes . . . ah, *bonsoir*, my dear Saint-Firmin! So you've decided to come out!"

The Baron stopped to shake the hand of a stout skeleton with a sympathetic appearance and a comfortable shroud, who was trotting along, smoking a cigar, on the heels of a pert individual whose shroud, coquettishly tucked up, uncovered a slender fibula.

"Yes, yes," replied the stout skeleton. "I manage to find my iliac—it's that little minx Clara who had hidden it." He dabbed his parietals with a flap of his shroud, and added: "It's warm this evening."

"And what a mist! If one had bronchi, eh!" the Baron remarked, wittily, making his stout friend burst into immoderate laughter, which made his entire solid carcass rattle. Monsieur La Rose continued: "But permit me to introduce a newcomer to you, who is a relative of mine, Monsieur Adhémar de Léonce, an accomplished young man."

"Delighted, Monsieur," said the stout skeleton, recovering his composure and bowing courteously to the young man while holding out his right hand, a set of knucklebones, which Adhémar shook, not without a certain frisson. "Delighted to have you among us. My dear Baron, I hope you'll bring Monsieur along to the Comtesse de Talk's twelve o'clock; he'll see all of society there, and we'll meet again."

"Yes, undoubtedly," the Baron replied, "but I don't want to keep you, my dear friend . . ."

"Hmm . . . I'd like to stay, but excuse me . . . a find, a marvel, my dear chap, a little charmer—plebeian, no doubt, but slim, light, clean, polite . . . and coy . . . I fear that she might escape me . . ."

And bidding farewell with a gesture, he drew away hurriedly on the track of the pert shadow, which seemed to be taking pleasure in allowing that pursuit, doubtless not being as coy as Monsieur de Saint-Formin would have liked to think.

"What a charming man," said the Baron. "Ever young, ever amorous, always in quest of new adventures, but obliging and courteous too. Oh, he takes death cheerfully, that one—long and good, he says, and my word, he's right. In accordance with his advice, my dear chap, I'll take you to Madame de Talk's soirée, and you'll see that we aren't boring . . . but forgive me; I'm talking about pleasures when you have an affliction of the heart . . ."

They took a few steps in silence. The skeleton seemed quite satisfied with himself and others, although he seemed sincerely sympathetic to his companion's pain. As for the latter, one could not begin to fathom his thoughts, but they were somber—that was obvious.

"Forgive me," the skeleton said, suddenly, "if I'm stirring up your grief, but has your fiancée been among us for long? I don't remember her."

"Twelve days," moaned the young man. "The misfortune happened while I was traveling. I learned of it when I returned. I thought I would go mad, and I was closely watched. This evening, I was able to evade the surveillance. But why do you ask?"

"Oh, no reason, but you know . . . women . . . and as she can't hope to see you again very soon . . ."

"What are you getting at?" the living man interrogated, in anguish.

"Well, my God, it's delicate . . . I might be mistaken but I'd like, out of friendship, to avoid the overly rude blow of a new dolor. And the demoiselle, of course, must have thought that if you'd wanted to follow her, you'd already have done so, and not having done so, would sooner or later console yourself with the living, your peers . . . And it might be that she . . . one gets bored when one has nothing to do, and there's no lack here of . . . consolers who know their business, especially with a pretty newcomer."

"What horror! What an idea! I'm sure of her," the young man declared, peremptorily.

"So much the better, so much the better," said the Baron, who seemed skeptical. "But I thought I ought to say something." He pointed to a melancholy young skeleton wandering in a deserted pathway around a little chapel that was closed. "Look, there's a poor fellow who, like you, is suffering from love . . ."

"Oh," said the young man in mourning-dress, sympathetically, darting a glance at the unfortunate who had been indicated to him. "Has his fiancée left him?"

"No, not exactly, but it's a sad story, which shows how sentiments can be modified by a separation. It's him who left his fiancée, in ceasing to live a few years ago. So he was here, lamenting, full of love and thinking about the one he left behind in the degrading and transitory jail they call the world of the living, and he was jealous, suffering a thousand lives at the thought that she might have forgotten him and fallen in love with someone else. Those sentiments are terrible here, you see, for they're so impotent . . . I'm sure that if he'd been able to do it, he'd have gone to kill her, in order to have her with him . . .

"Fortunately, newly-arrived relatives told him that the little one had remained faithful to him and gone into a convent. That was a great relief for the poor fellow, and he continued to wait, passionately, but suffering less intensely. That didn't last very long, because she came here not long after him. When he saw the funeral procession arrive and found out that it was her, his joy scared us all . . . but the young woman had been seriously touched by religion, it appears, and never wanted to return his love on seeing him here. She loves him like a sister, she says, and not otherwise—so he's fallen into a frightful despair from which nothing can extract him. Every day, he comes to prowl around her chapel. She never opens the door, perhaps for fear that she might weaken, and they talk through the little grille, him begging her to have pity and love him a little, her exhorting him to tame his passions and lead a resigned and virtuous death . . . but shhh! Here he is."

The young skeleton had, in fact, arrived close at hand in the course of his mechanical wandering.

"Well, my poor friend," said the Baron, sympathetically, gently putting the tips of his phalanges on his ulna, "are you still as unhappy?"

"Oh, I'm going out of my skull!" replied the poor young skeleton, dejectedly. "I love her too much, you see! I adore her with all my soul, madly! I spend hours, prostrate and tortured, at that dear accursed door, which never opens to me! I burn, I beg, I suffer . . . oh, how I suffer! And she . . . never a word of love, never a surge of emotion. Always calm, always cold, always insensitive . . . and so lovely, so lovely!

"Sometimes, through the grille, in the mauve shadow projected by the stained-glass window, I catch a glimpse of her, upright, elegant and proud, finely outlined in her light form by the rays of moonlight that kiss her little polished bones so amorously! Oh, I'd give anything in the world to touch the hem of her shroud!

"Her teeth shine and drive me mad, and the mysterious hollows of her wide orbits seem to me to be a divine and deceptive abyss into which my passion plunges, is lost and is reborn, a thousand times more ardent, returning to envelop me like a seething, furious, devouring sea!

"I can't forget her, nor flee from her, nor bend her will. What torture! She has no heart, I tell you! And me, me . . . !" He gripped the left side of his thoracic cage despairingly. "Oh, I'd rather be back in the time when I was alone here, when I was awaiting her coming, when I still had hope . . . I have no more strength, no more courage, no more hope! The day before yesterday, I tried in vain to hang myself. Oh, I miss life—at least one could die!"

The unfortunate fellow's agitation had declined. He drew away, dejectedly. He went to sit down on a black tomb and, detaching his left tibia, which he had pierced like a flute, he played a melancholy, soothing and amorous tune on it.

"That's the song they once both loved, in the time of their love and their life," murmured the Baron to his companion, who was moved to tears.

They drew away, and the plaintive sound floated after them.

"Are we nearly there?" asked Adhémar, in a faint voice.

"Yes," said the Baron. "The yew crossroads is at the end of that path to the left."

"My God, my God!" moaned the young man. "To see her tomb!"

"Be careful," said the skeleton, suddenly. "Quick—let's hide in here!"

The young man in mourning-dress allowed himself to be dragged into the shadow of an old chapel. From a side-path, a tall, frantic half-naked skeleton emerged into the pathway, brandishing an iron bar, which he was whirling around, shouting furiously.

"I'm alive," he howled. "I'm alive, for God's sake! Help! Help! I'm alive!"

He disappeared at top speed, brandishing his weapon. His cries became inarticulate. Two other skeletons launched in pursued, passing by at a run.

"What's going on?" asked Adhémar, trembling.

"He's a madman," said the Baron La Rose. "A dangerous madman, whom his guardians are trying to recapture. Let's go . . ."

They advanced rapidly along the pathway.

"As you heard," said the Baron, "his madness consists of believing that he's alive. We all dream sometimes that we're alive, especially in the early days, and believe me, it's a frightful nightmare—meaning no offense. But he, poor chap, believes it all the time, and he's completely insane. It's true that he's gone through a rather harsh ordeal. He was brought here and buried alive."

"Alive!" said Adhémar, with a start of horror.

"Yes—he was cataleptic. Once buried, he woke up. You get the picture? He was in his coffin for seven whole days, howling. The living couldn't hear him, but we could hear him very clearly. He howled as he was howling just now, and it was enough to chill your bones. He ate his entire right hand before . . . before becoming tranquil . . ."

"But why didn't you rescue him?" Adhémar exclaimed, alarmed by his companion's calmness.

"My God," the skeleton replied. "That's nothing to do with us. We don't like getting mixed up in your business, in general; we're afraid of being betrayed. And really, once one's here, one might as well stay. A little sooner, a little later . . . we never intervene in such cases."

Adhémar flinched. "In such cases?" he stammered. "You mean it happens often?"

"Often enough," said the Baron. "It's easy, you know, to bury someone alive. Obviously, it's not very pleasant for the individual concerned, but when the painful moments have passed, they generally don't regret it—on the contrary. As for that one, we liberated him as soon as he was one of us, but it had gone on too long and he was a nervous type—he was raving mad."

"I can understand that, poor fellow!" stammered the young man in mourning, who plunged into meditation.

"We're here, my dear chap," said the Baron, suddenly touching his arm.

"My God, my God!" moaned Adhémar, putting his hand on his heart and stopping. "We're near to her . . ."

"Lower your voice," instructed the Baron, "and if you trust me, let's approach without being seen. The Larivière family monument is over there, behind that bush—let's slip into the shadow of the yews without making any noise."

Stifling the sound of their footsteps as much as possible and ducking under the branches of evergreen foliage, they advanced to the vicinity of the monument. Then, without being able to make out the interlocutors, they heard two voices whispering in the shadows.

The young man had a spasm. "It's her voice," he whimpered, panting. He seemed to be on the brink of dying.

"Shh!" breathed the Baron, supporting him; he seemed keen to see the investigation through to the end. Without being able to retain a muffled snigger, he added: "There's also a man's voice. Let's get a little closer; they won't hear us."

Silently, with the prudence of a serpent, they crept closer.

"Stop here," murmured the Baron. He recognized the masculine voice. "Ah! That's Henry de Livry, one of our best Don Juans."

"It's her, it's her," moaned Adhémar, feebly, perturbed to the utmost depths of his vital spirits.

"Shh! Listen!" the Baron ordered, almost imperceptibly, lying flat on the ground and obliging his companion to do likewise.

"Henry," murmured the feminine voice, which was soft and musical. "Why are you here? I begged you not to come back."

"Forgive me, Louise. I love you so much. I thought I could, for one more night . . ."

"But I'm becoming ugly, and I don't want you to see me like this."

"Ugly! You, my love? But you're more beautiful than ever. Less beautiful, to be sure, than you will be later, but already so beautiful. Your skin is taking on charming tones, your eyes are more profound, your silky golden hair . . ."

"Soon I won't have any. It's already going . . ."

"You'll only be more beautiful. My love, since the first evening I saw you here, in this poetic and deserted spot, since the first evening when I fell in love with you, every evening, I've followed the exquisite marks of transformation on your face passionately. What I see in you are not the gross charms that pleased the living, which I see coming to an end. What I love in you is the promise of your true beauty, which I sense ready to emerge, to blossom, to shine radiantly in all its elegant purity. Beneath that flesh, which I hate because it is delaying the hours of our happiness, because a man has loved you in it, beneath that flesh, which is ceasing to be yourself and which you are allowing to fall away like an excessively heavy cloak, I divine your real, adorable personality, as indestructible as our love . . ."

"You're sure of that, Henry? It astonishes me so much."

"It's the last memories of the errors of life that are still troubling you. Look at me, my love. Am I not as you will be, and don't you love me thus?"

60

"Oh yes!"

"Would you love me more if I had flesh, hair, all the bother of a weighty, thick, suffering body, becoming more dilapidated every year as it approaches its end?"

"No, no, Henry! I understand very well. But what do you expect? It's been such a short time since I changed. I'm still almost alive."

"Yes, that's true. My God, it will be a long wait . . ."

"Alas, Henry—how long?"

"Oh, that depends. One can't tell in advance . . ."

"Oh, I'll hurry . . . it doesn't do any harm, does it?"

"No, no harm. One gets bored, that's all, but one interests oneself in the work that liberates us . . ."

"Of, if I could beg them to make haste . . . so many long hours without seeing you . . ."

"You'll think about me?"

"I'll only think about you. The memory of your love will never leave me. My God, when I think that, as soon as I'm free, beautiful, like you, I'll be able to throw myself into your arms. You won't forget me for someone else, between now and then? I'll be here, alone, shut in, while you . . ."

"My beloved . . ."

"Henry . . . But go—it's late, my grandmother might come back . . ."

"No, my darling, you know that she's in the chapel, and that she'll stay there until morning."

"Yes, but I'm in haste to begin my reclusion. I'm in haste to surrender myself to them, in order to resemble you sooner."

"They take hold of us even before the funeral, my love, and as soon as we're here, we belong to them and their work begins . . ."

"Oh, my God, Henry, go! I don't want, before you . . ."

"One more word, Louise: that fellow, that living man—your fiancé, in brief—you no longer love him, do you? You no longer think about him?"

"Henry, I've already told you . . ."

"But I need to hear it again! Especially at the moment of such a long separation . . . I'm jealous . . . not of the kisses he's been able to give you—your flesh isn't you—but I'm jealous of your love, of your thoughts. You no longer love him, do you? You no longer love him, that gross human larva, lumpen, stupid, adipose and hairy?"

"No, I swear to you, since I've seen you, the memory of his gross face is repugnant to me . . ."

"Oh, Louise, let him never attempt to dispute you with me!"

"You're mad! He's a robust and healthy man. He'll fall in love with someone else who's like him, and continue his dirty living existence with her. May he become very old, and never come here . . . that's all I wish for him . . ."

"Is that really true, Louise? You don't want to see him again? If he were to die, that wouldn't change your sentiments for me?"

"Oh, God no! I scarcely loved him, without knowing anything, like a crazy living little girl—but you, Henry, I love you profoundly, like a woman, like a dead woman . . ."

"Louise, I adore you!"

The voices melted away, becoming lower still, and tender, in amorous whispered endearments that were suggestive of speech and kisses.

✻

That was too much for poor Adhémar. With a sigh, he collapsed on the Baron's hospitable clavicle.

"Damn!" muttered the other. "He's got worse! It's true that it's a rude blow for the poor fellow." He shook him, tapped his hands, and having brought him partly back to his senses, with a strength one would not have suspected in such a thin being, muffling his footfalls, he carried the unfortunate man outside the clump of yews in which the blackest of treasons had just pierced his heart.

"My God, my God, the vile woman!" moaned Adhémar dully, dazed by dolor.

"It reminds one of life, eh?" observed the Baron, with a bitter smile, forgetting that his companion was not entirely like him. "But don't attach too much importance to that, my friend. Have courage. It's a hard blow, but take it like a man."

"My God, my God!" moaned Adhémar, spasmodically. "What horror! And her grandmother, who goes to the chapel instead of watching over her! My God, my God, I'm choking!"

And suddenly, letting himself fall on to an old mossy slab at the corner of a deserted pathway, he burst into convulsive sobs.

"Weep away—no one can hear you, and it'll soothe your pain," murmured the Baron, sitting down beside him. "Weep, poor childish heart, broken by the cruel heart of a woman." Pensively, he added: "It's a long time since I've seen real tears wept. We sometimes sweat when the weather's damp, but it's not the same . . . it's very moving and a trifle ridiculous."

Adhémar wept for a long time.

The Baron remained sitting by his side, without saying anything more, until he saw that his companion's sobs were diminishing in violence. Then he got up and, with gentle firmness, constrained him to straighten up and listen to him.

"My friend," he said to him, "you've wept as much as a man can and must when he's sensitive and great suffering strikes him for the first time. I've respected your grief. But it's not appropriate to yield to your sentiments like a child devoid of energy. Envisage the situation frankly and accept it. That young woman no longer loves you, and if you want my opinion, which is only what she said herself, she never loved you, even when she was alive."

"My God," moaned Adhémar.

"No, for sure," said the Baron, forcibly. "It's necessary to cut to the dead—pardon me, to the quick—and not cradle oneself with illusions. We're going to leave this deserted and not very comfortable place without further ado. We'll take a little walk, to enable you to pull yourself together, and then I'll take you to the Comtesse de Talk's."

"To a party! Never!" said Adhémar.

"Yes," said the Baron. "Do that for me. It will change your ideas and bring you back to yourself. Afterwards . . ."

"Afterwards?" stammered the comatose Adhémar.

"You can do as you wish," said the Baron, negligently, who seemed to have a thought at the back of his skull, "but let me tell you right away that I consider you to be a gallant man, for whom I experience a keen sympathy, and whom I'd be happy to have as a best friend."

"I too like you very much, and I'll do as you wish," sighed Adhémar, shaking the worthy skeleton's phalanges feebly.

"No more sighs, then," said the Baron. "Be sad, but don't show it. Anyway, damn it, at your age, when one loses a woman, one finds ten more . . ."

"Oh no!" Adhémar protested. "Women—I hate them!"

"That's because you love them too much," said the Baron. "Or, rather, because you only love one of them. Love several at the same time, and . . . tell me how it works out . . . But let's go. We'll call in at the great market, which is a curious thing to see, take a turn down below and then go see the dear Comtesse. We'll arrive just as the party's warming up."

They left, the Baron cheerfully whistling a funeral march and, from time to time, making a witty remark, a pun or a deft and mordant quip to distract his companion, who was walking with his head bowed and shoulders slumped, depressed as he was by dolor and the dark thoughts he was mulling over.

At a junction of the path, in a large isolated crossroads near the enclosing wall, they saw several skeletons together, conferring gravely. Two of them, separated from the group and from one another by the whole breadth of the crossroads, seemed to be waiting with a slightly feverish dignity. Another was measuring distances on the ground, Long hard objects wrapped in green serge were lying on the ground.

"Look," said the Baron in a low voice. "They're making preparations for a duel. One of the gentlemen—the tall one with the embroidered shroud who's standing apart on the right—has been accused by his companion of cheating at cards. He's just had an extremely fortunate bank at baccarat—too fortunate, it appears. Anyway, he's a sort of flashy Brazilian who poses as a man of the world and who never ought to have been allowed into a respectable club like *Les Racines*, where the quarrel took place. His adversary had some sorry adventures in his youth, and isn't much better than him. The duel will be serious, because there are scores to be settled. They're caught by the hair, if I might use the expression, and no one's more jealous of his honor than someone who has none. But let's make ourselves scarce—reporters are arriving, by invitation, and photographers, and I don't want to be recognized, because I refused to serve as a second. It's a shabby affair, in which a real man of the world can't get mixed up."

"With what weapons will they fight?" Adhémar asked, who was visibly thinking about something else.

"Flat swords," the Baron replied, drawing away with him. "But please, my dear chap, pull yourself together and make an effort to shake off your sadness. You're getting deeper into it by the minute and chewing it over. It's true that it's very recent and that, before having seen your mistress again—or, rather, having heard her—you were only suffering in your heart, whereas now it's your self-esteem that's afflicted . . ."

"Perhaps," said the young man. "My suffering is certainly more painful now. Just now, I was able to weep for my lost love and that adored woman, whom

I believed to be pure and sincere, without any further thought. Now, you see, my injury is crueler, my wound more envenomed, for not only has the woman I loved been stolen from me forever, but I can see her in the arms of another, I know that she didn't love me, and shame, scorn and bitterness are rendering my tears more scalding."

"Undoubtedly," observed the Baron. "Nevertheless, a little while ago you were able to believe that you had lost the exquisite exception that one never finds—a loving, frank and faithful woman—whereas now you know that her soul was the eternal feminine soul, flirtatious, fickle and capricious, which enjoys doing us harm and laughs at our avowals. Let's not be hasty to condemn, though . . . she was very young to be in love when you knew her, and perhaps she really has encountered in Henry de Livry her predestined amour."

"Ah!" the young man exclaimed, "I should have killed myself when I learned of her death. I would have come here. I would have been ready, later, at the same time as her . . . and she would still have loved me. It's my fault . . ."

"Undoubtedly," said the Baron, with a smile. "You seem to me to be one of those true lovers who don't want to see the defects of their lovelies, and who always accuse themselves of the sins they've committed. But let's pass on. It's too late now. You'll never be able to efface from your memory what you heard just now, and she'll never love you again. Shake off the memory of that lost love, accept the inevitable and be a man . . ."

"You're right," said Adhémar. "Excuse my weakness. I'm going to get a grip on myself. I'm very lucky to have found, in my misfortune, a friend like you . . ."

"Very good," said the Baron. "I'm glad to see you like this. We're going to distract ourselves."

"Yes," said Adhémar, who seemed resolute. "We need distraction. But explain to me, I beg you, something you said just now. You mentioned reporters. Is there a newspaper here, then?"

"There are three," said the Baron, "and naturally, each one has a different opinion. The issues are written in chalk on slates, which are passed around and fixed outside. First, to begin at the bottom, we have the organ of the common people: an infamous, pretentious and bilious rag that devotes itself, under the pretext of denouncing abuses, to the most atrocious blackmail. It's stupidly entitled *Le Corbillard des Pauvres*, and delights in dragging the most eminent dead through the mud. Its editor is an ignoble individual who signs himself Le Mort Maigre. He's a universally-scorned renegade who poisons the people with criminal slanders and invites the communal graves every evening to rise up *en masse* and march against us to claim their mortal rights. Pooh!

"Next, at the opposite end of the spectrum, is *Le Monitor des Os Blancs*, respectable, to be sure, but unbearably tedious. Only the staunchest conservatives read it. I must confess that, for myself, I don't have the courage. It's edited by a kind of historic ruin who dates from the *ancien régime*, and prints any tedious and stupid tidbit to please his clientele of dowagers and backward curés.

Finally, there's *L'Écho de Minuit*, the only readable paper, which reports society events and parties, the night's news, and the names of new arrivals of note. In its supplement, *Le Mort Pour Tous*, it also publishes articles signed by the most notable literary and political celebrities we have among us, and who obtain glory by contributing to it. The paper is very interesting and its editor, who's a friend of mine, is a remarkable intelligence, fond of art and letters. He's thinking of founding a theater, using the great public cenotaph as an auditorium, but he needs subscribers. The great artists who are resident here would like nothing better than to lend their collaboration, in spite of the jealousy that they experience for one another . . ."

The Baron interrupted himself, for they were leaving the narrow pathways, propitious for conversation, and emerging into a vast artery that was almost tumultuous.

"What a crowd!" remarked Adhéma, astonished.

"Let's join in," said the Baron, "and observe what's happening around us. It's very busy tonight. The majority of the merchants you see are Jews—their cemetery's over there to the north. They maintain the traditions of their race intact, I can assure you. Here's one—you see, that old man with the sordid shroud who's scraping dried mud off his ankles with a fibula. He's one of the biggest capitalists we have here. He's made a veritable fortune solely by selling metal plates that he hammers himself. It was fashionable a few years ago to line one's lower jaw like that. It was all the rage for a long time. According to one's fortune, one employed gold, silver or lead. The lower class, always ambitious to ape the ridicule of superiors that they imagine they can equal in that way, made use of the lids of sardine-tins on a massive scale. The vogue passed, as all vogues do, but a lot of merchants got rich on it."

Adhémar listened to these explanations while making his way, with some difficulty, through the dense crowd surrounding him. On each side of the avenue there were displays, behind which, squatting like tailors, were merchants fashioning articles animatedly and agitating all their bones wildly over the slightest objects. Save for rare exceptions, the merchandise was not very attractive, and would doubtless have been considered by the inhabitants of living world to be mere junk, only good for putting in the cellar or throwing into the gutter, but it was hotly contested nevertheless.

Adhéma observed, regretfully, that the transactions were not all made in entirely good faith. One skeleton especially, who seemed to be drunk and who was accompanied by a young woman of loose morals, was odiously deceived by a young dealer in detached bones. The latter, before Adhémar's very eyes, robbed the drunkard of his own clavicle and then sold it back to him at an exorbitant price, with the manifest complicity of the girl, who protested to the poor soak that she could not love him much because he was incomplete. Indignant, Adhémar wanted to intervene, but the Baron dissuaded him urgently.

"Be careful not to get mixed up in anything whatsoever," he told him. "These are the dregs of the population and you'd be looking for trouble. Let's remain spectators, as prudence demands—and it might be better for us to retire. We've come a little late. At this hour, roguery rules and prostitution triumphs in these ill-famed locations. Let's go; I wanted to show you a gracious child who's usually here, selling fire-follets or glow-worms, which ladies buy to make into ornaments, but her place is vacant already, so we'll have to leave it for another time."

As they withdrew, they were subjected to tenacious propositions from low-class hetairas and the insulting remarks of several skeletons of shady appearance. The Baron's firm attitude imposed itself upon them, and Adhémar, who was beginning to feel some anxiety, breathed more freely when he and his companion turned into a tranquil pathway.

"What villainy!" said the Baron. "It was time to go. That's how riots start. Let's go to the Comtesse's—her luxury and grace will seem all the sweeter after that ignoble spectacle."

Without further discussion, they hastened past neatly-formed chapels and regular gravestones. The denser mist limited visibility and stifled footfalls.

"Oh!" Adhémar exclaimed, suddenly. "A man!" his arm indicated a fleshy apparition emerging from a chapel.

"Could it be a burglar?" Monsieur La Rose advanced swiftly. "Oh, no," he added. "I recognize him. He's one of ours—but what is he doing?"

"What am I doing?" replied the individual, angrily, in whom Adhémar was able to recognize a body that was still almost entire, and not even too dilapidated, but was visibly as dead as anyone else. "What am I doing? That's none of your business, is it?"

"Monsieur!" protested the Baron.

"Ah, it's you, Baron!" And the dead man assumed a less hostile attitude. "Pardon me—I didn't recognize you . . . the fog! And I'm annoyed. For an hour I've been working to clear my chapel of the funerary ignominies with which my wife stuffs it every year under the pretext of souvenirs. It's not enough that she poisoned me . . ."

"Poisoned!" said Adhéma, terrified, paying no heed to the nudge in the ribs that the Baron gave him. "Your wife poisoned you!"

The dead man looked at him. "Indeed," he said, dryly. "She poisoned me in order to marry my best friend. That's the way of things. It makes me mad! I'd rather she hadn't employed, under the pretext of caring for me, that filthy arsenic, which has conserved my flesh for years without me being able to lighten myself like everyone else. But all in all, I could let that go, having never had any disposition to play the rake. No, what disgusts me is these wreaths, which she persists—God knows why—in sending me every year. If they were even something artistic, with natural flowers and nice ribbons, but look at this! Look at this cheap rubbish in iron wire and glass beads! Every year it's the same. She gives the job to that drunkard François, my former valet, and he buys filth to his own taste and hangs it up all over the place, sobbing, too drunk to see clearly any longer! For God's sake!"

"Calm down, now," said the Baron. "You're expressing yourself rather violently. Distract yourself rather than shutting yourself away—go out, see people. That will change your ideas."

"Pooh! With the face I have? Go out? No thanks! I look like a spoiled mummy. I'd prefer not to show myself. Then again, I'm too old for partying. I prefer sleeping or reading peacefully. I wouldn't have got up, except for these infamies, of which I had to rid myself as soon as possible. What do I look like, I ask you, when I have this on my grille?"

And with a kick, he sent a wreath flying twenty meters.

The two friends bade him farewell and went on their way. "His wife never poisoned him, you know," said the Baron, when they were some distance away. "One of his cousins told me the whole story. The unfortunate woman suffered ten years of marriage and martyrdom with that misanthropic and alcoholic old fool. He did indeed take arsenic medicinally, and that's what conserves him, but he died quite simply of his illness, and if his wife has remarried and tasted a little happiness, it's only just.

"I hope the unfortunate woman never comes here—he'll resume tormenting her, and he'll reproach her all the time with that fantastic tale of murder, which he's invented wholesale, but which he's ended up believing to be true. It wouldn't be a death for the poor woman. But we're getting back to the classy quarter now. What a pleasure to find oneself at home, in the comfort of one's habitual environment. Will you do me the honor of coming to my place when we leave the Comtesse's?"

Suddenly a cheerful voice broke in: "Here you are, then!"

They turned around and saw the stout skeleton that they had run into at the beginning of the evening. A middle-aged dead man, who seemed to have quit life only a few days previously, clad in a beautiful brand new shroud, was walking beside him, seemingly prey to an ill-concealed alarm.

"My first cousin," said the stout skeleton, making the introductions. "He hasn't been here long, and it's his first outing. "I've only just gone to fetch him, and he's still half-asleep."

Adhémar seemed interested by this cousin, who was fairly similar to him, save for the bagatelle of the change of state.

"Have you . . . slept well?" he asked, for something to say.

"Yes, yes," murmured the cousin. "It's good to sleep as one does here—my God it's good . . ."

"Isn't it?" remarked the Baron. "Especially after all the bother you've just been through. All the bustle of funerals wears you out with fatigue and annoyance!"

"Did you suffer much before? Did the thing itself give you a lot of trouble?" asked Adhémar, with an ardent and tremulous curiosity.

"Shh, my dear chap!" hissed the Baron, digging him in the ribs. "One doesn't ask that sort of thing; you'll give yourself away."

"I d . . . don't really remember," stammered the cousin, who seemed anguished. "My daughter wept so much . . . I've left her alone down there, and that torments me . . ."

"Come on, come on—the Comtesse will think we've abandoned her!" To break off the conversation, the stout skeleton pushed him forward. "We're very late," he added. "I was held up. Delightful, believe me, delightful . . . such grace and charm . . . ha ha!"

They soon arrived. The party was in full swing. The Comtesse's monument was very elegant, decorated with perfect taste, as were the vast vaults where a soft phosphorescent light reigned.

The mistress of the house welcomed the newcomers with a marked favor. Her capacious silk shroud, slightly low-cut, allowed her pearl necklace to be seen, and fell in broad pleats around her slender form. Very gracious, coiffed with chrysanthemums, gloved in white to the elbow, she took a step toward her guests that revealed the fine phalanges of her child-like feet, laden with rings.

"I was almost despairing of seeing you, Baron," she said, with a delightful amiability, playing with her fan while Monsieur La Rose leaned over to kiss her hand. "You and Monsieur Saint-Firmin are ever faithful, though." Welcoming the newcomers, she added: "In any case, the presence of these gentlemen explains and excuses your lateness."

"A thousand thanks, Madame," stammered Adhémar, bowing deeply.

The stout skeleton and his cousin, who still had a rather sad expression, also presented their homages, and then went to mingle with the guests, who were not very numerous but all individuals of the highest society. Adhémar, somewhat out of place, moved a few paces away and leaned to a marble column, pensively.

"What a charming fellow," said the Comtesse to the Baron, who had remained beside her. "He's well worthy of being your relative, but why has he maintained those hideous vestment of existence?"

"He didn't know that he'd have the honor of being introduced to you, my dear Madame," the Baron replied, a trifle embarrassed. He lowered his voice: "But allow me to tell you that I've never seen you looking so lovely . . ."

"Bah!" The Comtesse seemed to smile softly. "You say that every time we meet."

"Doubtless because it's true every time," said the Baron, amorously, leaning toward her. "Your headgear this evening suits you delightfully. Those heavy flowers, on the polished white of your temples! My God, you're seductive!"

The Comtesse seemed to smile again, and, turning toward him, with a movement that was simultaneously chaste and provocative, she opened the top of her shroud momentarily. Through the fine trellis of ribs, the intoxicated Baron saw a fire-follet glowing in the location of the heart.

"It's burning for you," she said, with adorable coquetry.

"My love, my queen," murmured La Rose, transported.

"Shh! Someone will hear you. Let's go rejoin your young relative. That terrible Vidame[1] Hilarion is going to bore him with his stories of the other world."

"Let's go—but I beg you, tomorrow night at my place?" pleaded the enfevered Baron.

---

1 Vidame, from the Latin *vicedomus*, was one of the more esoteric titles in the French feudal system, originally referring to an official appointed by a bishop to further the Church's worldly interests. The rank was equivalent to the secular rank of Vicomte, and was eventually absorbed into it; the character's retention of it would have been an anachronistic affectation even in life.

"Perhaps," the Comtesse murmured, softly.

The Baron offered her his arm, and they both advanced toward Adhémar, who was, indeed, the prey of the Vidame Hilarion, an old skeleton dressed in the antique style, finicky and passionate, who had been introduced to him by Monsieur Saint-Firmin, doubtless desirous of getting rid of him.

"Yes, Monsieur," he was saying to the young man, in a shrill voice, holding on to the lining of his jacket. "Yes, it's incredible, and yet I affirm it to you! I read it in a newspaper of the living, which had been forgotten near my residence, the inept opinion of one of their doctors regarding our modifications. Well, would you believe that the donkey with a soft brain and dirty skin dares to write that *they* don't exist! That they're a legend! That we disaggregate on our own without anyone undressing us! What stupidity! What impudence! What blasphemy! Does he think, that shameless idiot, that we're disposed to retain indefinitely the ignoble charnel burden that makes us resemble larvae like him! Which dishonors us as much as if we were wearing a rag! Which buries the nobility of your physiognomy, Monsieur, and will deprive us for a long time of the pleasure of seeing you! *They* don't exist! Truly, it's revolting! And do you know what they're doing at this very moment?"[1]

Adhémar started. Fortunately, the Comtesse, on the Baron's arm, arrived beside them.

---

1 This joke assumes a pun that does translate into English although the relevant terminology is less esoteric in French than in English, linking the insect larvae that devour the flesh of dead bodies to the "larvae" [ghosts] whose existence is denied by living skeptics.

"Come, come, Vidame," don't get angry." Madame de Talk had an ironic expression. "What is it now?"

"The living, Comtesse! The damnable breed that's always making things up about its superiors, and leaving infamous newspapers lying around in our abode expressly to insult us."

"That's of no importance," said the Comtesse, negligently. "Don't forget, Vidame, that we descend from the poor living . . ."

"Alas," groaned the Vidame, "it dishonors the dead, to be produced by the living."

"Bah!" said the Comtesse. "I don't feel dishonored, myself. And I don't deny at all what I was before coming here. But how are your charming daughters, Vidame? I don't see them this evening."

"My God, Comtesse, the older one was obliged to stay at home to keep my son-in-law company; he had a dorsal fluxion—I'm instructed to give you their apologies and regrets—but Adrienne's with me; here she is now."

And the Vidame indicated a young person of virginal appearance, whom Adhémar, his esthetic sentiments being strangely modified, found utterly charming as she came forward, gracious and, it seemed, blushing. The Comtesse kissed her tenderly on the forehead and sat her down beside her.

A conversation was engaged, becoming lively and animated. The Baron was the soul of it, by virtue of the finesse of his remarks and the witty charm of his repartee. Adhémar sat down next to the young Adrienne and, from time to time, made some banal remark to her, obtained at the price of a furtive emotion of which he was unable to take clear account. The child's timid and simple responses and the sincerity of her youthful voice, however, made an increasingly deep impression on him, and in his heart, wounded by the recent and cruel disappointment he had suffered, a kind of tender seduction blossomed, like a balsamic flower whose fresh perfume put pain to sleep . . .

There was dancing toward the end of the soirée, and when Adrienne placed the light bones of her little hand on Adhémar's shoulder, and when he felt, in the grip of his arms, the flexible vertebrae of a wasp-like waist fold softly, a strange intoxication invaded his entire being, and he shivered profoundly, agitated by a passionate emotion that the circumstances rendered very curious. Then, forgetting a great many things regarding himself and the world, just as he had once looked into the living eyes of his first beloved in search of her dream, he leaned tremulously toward the timid and troubling companion enlaced by his arm, and in the profound orbits, full of a great shadow unknown to mortals, he dared to pursue, with a bewildered ardor, a similar and new dream.

He thought he saw in that shadow a response to his desire; an immoderate joy saturated his feeble heart, and, abandoning himself to the whirlwind of unconsciousness that carried him away as the autumn wind carries away a willow-leaf, he murmured phrases passionately, which were no longer phrases of indifference but which strongly resembled, although they were more ardent, the phrases of love with which he had once captured, during his terrestrial interval, the heart of the girl with long hair and supple skin who had betrayed him, and whom he was betraying in his turn . . .

His tender words doubtless found some echo in the new object of his desire, for Adrienne, now, no longer dared raise her forehead toward him, which seemed to have reddened, and she trembled with emotion in his arms. Such symptoms delighted Adhémar and increased the strength of the sentiments as well as giving free rein, fervently and persuasively, to their expression.

However, the soirée was reaching its conclusion; the majority of the guests had already retired, and the final refreshments were being handed out.

"Tell me, Baron," remarked the Comtesse, who, while leaning on her faithful friend's arm, was observing with interest the smiling Adhémar and Adrienne, now sitting side by side pensively, exchanging long, troubled glances, "don't you think that your young relative seems rather taken with my young friend Adrienne?"

"But . . . it doesn't seem to me . . ." stammered the Baron, who had indeed noticed it, and was as astonished by it as he was annoyed.

"Come, come, Baron, there's no need to be disturbed by it," protested the Comtesse, mischievously. "It's perfectly evident . . . and it's very good. Your young relative is accomplished, that's obvious at first glance, and as for my little Adrienne, she's worthy, as you know, of being loved by a gallant man."

"Yes, certainly," murmured the Baron.

"She's as virtuous as she's beautiful," the Comtesse continued, "and has never lent herself to those girlish flirtations that sometimes go a bit too far. It's obvious that Monsieur de Léonce has made a deep impression on her. Anyway, here comes the Vidame—who, in spite of the habitual blindness of parents in these matters, must have noticed it. Isn't that so, Vidame?"

"Comtesse?" The Vidame, who was a trifle deaf, turned round.

"Doesn't it seem to you, as it does to me, that your daughter and that charming young man, the Baron's relative, are getting along very well?"

"Oh! So much the better! I don't mind at all, to tell the truth." The father, who had not noticed anything, seemed perfectly content. "She doesn't want to accept the homages of anyone, the silly girl, and whenever I press her to make a choice among her suitors, of whom there's certainly no lack, she refuses squarely, under the pretext that she doesn't love any of them, and wants to wait for the chosen one, who'll certainly come along. I no longer know what to do. If Monsieur de Léonce is the chosen one, I'll be delighted. He's the Baron's relative, and that says it all from the viewpoint of rank and fortune. I also remember that I knew his great-uncle, the general. Adrienne de Léonce! A fine name, to be sure! So much the better, so much the better! It's an embarrassment, you know, to have a daughter to marry off."

"Don't go too quickly," the Baron protested, seriously alarmed by the turn the adventure was taking. "Nothing's happened yet!"

"Bah! We'll fix an engagement tonight!" And the Vidame Hilarion rubbed his phalanges joyfully. "We'll go quickly and true—here, we know how to take advantage of good opportunities. We're not like those imbeciles the living, who use up their dirty little existence speculating about a future happiness that they never attain. We have the time to wait, and that's why we don't!"

Thinking that he had said something profound, he laughed like a creaky church door.

"Although," the Comtesse remarked, "Monsieur de Léonce won't be ready for some time. But I know Adrienne and the rectitude of her sentiments. That delay, far from diminishing her love, will increase it.

"Indeed, indeed—and it will be a great marriage," the father remarked, proudly.

Baron La Rose no longer knew what to say. "Permit me to go talk to Monsieur de Léonce," he stammered.

He went to join the amorous object of his concern.

Adrienne and Adhémar were still sitting side by side, their voices stifled by the timidity of passion, exchanging eternal oaths. Monsieur La Rose sent the young woman to speak to the Comtesse and took Adhémar's arm.

"My dear chap," he asked him, rather abruptly, "have you any idea what you're doing?"

"I'm in love," Adhémar replied, seemingly in the seventh heaven and smiling with interior joy.

The Baron was flabbergasted. "Word of honor, you're admirable! What! Two hours ago you were sobbing on my sternum because of your lost love, and I had all the difficulty in the world sustaining your despair, and now I find you smiling, drunk with joy, and when I ask you to account for the compromising follies you're in the process of committing, you reply: 'I'm in love!' with an ecstatic expression, as if it were the most normal thing in the world!"

"I didn't love the other one," replied Adhémar, calmly, still in the bosom of his enchanted dream. "I thought I loved her but I see now that I was mistaken.

Don't remind me about those moments of gross dementia. I've banished them from my memory forever. Adrienne, I adore! I adore her, I tell you! Celestial angel, river of delights, intoxicating soul, divine purity! I adore her! How feeble and insufficient that word is! You can't understand . . ."

"Naturally!" The Baron seemed furious. "Love, in truth, renders people idiotic. But have you thought about the person with whom you're in love, the unfortunate child? Have you thought about that?"

"I love Adrienne!" Adhémar replied.

"I know that. You've already told me that. But do you know what Adrienne is? Do you know that? She's one of us. One of us! Do you understand? Get a grip on yourself! She's one of us! And you're alive, damn it!"

"What does that matter?" the imperturbable and ardent young man replied. "I love her!"

"What does it matter? Word of honor, it's stupefying!" the exasperated Baron almost shouted. "It wouldn't matter at all if you loved her without her suspecting it—that wouldn't worry me at all—but it also seems that she loves you: that's the problem!"

"She's been kind enough to make that sweet admission to me," Adhémar replied, proudly. "That was a divine moment for me, and my happiness is complete."

"But what about the situation, wretch!" groaned the Baron. "The situation! Your situation! Mine! What are we going to do? What am I going to do? Me, who was mad enough to bring you here! Me, who's responsible for you!"

"You'll have no reason to regret it, Baron," Adhémar put in, with a noble expression.

"But what do you expect me to do? Think for a moment, will you? If I tell the truth—and how can I not tell it?—I'll be dishonored in the orbits of our entire society, which I've betrayed out of weakness for you. All doors will be closed to me, and I'll have to fight twenty duels with the Vidame and all his relatives. That's nothing, though—how will the Comtesse take it? What will she think of me? And that poor little Adrienne, whom you love! Who loves you sincerely, as her first love! Poor child, compromised by you! By a living man! With my complicity, for I'm an accomplice! What a situation! What am I going to do?"

"Tell the truth," replied Adhémar, tranquilly.

"Tell the truth! Yes! It's necessary! And without further delay. But what shame for me," murmured the Baron, disheartened.

"Not at all," said Adhémar, serenely. "Let's go!"

He shoved the Baron toward the group that had formed confidentially around the Comtesse and Adrienne, with the Vidame not far away.

The latter, on seeing the two friends approach, could not contain the delight caused in him by the thought that he was about to get rid of his daughter. "Very glad to see you, my dear Monsieur de Léonce," he said, coming forward and taking Adhémar's hand, which she shook cordially between his hard phalanges. Astonished, he remarked: "Why, how warm you are—and how your eyes shine!"

"That can be explained," Adhémar replied, politely. "Monsieur le Baron La Rose has something to tell you."

"Very good!" said the Vidame.

"Any communication on the part of Monsieur La Rose will be very agreeable to us," said the Comtesse, taking a step forward, while Adrienne, who seemed confused, stayed behind. Madame de Talk added: "In any case, my young friend has allowed us—the Vidame and myself—to anticipate what it might be."

"I . . . I don't think . . ." murmured the Baron, who had a light sweat on his forehead, so anguished was he.

"Yes, yes, I believe . . ." The Comtesse put on a cheerful expression. "Come on, Baron, speak—you can do so freely. All my guests have gone, and we're all family now . . ."

"Yes, speak, Baron!" said the Vidame supportively, striking the pose of a noble father—which, of course, he was.

"Oh well . . . well . . . I don't know how to confess . . ." Monsieur La Rose truly seemed to be suffering. "Well . . . I've betrayed you, Madame! I've betrayed our entire society! Monsieur de Léonce"—he pointed at the individual in question—"is alive!"

"Alive! O horror!" cried the Comtesse, with a spasm of disgust.

"Alive! One of those wretches among us! With my daughter!" roared the Vidame. "Baron, you'll reckon with me!"

"Alive! Him! My God!" sighed Adrienne, in a desolate voice.

That was the only one that Adhémar heard. He leapt forward to catch the poor child in his arms, as she sagged like a flower whose stem has been broken by a hurricane.

"Back!" cried the Vidame, launching himself forward. "No living person shall touch my daughter!"

"Calm down!" Adhémar, whose left arm was sustaining the fainting Adrienne against his heart, made a gesture with his right whose dignity imposed itself even on the furious Vidame. "Calm down," he repeated, with all the honest frankness of youth and with honor on his brow and in his eyes. "Alive? I certainly am! It would be bad form to deny it, and no lie has ever soiled my lips. I'm alive, but, if the Baron is guilty of introducing me among you, be sure that, in accordance with the grandeur of his character and his virtues, he has been guilty of nothing except nobility of soul and generosity. He has put his faith as a gentleman in a gentleman who is not undeserving of it, believe me! I am now alive, but that's of no importance, for right here and at this very moment, I shall cease to be!"

"What?" said the Comtesse. "You want to?"

"Generous friend!" cried the Baron. "I hoped so, but my delicacy forbade me to mention it to you."

"Good, young man!" said the Vidame, blowing his nose.

"My noble Adhémar," sighed Adrienne, who had partially recovered consciousness

"Angel," said Adhémar, with infinite tenderness, amorously pressing the charming child's flexible ribs against him, "Angel, to win you, it's the only thing I can do. Anyway, the sacrifice isn't one—far from it. I've had enough of life and its gross treacherous women! Here, I've found honor, love and friendship! I'm staying!"

"What joy it will be to keep you!" exclaimed the Comtesse. "Your entry among us is truly romantic, and you will do us honor, Monsieur."

"My friend, I weep!" The Baron kissed Adhémar on the cheek, and the Comtesse too, in the midst of his disturbance.

"My son!" And the Vidame kissed Adhémar on the other cheek. "Those imbeciles," he added, "wouldn't want to be alive any longer, if they could see the happiness we enjoy here."

"I love you," murmured Adrienne, so softly that only Adhémar's heart could hear it.

"Let's act without delay!" cried the intoxicated man.

"Perhaps it would be better if the ladies retired," the Vidame suggested.

"You can't be serious," protested the Baron. "It can't happen in Madame de Talk's residence. Propriety demands that it take place outside. We'll go out."

"Indeed," said Adhémar, utterly excited. "Let's go out!"

"*À bientôt*, Monsieur de Léonce," said the Comtesse, emotionally, to the young man. She added: "Let him go, my dear Adrienne," for the young woman, clinging to her beloved's neck, did not seem to be able to tear herself away.

"One kiss," Adhémar begged, holding her back. She allowed him to take it with a sob of delight, and the Comtesse drew her to her side.

"Is it going to hurt him?" whispered the tender child, in a voice full of anguish, as she let herself fall, swooning, upon Madame de Talk's clavicle.

"No, it's nothing," the latter stammered, supporting her, deeply affected herself and going pale.

※

Adhémar, Monsieur La Rose and the Vidame went outside. As morning approached, the fog had become glacial and its heavy folds were trailing like a livid crêpe. Adhémar shivered slightly.

"An old residue of the infirmities of that dirty life!" the Vidame muttered, between his false teeth.

They arrived at a comfortable bench at a little cross-roads that was entirely deserted, and sat down.

"What means are you going to employ, my dear friend?" asked the Baron, affectionately.

"I brought various different things," Adhémar replied, "for I had no intention, when I came here, of leaving again. The cowardly despair that drove me then appears very undignified and ridiculous now, but at least, in consequence of it, I have everything that I need."

He took out of his pockets a revolver, a dagger, several small phials and a letter. "This piece of paper," he said to his companions, "contains what the living call my last will and testament. In it, I order that I should be placed here, in a monument, in perpetuity. As I'm rich and have no close relatives, that will not encounter any difficulty." Speaking to the Baron in confidence, he added: "The world can believe, if it wishes, that I'm quitting life in despair, because of the little slut whom you know, but that doesn't matter to me."

"The opinion of the living is of no importance," the Baron declared. Aloud, he added: "With regard to your habitation, though, right next door to me, a little way from here, there's a property for sale. Specify, then, path D, number 28. It's very well accommodated, and will be perfect for a young couple."

"And order two coffins, lead and oak," remarked the far-sighted Vidame. "One sleeps better—but not quilted; it frays and makes one cough."

"Good," said Adhémar. He reopened his letter, and, although scarcely able to see it in the soft and livid light, resting it on his knee, he traced a few lines in pencil. When that was done he stood up, resolutely, but a trifle pale and shaky all the same.

"Now, friends, I'll become one of you!" he said, emphatically, putting the revolver to his forehead.

"Not like that!" exclaimed the Baron, grabbing his arm. "You're going to shatter your skull! Adrienne would be desolate!"

"Oh, of course!" said Adhémar, redirecting the weapon toward his breast.

"Be careful of your ribs!" remarked the Vidame in his turn. "It spoils the look if they're broken."

"What shall I do, then?" asked Adhémar, troubled, looking at the revolver as if asking its opinion.

"My dear chap, are you particularly enthusiastic to make use of that brutal and noisy implement?" asked the Baron. "I saw a certain little phial in your hand a few moments ago . . ."

"Poison?" said the Vidame. "That causes suffering, is rather disgusting and can go wrong. No—believe me, young man, employ the clean weapon—the dagger. That's the only one, you see. The pure and faithful blade of our ancestors! One slices through the heart frankly, and that's it!"

"You're right, Vidame!" the Baron exclaimed. "The dagger! It's noble, and one knows what one's doing!"

Adhémar unsheathed a charming little dagger with a sharp blade and a coat of arms on the hilt. "Do you think," he interrogated, with a slight spasm, "that I'll be able to do it? All alone? At the first thrust?"

"I'll gladly render you that small service," the Vidame proposed, hastily, taking possession of the dagger, whose point he tested on the first phalanx of his thumb.

"Choose the place carefully, and plunge it in with a single thrust, while I support our dear friend." So saying, the Baron stepped behind Adhémar. He told him: "We'll place your testament beside you, on the bench, and the groundskeepers will find you when they make their first round. We'll doubtless have the pleasure of seeing you again in two days, for you'll surely be put here provisionally."

"Let's get on with it—dawn's approaching," said the impatient Vidame, brandishing the dagger.

"Yes, let's get on with it," stammered Adhémar, nervously, whom the Baron was holding under the arms, firmly.

"With your permission, I'll move the garments aside," said the Vidame, unbuttoning the jacket and waistcoat. He took up a comfortable position and placed the point of the dagger on the uncovered breast level with the heart. "Whenever you please!" he said, with a courteous politeness that was not exempt from a certain unconscious ferocity.

The living man swallowed his saliva convulsively.

"G . . . go!" he said.

"Aah!" he groaned, having been obeyed, with a vain twitch and a final hiccup. "Aah—life!"

As he quit it, a cock crowed.

THE SECOND LIFE

by Charles Asselineau

Sic postquam fata peregit,
Stat vultu moestus tacito, mortemque reposcit.
Lucan.[1]

I

SINCE we are dead now and we no longer have any-thing better to do until the day of resurrection but tell one another stories until we are sated, O my dead neighbor, do as I do: sit down unceremoniously on your tomb and listen to my account of my adventures in the world of the living.

It will not amuse you very much, I fear, the first time, will bore you the second, and send you to sleep the third, but as I am menaced on your part by the same procedure, I beg you in our common interest to be patient. Know, too, that I have died twice, which gives me a definite advantage over you.

---

1 The quoted lines are from book six of the *Pharsalia*. An approximate translation is: "After he has thus revealed the Fates, he stands there glumly, saying nothing."

It is a beautiful night, although cool, and we no longer need dread catching a chill . . .

So, while our colleagues hold a conference up there on the hill, around the chapel, or lament the memory of their past amours and lost riches behind the yew-trees, listen, my dead neighbor, to how I drowned myself, the first time out of despair, and how, having returned to earth conditionally, I came to return by the same route after a short interval, to occupy the tomb next to yours, where I find myself so ill at ease between sunrise and moonrise.

My name, on earth, was ***. I was the issue of an aristocratic family, rich rather than comfortably off. I was young, since my definitive act of mortality gave me no more than twenty-four years of age. I was handsome, I was rich, and yet I was not happy . . .

You find that sentence commonplace, neighbor, I can see; have patience nevertheless, I beg you, for I intend to prove to you that, if my statement is vulgar, my woes were not.

Young, handsome and rich, it might seem that, in order to be happy, I had only to follow the ready-made pathways of life. Besides which, that triple advantage of youth, beauty and wealth had the particularity, in my case, of corresponding to the three principal vices of my nature: I was lazy, and was thus able to do nothing; I was vain, and was thus able to obtain vanity from my appearance; and finally, I loved living, considering the sunlight and idling in the woods and the streets with no particular purpose, and I had long years before me to devote to that penchant.

I do not know, my neighbor, whether, in the course of your existence, you have ever reflected—that doubt, of course, cannot be an insult on my part, for it has not yet been demonstrated to me that a man who thinks is worth more than one who conserved the virginity of his rational faculties—but at any rate, if you have done, have you not been struck by the utility of misfortune in human life?

The sage who first said that life is a battle was profound. There is in the life of every human being—have you not noticed it—between adolescence and the age of virility, a period of malaise and inertia, during which the faculties remain as if in suspension: belief being fixed and development accomplished, numbed thought evaporates is vague and sterile reveries.

It is, so to speak, a time of stasis, during which a man assures himself internally of his strength and seeks to anticipate the direction from which the enemy will come. Sometimes, he marches to intercept him; as soon as he perceived him, he runs toward him; the struggle commences, and life with it. Until then, he has only been vegetating, arming himself for the battle.

The inert bliss of Paradise was not a tolerable life—a human life, that is—and so our first father could not maintain it. To escape that stupid Eden he only had a hole as broad as a hand, still completely obstructed by menaces and maledictions, but he hurled himself into it, so natural was it for him to prefer a life of misfortune to that lethargic felicity.

If I did not fear scandalizing you, I would add that, in acting thus, he was only obeying the will of the Creator without knowing it. If the fall of humankind had not been intended by God, why did He not charitably attach the fatal fruit to the top of an oak-tree, instead of suspending it from the branches of a paltry apple-tree? But no! He wanted to give humans knowledge, and, moreover, the merit of collecting it themselves. Thus, in the Mystery of *Paradise Lost*, the serpent was merely an accomplice.

Be sure, by way of conclusion, that if all the evils if the world went back every year into Pandora's Box on the feast of Saint Sylvester,[1] it would be broken again, without fail, on the first of January.

But let us close the parentheses and resume my story.

Whence might misfortune come for me, surrounded as I was by all the external forms of happiness? I had but one resource, and that was to find it within myself.

At this point, my dear neighbor, permit me to interrupt myself and mark with an epic pause that solemn hour when life, true life, commenced for me.

You were, you have told me, a Parisian like myself; you must, therefore, have a memory of those pale young faces suspended on curved spines that you have often glimpsed passing slowly through galleries and along sidewalks. The laborer who brushes past them only sees their black coats, which are more expensive than his own, and which he envies. He is offended by the sterile fatigue of those mechanisms rotating in the void, and calls them: happy!

Oh, you are a thousand times happier than they are, who, at least, only have to struggle against visible and tangible objects—you, for whom every blow of

---

1 i.e., New Year's Eve.

the hammer is a conquest, and who go to sleep every night with your forehead bathed in the salutary sweat of labor!

Pale faces! Black coats! The livery of despair and impotence—oh, how well I know you! How many times have I exchanged a sympathetic glance with you! How many times has my elbow made contact with your fraternal sleeves! Our fathers have wearied us with accounts of Moscow and the Berezina; they have exploited the glory thereof usuriously. But no brush will ever retrace that terrible retreat from Russia, the frightful descent from Courtille, executed by a generation of scarecrows, casualties of thought: Prometheuses in dirty underwear, Sisyphuses in threadbare clothing. But what rock would not seem easy to roll to those poor souls, crushed for an entire lifetime between those two terrible cylinders, ambition and impotence?

I don't know, my friend, whether you have understood me fully; I doubt it. But in sum, I was one of them! I too had to hide the fox beneath my tunic, interrogate the walls with dull eyes, and demand an explanation from God of the inequality of my strength and my desires.

My clothes were perhaps less dilapidated, because I had the money to renew them, but what did that matter?

One friendship, one love, one hatred; that is the triple complement of every life. I had a mistress, a friend and an enemy: my good friend, my blond Schmidt, the painter; my mistress, Baronne Lydie, a coquette; my enemy, the pianist Gatien, an undistinguished and malevolent animal.

If, after that, you expect a love story, especially of ordinary love, you're mistaken. Among us, love only really has a place in life by virtue of the contingent sentiments it develops. For me, from the day when I fell in love with Lydie, it gave me for a rival and enemy the musician Gatien.

I shall do myself justice, neighbor, this being neither the time nor the place for coquetry. In truth, I was incomparably more handsome than that Gatien. He had a face like a kestrel, the eyes of a lobster, and the hands of an ox. Mine, incessantly rubbed with fine almond paste, were as white and smooth as those of a duchess; the oval of my visage was perfect, my hair abundant, my neatly separated eyes drowning in the line of my artistically-designed eyebrows.

Let us say, to complete the portrait of Gatien, that, according to the custom of his colleagues, he had in his fingertips the intelligence that honest men usually have in their heads. Personally, I dressed artistically, and had many things beneath my scalp that were not in Gatien's fingers. How many times, how many times, I said to myself: *If I were a Baronne, a pretty woman, and an intelligent one, well, I would want me for a lover!*

And in fact, by taking me, she would not have been too unhappy.

She wanted to be. I don't know what fatality caused her to be seized by the strangest caprice for that wind-up mechanism, that cylindrical bird-organ who dressed in the evening in a blue coat with gilded buttons and alternated the variations of Thalberg and Moscheles[1]—

---

1 The composer/pianists Sigismund Thalberg (1812-1871) and Ignaz Moscheles (1774-1870).

an inexplicable whim! Very often, during our morning walks, along the flowering avenues of lilac, I saw her soften at my words; her languid gaze seemed to say to me: "You're wittier than Gatien!"

But in the evening . . . oh, the evenings were fatal to me. The cylinder began to rotate and draw into its sphere of activity, as a mill-wheel draws a swimmer, the heart and thoughts of the Baronne.

One night I dreamed: I saw myself in a magnificently-illuminated drawing room, in the midst of a numerous company. Gatien and the Baronne were there. I was sitting beside Lydie and was playing, while talking to her, with the extremity of her sash.

Suddenly, there was a great stir in the crowd; Gatien was sitting down at the piano.

The Baronne swiftly withdrew her sash; *he* had looked at her!

My enemy spent some time over the preliminaries. His stupid face was blooming at the idea of the success he was about to reap.

He began—but from the very first measures a singular malaise took hold of the audience; everyone exclaimed; the most timid looked at one another. The instrument was not resonating!

Every key struck by Gatien rendered beneath his finger the dry and dull sound of a piece of wood struck by a hammer.

The bewildered musician tried in vain to struggle against that resistance: his fingers were clenched and splayed, his face contorted; but nothing! The most savant and most complicated scales only reproduced the strident noise of a craftsman at work.

Standing at the back of the room, I saw the heads of the audience swaying in a uniform and rhythmic motion, in a sign of discontent. The mistress of the house, a charming young woman with her hair bound in silken nets, went from one to another as if to stifle the murmurs.

Soon, the keyboard, still resistant, began to rise up, lifting the hands of the player to the level of his chin; a rumble like that of distant thunder emerged from the case of the instrument.

The swaying of heads became furious, and above that sea of moving skulls the gracious visage of Madame C*** floated, smiling and agitating her silken nets.

Gatien was still struggling. His face passed from the expression of the most vivid terror to the most grotesque grimaces. The least of them projected his nose and jaw forward, rounded his eyes and made two long hairy ears stick out beneath his temples, between which Madame C***'s head, still floating, came to settle, saying with a smile that showed off her mother-of-pearl teeth: "A donkey! It's a donkey!"

At that moment, I don't know what supernatural force transported me to the corner of the piano. Gatien had disappeared, and in his place I saw a stranger with a peculiar appearance, who said to me in bad German: "I'm at your orders."

Indeed, without my being able to explain how, there was a violin in my left hand and a bow in my right.

"*Geh!*" cried my accompanist—meaning "Go!"

I applied the bow to the strings. I played.

I played, Monsieur! Or rather, I sang, I spoke—for it seemed to me that the sound departed from my lungs to pass through the instrument. Soon, there was no longer any violin or bow; my right arm, passing over my left, executed scales and arpeggios. Remember that what I was playing was not music; I was speaking! The Baronne, Gatien, my love, my jealousy and my hatred could all be inferred from the impetuosity of the passion, the facility of the discourse.

Sometimes, I addressed tender reproaches to Lydie, reminding her about our pleasant walks in the garden of her house; sometimes I humiliated her, mocking her insensate liking for an animal of the vilest species; then I overwhelmed her by drawing myself up to my full height, and then I intoned, in the most elevated style, the hymn of heroic passion. And Lydie subjected successively to the empire of the sentiments that I expressed, sometimes she smiled at me tenderly, sometimes she sank down in humiliation, and sometimes she implored me with tears.

I continued thus for a long time; in the end, succumbing to the very violence of my emotion, intoxicated and delirious, I stopped and went back to my place, in the midst of frantic applause.

Lydie was waiting for me, delighted, tamed and suppliant. "Oh!" she said to me. "Love me; I love you; let me love you."

She loved me.

How can I describe the thoughts that assailed me when I awoke? Was that dream a premonition, a revelation? Or was it merely a bitter mockery of hazard?

I wanted to put my mind at rest on that score, and, in the days that followed, I devoured all the treatises on oneiromancy that I could find.

I paused at this passage from the *Symbolism* of Pernetius[1]:

"During sleep, the soul quits the body it inhabits and goes where it pleases. What we call dreaming is merely the vague and incomplete memory of that other life. It is thus that we glimpse, in sleep, countries that we have never visited. It is for the same reason that we remember having done, while dreaming, things that we know we have not done, but would doubtless be able to repeat tomorrow, if our memories were less incomplete and more precise."

Thus, if I could only render to my fingers the memory of what they had done the previous night, I would become in reality the virtuoso of my dream?

That idea never left me.

I told Schmidt about it one day, while he was sketching a charming landscape that I can still see.

It was, I recall, a beautiful day in April. A fresh and cheerful light inundated the studio; a bouquet of lilacs, set on the window-sill, was stirring in the wind, sending us a gust of perfume at every quiver.

Schmidt was working enthusiastically, his eyes ardent, his forehead damp and his lips moist. His hand was flying over the canvas, boldly and without hesitation.

"Schmidt," I asked him, "is what you are doing now very difficult?"

The question did not merit a reply.

"Do you think," I added, "that I could do as much?"

He smiled.

---

1 This author is fictitious; the thesis supposedly appropriated from him is presumably Asselineau's own invention.

I explained the theory of Pernetius to him then, and tried to prove to him that if, during the night, my soul had gone to inhabit the body of a painter, and had kept until the next day the memory of what it had been able to do, I would have found myself, on waking up, as skillful as he was.

Schmidt, as illiterate as the landscape painter and as positive as the dogged worker that he was, considered Pernetius to be a visionary and raised the objection of his ten years of labor, which, according to him, had not been a dream.

"But," I persisted, "although it took ten years to learn what you know, can you not imagine that, by concentrating the effort of those ten years into an instant, you would have been able to learn it instantaneously? How long would it take a mediocre individual to arrive at an understanding that Michelangelo realized in a moment? It is said that genius is patience, without taking into account that patience is merely what brings it into the range of the stubborn and the stupid. Genius is concentrated will."

I unraveled the metaphysical skein at such length that Schmidt, German as he was, ended up begging me either to change the subject or go away.

I went away.

But that conversation had changed the direction of my thoughts; it was no longer a matter of dreaming, or peregrinations of the soul, or of gasping a confused memory. Equilibrating the power of will, combining in a single supreme leap the effort of ten years, that was the problem henceforth.

And in fact, I thought, is it not ridiculous to believe that men, more divine for us than the gods themselves, such as Raphael, Columbus, Milton and Galileo could have found a corner of the universe into which their penetrating intelligence would not have been able to expand? What! Raphael, holding a bow and a violin in his hands, would not have been able to make use of them, when the meanest guttersnipe in Rome, after six months of study, could extract satisfactory chords therefrom!

Perhaps you will think that, from then on, there was only one thing for me to do: to buy a violin and use it to help me try out my theory? Oh, how wrong you are! The proof would doubtless have been easy, but it would have been decisive, and I was afraid.

I often caught myself, in solitude, taking the pulse—so to speak—of my will; and if in those moments I happened to find a certain degree of forcefulness, then, I'm ashamed to say, I got up, bent my left arm, extended the right, and performed in the void. A violin! But my love, my happiness, my vengeance, my entire life had passed henceforth into the violin; it had become the motive for my hopes and fears. Thus, I had the sentiment of superstitious distance therefrom that the negroes of Guinea have for their fetishes; the sound of one made my hair stand on end; the mere sight of an instrument in its case gave me vertigo; its rounded hips, its mocking waist and its cambered sternum moved me more violently than the Venus de Milo, posing before me alive and naked, would have done.

On the other hand, the Baronne, increasingly infatuated with her pianist, treated me more unkindly with every passing day.

And, as is logical, every day I loved her more.

One day, I received an invitation to an imminent soirée. As I had some reason to suppose that Lydie would be there, I decided to go.

But the note bore a postscript: *There will be music.* Gatien! Always Gatien!

By dint of reflection, I believed that I could see, in the fatality that incessantly brought us together, a provocation: a challenge that destiny was throwing down before me, to force me to put an end to it.

What was I risking, in fact? Had not the measure of my unhappiness reached its peak? I could not live without Lydie's love, and, in order to be loved by her, I had but one resource: to destroy in her mind the false superiority of my rival. The means to which I had recourse was terrible, and, in case of failure, there was nothing beyond it but death.

But what was living, save prolonging the nightmare against which I had battled for so long? Who could tell, in any case, whether the gazes of the crowd, the dread of mortal ridicule, in the presence of my mistress and my rival, were not so many obstacles necessary to exalt my will? I would therefore make the trial, before their eyes, before her, in public; there was the supreme peril; there, perhaps also, the supreme triumph.

Once the resolution was made, I entered into the state of sinister calm that precedes great coups. I watched myself living. I observed my most trivial actions with the interest that the final gestures of a dying man acquire. When the day came, I dressed myself with solemn slowness: the costume of the condemned! During the journey, I was astonished not to hear the noise of cavalry around my carriage, so strongly did it seem that I was marching to an execution!

When I arrived, the reception rooms were already full.

I searched for my Baronne with my eyes; a place was vacant beside her; I ran to it. When I sat down, it was as if I were thunderstruck by a singular revelation: the room in which I found myself seemed to be identical to the one of which I had dreamed some time before; everything, including the accidents of the lighting and the distribution of the groups, coincided with my memories. I even recognized certain faces that I was sure I had never encountered anywhere but in my dream. Finally, the place I occupied next to Lydie, and her costume, were the one that I had occupied and the one I had seen her wearing that night.

Did someone or something will it thus?

One last circumstance remained for me to verify before making a decision: was Gatien here? Would he come? Would he try to play, and would his pretention turn to shame? Such were the thoughts that were preoccupying me while my neighbor, astonished by the state in which she found me, and even more surprised not to obtain any reply to the remarks she probably addressed to me, considered me with a kind of dread.

Gatien appeared. I don't know whether it was the effect of my preoccupation, but it seemed to me that his face was pale, his countenance embarrassed. Nevertheless, he sat down and ran his fingers over the keys. Silence fell. Two or three times, my rival turned his gaze in Lydie's direction, and encountered my gaze every time, which caused him to lower his own.

It is certain that, from the beginning, he seemed out of sorts. Suddenly, as if abruptly taken ill, he interrupted himself and leaned over in his seat, murmuring a few words of excuse.

I stood up. An army general giving the signal to attack could not have been more emotional than I was; I too was about to deliver battle. I took three steps forward; everyone in front of me stepped back, as if I had the head of Medusa on my shoulders. The conjuration of hazard lasted until the end; the first object I perceived on approaching the piano was a violin deposited on its stand.

I seized it; I placed it on my breast. At that moment, I felt all gazes fix upon me. The emotion caused by Gatien's fainting fit calmed down.

I attacked, vigorously.

A cry of fright burst forth in the audience. I dared to continue—but this time the rumor was such that the instrument escaped from my hands and fell to the floor, rebounding with a groan.

At the same moment, an arm slid under mine, and, yielding to a strange impulsion, I headed toward the door.

Women fled in terror as I passed by. One of them, young and pretty, watched me leave with an expression of compassion, and I heard her say: "Poor young man! He's mad . . . what a pity!"

II

Mad? Was I, in fact? You will understand shortly why I can no longer have a clear idea of the meaning that people attach to that word.

The truth is that, for a certain time, I lost consciousness of my being.

When I came round, I was in the middle of the Place du Carrousel.

I perceived that I was bare-headed and that I was wrapped in an ample cloak, which I remembered having picked up as I passed through the antechamber, but which, I believe, did not belong to me.

I walked, I ran over the white dry paving-stones. In a matter of seconds, I had crossed the square, and I found myself on the bridge.

Dusk was extending its gray sheets over the quays and stifling the red lanterns of nocturnal merchants in their grease-paper globes; market gardener's carts were moving along, jolting noisily on their axles.

It seemed to me that it was a good time to take leave of the city and the world.

The Paris I knew, my own Paris, was asleep; the one that was still awake around me was as foreign as the people of Lima or Chandigarh.

I leapt up to stand on the parapet. A slight noise made me turn my head; it was the window of a nearby house opening.

The face of a woman appeared, still clad in soft white night attire.

By virtue of a supreme effort, my eyes could see her through the obscurity of the hour.

She was beautiful, and I think she was looking at me. I concentrated all the strength of the life that I was ready to extinguish in my gaze.

You, I thought, *who have been given to me to perceive me in my final moment, receive the adieu that I leave to this world that I curse, this life that I quit while loving it!*

And in less than a second, the sky of the most beautiful days, all that I had known and loved, was evoked in the darkroom of my mind:

Adieu!

I folded my arms beneath my cloak, which I tightened around me, and . . . *pouff!*

Glug, glug, glug, glug! The water resonated loudly in my ears. It seemed to see me and to be calculating the mass that I was displacing. Finally, the last breath of air that my lungs contained was exhaled, to go form magnificent circles on the surface. A wave penetrated my throat . . . and I felt nothing more until the moment when I found myself stiff and icy in my heavy garments.

I was in a dirty, low-vaulted room, somewhat similar, I imagine, to the antechamber of a jail or a morgue. A frightful lamp suspended from the ceiling projected a dirty glaucous light on to its oozing walls. All around the room was a wooden bench, on which I saw strange human forms in front of me and to either side, some rolled up in their clothes like me and others half-naked.

One, in particular, was horrible to see: the head was tilted back and the throat bore the trace of recent wounds, in which blood was coagulated.

After some lapse of time, I discovered that I was seated on the bench myself. Sitting, or posed—how? I did not know. I did not experience any contact. I was not suffering from cold or any pain. I was, instead, informed by an intimate consciousness that the vital heat had withdrawn from me and that my limbs were deprived of the springs that had once made them obedient to my will.

The eyes, which had conserved, uniquely, a little of their power, only existed now in the condition of a purely passive organ. The faculty of sight remained to them, but they had lost that of gazing. I mean that, like glass, they received the reflection of objects, but without the power to direct themselves or to express anything by themselves.

Then I noticed a singular individual leaning against a solid door, who attracted all my attention.

I was—yes, it really was—a man, or rather a giant, for he must have been no less than eight or nine feet tall. His broad shoulders, his thin limbs, his pale face—not the pallor of human faces, but of that matt white, arbitrarily tinted with pink and violet, that one observes on the masks of the drowned—and even his attitude, had something supernatural about them, which teased the imagination.

His costume, uniformly gray, narrow and tightly-fitted to the body, was cut off abruptly at the base of the neck, which gave him the appearance of a monstrous vegetable peeled at one of its extremities. His eyes, as red as an albino's, were fixed upon me with a bleak stare that fascinated me. I could no longer see anything but him.

At that moment, the sound of a rusty bell became audible at one end of the room.

The giant abandoned his nonchalant posture and called: "Number six!"

One of the bizarre phantoms next to me rose stiffly to its feet and headed for a small door situated opposite the first, which the giant carefully closed again as soon as it had gone through.

As he turned round, he attached his fixed stare to me again, slowly traversed the room and returned, without taking his eyes off me, to take up his post to my left.

Where am I?

These words were not articulated. I had lost the ability to express myself by means of sounds. Nevertheless, the giant had understood my question, and replied to it. I realized then that I was now able to express my thoughts without the aid of any organ; thinking and speaking had become identical processes. And it was in that fashion that a dialogue was established between the giant and myself.

I was—I am translating his reply for you—in the waiting-room of the clerk to whom all those dead by immersion would relate the voluntary or accidental causes of their death. That formality is a kind of investigation ordered in view of the last judgment.

The body is then sent back to float on the water in order to be collected and buried. That explains why the cadavers of drowning victims often remain submerged for a long time before returning to the surface.

The guardian—I shall describe him thus—successively indicated to me among the dead surrounding me an old man who had committed suicide for love, a young woman drowned by despair and poverty, and the wounded man I have already mentioned, whose throat had been cut by malefactors and had then been thrown in the river.

During these explanations, the giant had quit the door against which he had been leaning and had come to sit down beside me, his back rounded and his legs folded beneath him, his arms dangling, mechanically swinging a bunch of large keys with the negligent, amiable and teasing air that poor devils enslaved by tedious employments adopt during the intervals in their duty.

"You aren't wounded," he said, examining me attentively. "You bear no trace of violence or strangulation." He attempted to give his gaze an expression of commiseration, and added: "So you came here voluntarily? And so young! And your garments don't advertise poverty. If you had a wretched little fifteen-sou calico dress, like that unfortunate woman you see over there . . . oh!" He paused, and looked at me knowingly—and what a look! What intelligence! "You're in love?"

I tried to burst out laughing and was quite astonished at not having succeeded. Then I hastened to disabuse my interlocutor by telling him almost my whole story.

He seemed to be listening to me with interest, and I confess that I was not devoid of enjoyment at that small posthumous success. In fact, a man who drowns himself because he has been unable to seduce his mistress by playing the violin, without having learned to do so, certainly warrants some consideration.

It did not take long, however, for me to realize that what I had mistaken for interest was only surprise—less than that, stupidity. My listener had not understood.

I saw that the ideas I had expressed were colliding confusedly in his thoughts, without him being able to reconcile them.

"Music—making music? And if you had made the music, she would then have loved you, this woman?"

"I presume so."

"Well, you should have made some."

"I couldn't."

"Why not?"

I explained the mechanism of the violin to him and attempted to make him comprehend how difficult it is to make use of one.

"But who makes violins, then?" he asked.

"Men."

"And they can't make use of them?"

"They have to learn."

The giant seemed madly amused.

"Oh, a poor species! Crippled creatures! To speak, they need a tongue, to sing, they need a throat, to play the violin, they need fingers!"

"But you," I said, "can do all that without difficulty?"

"Of course," the giant replied, proudly.

"What! You can make music?"

"Of course! It's easy! Why, you, who have just rid yourself of all that mortal garb you call organs, are at this very moment infused by the science."

He was telling the truth!

"Oh!" I cried. "One year! Oh, to return to the earth for one year, knowing what I know!"

At that moment the bell recalled the guardian, who had to leave me again to call number seven; that was the last one.

I was already sufficiently accustomed to his strange physiognomy to notice, when he came back to me, that he was in a state of violent internal conflict.

He pulled himself together, visibly embarrassed.

"Listen," he said to me, directing all his will-power at me in his gaze. "You're an honest fellow; you're not like everyone else. In sum, you interest me; I like you, damn it! And then . . . so young! To deprive yourself, at your age, of a mistress and long years of pleasure! For I know that you had a long time to live; it's a harsh lesson. Would you be glad if it were possible for you to return up above?"

I wanted to shake his hand, but could not. "One year! One year!"

"There would be one condition—that would be to come back here by the same route." He lowered his eyes and added: "Otherwise, I'd be held accountable."

I completed his train of thought. On my return, the odd fellow would be proud of himself for having contributed something to my adventure: that would be his petty profit.

"Listen! Listen! You don't have a number. You were the last to arrive. No one knows that you're here. I can therefore send you back. But it's a matter of not dying of old age."

I promised; I promised with all the sincerity of my soul, and he was able to convince himself at a glance that I was not lying to him.

He therefore picked me up, made sure that there was no risk of our being caught, carried me away in his arms, opened the main door and . . . *hup!*

Again I felt the coldness of the water; at the same time, my limbs flexed, and . . .

I found myself on the sidewalk of the bridge again, safe and dry, in the very spot where I had made my final resolution.

It really was the same place, the same surroundings, but inundated with the rays of the rising sun, which dazzled me at first. To my right, the trees of the terrace of the Tuileries traced a line of verdure between the blue of the sky and the white of the wall. The gray waves of the Seine were speckled here and here by luminous dots, more luminous and closer together than the scales of a fish.

When I turned my head to the left, I had the puerile curiosity to search for the window at which the providential woman had appeared. The window was open; furry rugs were hanging on the balcony. It seemed to me that the room was empty.

Around me, the merchants were relaxing drowsily over their wares.

A few passers by were examining me, surprised to encounter a man in evening dress, without a hat, at that hour and in that place.

By my calculations, two hours might have gone by since the moment I had gone over the parapet.

But those mild sensations of awakening and life regained were soon succeeded by a more violent emotion, when I had collected myself. All my faculties, multiplied tenfold, were singing a hymn of omnipotence and genius.

I sensed in myself the Virtue and Faith that makes Columbuses and Galileos. My gaze overcame distance and pierced walls according to my whim; faces unveiled their souls to me. My ears immediately analyzed the slightest sounds. In a word, the universe revealed itself to me, no longer as a spectacle but as a system, whose laws and relationships I understood.

The novelty of my sensations delighted me. It was like a new birth, but in which intelligence enjoyed every manifestation like a conquest. Ten nights would not be sufficient for me to render you a full account of the surprises and the joys that I experienced in those first hours.

The first time I saw Lydie again—it was at another social occasion—and I remembered that it was for her that I had wanted to acquire a superhuman power, I was astonished. What I saw in her gaze made me indignant against myself. The recent events gave my re-entry into society a rather romantic interest. The word "madness," pronounced at my exit, had circulated. A servant in the house who had followed me, on his master's orders, had been a witness to my suicide. The silence that I maintained with regard to the latter event gave rise to the most fantastic suppositions. It was then assumed by everyone that, in a fit of madness, I had attempted to die, and that the Baronne's harshness was the cause of that resolution. Well, Lydie was charmed by that inter-pretation; that was what her first glance told me, and if that discovery had not led me to conceive an aversion to her, she mingled with it a desire for vengeance upon my thoughts of love.

That evening, Gatien, who was to be found every-where that I looked for Lydie, was playing as he usually did and with his customary success. I could not resist a desire to cool his joy. I sat down at the piano, and the originality of my improvisation left no memory of him but that of a technician.

My life's ambition was therefore satisfied; my dream was accomplished, for I did not doubt, given the success I obtained, that the Baronne's heart would pass to the victor.

Need I say that the triumph in question, by reason of the little that it cost me, seemed mediocre? Lydie was still beautiful, and I could not forget the sensations she had caused me. Each of the revelations that I extracted from her eyes, however, where the vanity of her heart and the frivolity of her mind were painted, diminished the prize of my victory with every passing day. In any case, what was the conquest of a heart that asked for nothing other than to surrender itself, to a being whose senses were reaching incessantly for the impossible?

Furthermore, the joys of triumph did not take long to be compensated by an intolerable torture; my organs, by virtue of the extreme sensitivity they had acquired, were offended at every moment of every day in the relationships that I had with human beings.

Thus, for example, the overture of *William Tell*, played by the orchestra of the Conservatoire, had the effect on me of a Carib concert; it tore my eardrums, irritated my nerves. Music, such as men had invented and perfected it, was for me an art in its infancy. To persist, as musicians still do to this day, in taking for the basis of tonality the seven notes of the scale, seems no less absurd to me than trying to calculate with four numbers or write with five letters. Seven notes! Why seven signs? Why not twenty-four, as in the alphabet, or nine, as in numeration?

Between one note and the next, my ear perceived entire scales. Every semi-tonal relationship embraced for me whole worlds of distinct sounds, which the human ear cannot perceive.

The first people to whom I tried to explain this contented themselves, by way of response, by repeating that I was mad. Two or three of the most knowledgeable scientists glimpsed something in the depths of my ideas, but, embarrassed by the difficulty of bringing what I told them into accord with their vulgar science, they concluded that if I were proved correct, it would not be for another two hundred years.

I did, however, find one intelligent listener of good faith; that was a German Israelite named Jeremias Klang. The man in question, having spent sixty years of life and a fortune in pursuit of metaphysical phenomena, was delivering himself in a garret to the quest for a new musical synthesis. He came to see me.

In that first conversation, he declared to me that what I had revealed to him was what he had barely glimpsed during his entire life, and that, if I were not mad, I was certainly a supernatural genius, for I had just revealed to him the absolute in music. A second interview completed his enthusiasm; I had all the difficulty in the world preventing him from kneeling down before me. He begged me to accept him as a disciple and to permit him to be the first to write and publish everything I told him.

I held science in too much scorn not to consent to what he asked of me. He therefore came to my home every day, and every one of our conversations formed the basis for a pamphlet, in which my pioneer predicted the advent of a revolution in art, which would shake the Conservatoire and the Institut to their foundations.

The torture that I mentioned soon rendered my sojourn in Paris intolerable; I then decided to buy an isolated pavilion at one of the extremities of the Bois de Boulogne, and to retire there with Jeremias, the only person who could now understand me.

However, I had become famous, thanks to the singularity of my adventures, the apocalyptic publications of Jeremias and the facility with which I improvised on instruments of every sort. That varnish of renown, which I had not sought, was like birdlime, in which the eccentric Baronne allowed herself to be caught. She did more: that woman, so haughty and so vain with regard to her beauty, who would have required you to count it a favor to kiss the fingertips of her glove, did not hesitate to give herself ostentatiously to me, by following me to my retreat.

Even though she made me thereby more envied than my manifest genius could ever have done, I was scarcely touched by that step.

That woman, ruining herself in order to obtain the right to be the sole lover of an artist in whose future she had faith, seemed to me as contemptible as one who would have surrendered herself for money. She understood that, and fell into a depression—but neither her tears nor her submission could vanquish the scorn that I had conceived for her; I relegated her, like a sultana, to the depths of my apartment, where I avoided even meeting her, and spent my time in the intimate company of dear Jeremias.

He never wearied of hearing my talk and writing to my dictation. The night served him to redraft the chromatic scale according to my new principles.

According to his calculations, he still had ten years to live, and that was more than he would need to complete his revolution. In a hurry to put it into execution, he begged me one day to compose a symphony.

The task was too easy for me to refuse it.

I therefore set to work. In spite of the improvements I had made to tonality we were obliged to invent a new system of notation (and for that, Jeremias' former studies were a great help to us).

While I worked, he observed that the music, as I had written it, was impossible to play with the customary instruments. It was on innovations of that sort that he had once spent a part of his fortune. He therefore persuaded me to establish a factory in the vicinity whose direction he would take on. Fabulous products came out of it. There were gigantic double basses that could only be played by means of a mechanical device, and miniature violins so small that it became extremely difficult, while playing, to position the fingers.

Jeremias took the opportunity to supplement his factory with an academy, whose pupils were educated in his method.

My family was disturbed by these enterprises. Thus far, my madness, in being madness, had seemed tolerable; it was, at any rate, a quiet madness—but when they learned that my mental disorder was going as far as to involve me in expenses of construction and exploitation, they became alarmed.

Singular rumors came back to me, according to which it was a question of nothing less than forbidding me. I treated it as a joke until the day when a deputation of my relatives presented itself one day at my home to remonstrate with me, for my own good. I had no difficulty proving to my excellent parents that the employment I was making of my fortune did not deviate from legal conditions. I ended up disconcerting them by translating their own thoughts to them, word for word—which, most of the time, contradicted what they were saying. They retreated, somewhat disappointed, and I heard no more mention of it.

Since he had become the director of the workshop and a professor, Jeremias was obliged to go to Paris on a daily basis to make purchases and deals, and a thousand other concerns. One morning, he left, according to his custom, and did not come back.

That absence had already lasted for four or five days when I saw Schmidt, the painter, arrive one evening. He was the only one of my old friends that had not made it necessary for me to send him away in disgust; I held him in high esteem, for never having found his speech in discord with his thoughts. The sublimity of his soul had raised him more than once to the level of genius, and although, for want of understanding, he often remained my adversary in the frequent conversations we had together, I can say that he was—after Jeremias, of course—the only person who had suspected something of the truth.

The conversation came round, as usual, to esthetics.

"Alas," Schmidt said to me, finally, after having listened to me for some time, "perhaps all this is too much for us; perhaps, by dint of raising yourself up, you have lost yourself in the impossible."

Then, making allusion to my recent discord with my family, he complained that I was making myself incompatible with all society.

"How can I not regret the state in which I see you," he concluded, "when I think that the only man who has been able to understand you is a lunatic?"

And with that, he showed me a legal document signed by a commissaire of police, which stated that J. Klang, having been arrested while haranguing passers-by on the public highway, had been recognized as a patient escaped from Bicêtre Hospital, where he, the commissaire, had had him interned once again!

Schmidt—even the best of men is not exempt from an atom of egotism—smiled as he showed me this authentic document, which seemed to him to win the cause of his argument over mine.

"Mad!" I cried. "Jeremias mad! Jeremias at Bicêtre? So the only one that I have encountered among you truly possessed of intelligence, knowledge and genius, you humiliate, depriving him of his liberty? Oh, it's because the proximity of genius is dangerous for you, limited minds, monsters who believe that you possess the secret of nature and don't even know how to depict its surfaces. Go denounce me to the police, then! For if Jeremias is a danger to you, I am even more so. He's not half as mad as I am!"

And I shoved the stunned Schmidt out of the room.

Schmidt's visit was prolonged, and it was late when I said goodbye to him.

Left alone, I gradually fell into a profound depression. What good had this knowledge acquired by despair done me, which had increasingly hollowed out a void within me ad around me? The only person in whom I might have been able to take an interest had been stolen from me. I had learned to despise glory;

love had gone too, along with faith and illusion. Finally, the man I had just chased away from me was my best friend.

I found myself alone once again with myself, with no other compensation for so much loss than a power without object. What would I do henceforth? What remained for me to do that was better than going to fulfill the promise I had made to the one who had resuscitated me?

I thought once again about Lydie, and for the first time, since I had begun to live again, my heart melted.

I got up, took a torch, and headed quietly for the room in which I had abandoned my conquest.

She was asleep. The scorn that I had expressed for her had damaged her health; her face, once so beautiful, had suffered. Poor woman! She had loved me as much as she had been able to do; was it her fault that I had wanted to force her to give me what she did not have, and that I had made a crime of an ambition by which anyone but me would have been flattered?

Young and beautiful, she might still be able to be happy, to bring happiness to another; was it not just to set her free?

I went back to my study cautiously and sat down to write to poor Lydie, to inform her of my resolution. I ended by advising her to marry Gatien.

That done, I went out of the house and headed for the river.

It was almost the same time of day as when I had taken my leave of life the first time, except that, as it was August, the night was warmer—which diminished the merit of the enterprise slightly.

I remained seated on the shore for some time, interrogating myself, trying to discover in the depths of my heart some regret for the life that I was about to quit—but my heart held nothing but ruins; I struck it hard; nothing emerged but a sigh.

I had, therefore, nothing left to do but to close my eyes, fold my arms and abandon myself to the current . . .

Neighbor, the daylight is chasing us away. The cock has crowed; let us go our separate ways. Tomorrow it will be my turn to listen. Try to make your story less tedious than mine, but just as instructive.

Another fourteen hours to spend beneath that frightful stone!

Until tomorrow!

A DESCENT INTO HELL

by Judith Gautier

ONE day, the beautiful Miou-Chen awoke from a long sleep. She was in a wild forest, lying on lotus flowers; a tiger the color of jade was asleep at her feet.

While she scanned her surroundings with a surprised gaze, she saw a young boy with shiny brown skin coming through the trees, who was carrying a flag that was flapping in the air and brushing the foliage.

The child approached and, setting the flagpole on the ground, bowed to her.

"I have come to you by command of the Lord of the Hells," he said. "The great Jade King admires your wisdom, and if your courage is unfailing he will consent to let you pass through the gate of the terrible city of Fou-Tou-Tchan and visit his realm."

Miou-Chen rose to her feet without trembling, and gazed at the narrow strips of blue sky through the dark foliage.

"Wherever I am, so long as my virtue does not weaken," she said, "the Master of Heaven will protect me."

"Come, then," said the boy, lifting up his bloody banner. "The King of the Ten Hells is waiting for you at the golden bridge of Pou-Tien."

He cleared a path through the branches noisily, and Miou-Chen followed him.

They emerged from the forest and entered a solitary valley. After having walked for some time, Miou-Chen perceived a man sitting on the ground at the entrance to a cave, and stopped in surprise, for the man was surrounded by a band of demons who were attacking him, while scorpions scaled his body. To his left were beings with the bodies of leopards and frightful faces, stirring red-hot chains and shaking furious serpents. A frightful she-devil, her breasts pendulous, her head shaven and her muscles stripped of flesh, was holding a frog by the foot, and was jiggling it in front of the victim's eyes, laughing stupidly and toothlessly. To his right, two young women of superhuman beauty, magnificently ornamented, but allowing foxes' tails and deformed feet to be glimpsed beneath their robes, were displaying the gleam of their beautiful smiles and seductive gazes, while their rosy lips murmured soft words.

Miou-Chen said to the King of the Hells' envoy: "Who is that unfortunate man?"

"That man is the sage Ma-Min. The great Jade King has sent his devils to tempt him."

Then Miou-Chen drew nearer to the sage. "O Ma-Min," she said, "I see your immaculate thought rising from your forehead like a vapor and forming a glorious cloud that will raise you up to the realm of the immortals."

Then the young woman continued on the route toward the Hells. She arrived in the province of Sée-Tchoen, and reached the golden bridge that ends at the Gate of Hell. As she was about to cross it, she was forced to retreat by a tumultuous host of men and beasts, which was running from the other end of the bridge.

As she stood there, astonished, her young guide said to her: "You see here those who are returning to life in a new form. These superb kings were once poor and virtuous; these deformed beggars were once full of pride; these reptiles crawling and hissing have been envious and crafty men; these birds were young fools with light and careless hearts; as for that herd of donkeys rushing and braying, they're mostly former functionaries devoid of probity."

When the noisy troop had drawn away, Miou-Chen went over the bridge and found herself in front of the arched gate—yellow, like an imperial gate—of Fou-Tou-Tchan, the Severe City. To either side of the entrance two demons, one with the head of an ox, the other with the head of a horse, were posted as sentinels; a third being, the color of soot, whose head was made of iron, was sweeping the threshold. As the young woman approached it drew aside and the gates opened. She went in; the two heavy battens closed behind her, with a plaintive clang.

She went along the broad streets of the City of Justice, following the crowd of the newly dead, whom soldiers were driving toward the Palace of Supreme Judgment. At the corners of the crossroads she saw, along with heaps of useless debris, old torn-up account-books and instruments of torture worn out by over-use and no longer good for anything. Further on, however, active blacksmiths were hammering their anvils and twisting iron.

The boy who was guiding Miou-Chen went into the hall of a vast palace, and the young woman followed him. Then she perceived the Jade King on his throne. She admired his head-dress fringed with pearls and his face, the color of a ripe orange, exhaling honesty and equity. Facing him, on a platform, stood the ultimate tribunal, where the great judge Loun-Yo was seated, beneath two banners flamboyant with stars, assisted by numerous servants riffling through and setting in order the dossiers of the summoned dead. All around the hall were the mandarins of Hell: Fou-Chou, the bearer of the three-pronged lance; Pen-Tchan, the gourmand, the pou-sah of good cheer; Ti-Tsan, the priest of the infernal cult; and Ta-Tcha, the nocturnal spy who records insomnias and criminal dreams.

The Jade King bowed to Miou-Chen and said to her: "Would you care, young woman, to descend with me the seventy-two stairs of Hell?"

She made an affirmative gesture and the king got up from his throne. Then Miou-Chen saw a yawning gulf in the middle of the hall, and the first steps of a stone stairway. The king began to descend; she followed him, pale and trembling, and plunged into the heavy darkness of Hell.

Soon, howling and sobbing rose up like a bitter wind. The young woman saw a precipice beneath her, populated with serpents, dragons and furious monsters; a narrow bridge traversed it, guarded by the demon of that hell, assisted by a warrior with the head of an ox, bearing a placard one which was written: *Good and Evil.* The damned were driven toward that bridge and, stumbling, full of terror, they fell, with cries of horror, into the gaping and avid mouths.

"This is the first region of penitence," said the king. "You can see the ambitious, the cruel and those swollen with pride."

And he continued the descent.

She then saw a pale and motionless demon sitting on a throne of ice, its body covered in snow, and, as if caught in crystal shackles, the reddened heads of condemned individuals, whose teeth were chattering with a sinister sound, passing at regular intervals over the hard surface of the pool.

Miou-Chen wept, and her tears froze on her lashes.

"These men are the avaricious and the implacable rich, who allowed supplicant mendicants to die at the doors of their palaces," said the Jade King.

They reached the third hell, where women attached to stakes were being tortured. Several demons with bloody bodies were tearing out their entrails and replacing them with hot coals, then sewing up the skin again.

"Those are adulterous wives. Let their guilty entrails be subjected to burning remorse."

And the king plunged on toward the fourth region. There was a vast sea of blood therein, in which a host of men and women were fighting, while the gondola of that hell's devil sailed its thick waves. The devil in question was entirely clad in white and wore an immense conical hat on its head. When the damned approached to climb into the boat, it gouged out their eyes, ripped out their tongues, and writhed with laugher as it repelled them with kicks.

"You're witnessing the torment of debauchees and women of loose morals," said the king. "That white devil is Ti-Fan, who presides over storms."

Miou-Chen went down a few more steps and saw the fifth hell, the floor of which is paved with trenchant blades, over which the demons cause iniquitous judges and calumniators run incessantly.

The sixth hell was the most terrible. The devil that ruled it, with his one-eyed face the color of ebony, bristling with red hairs, was the most redoubtable of devils. Under his orders, the damned, imprisoned in wooden troughs are slowly and methodically sawed by toothed implements.

On penetrating into that region, Mious-Chen sighed, and put her hand over her eyes, but the Jade King said to her: "Don't groan like that, young woman, for these men are parricides."

They went rapidly down the lugubrious stairway and reached the seventh hell, where the victims were howling in boiling oil. They were poisoners.

The young woman, her heart full of sadness, shedding floods of tears, arrived in the eighth circle, and saw that an enormous cutlass, rising and falling, was slicing the bodies of thieves and murderers into a thousand pieces.

In the ninth infernal region iron mills were crushing arsonists, while furious dogs were licking up the blood and tearing shreds of flesh from the victims.

She finally reached the last of the ten hells, where the teeth are broken in the mouths of liars and their tongues are torn out with red-hot pincers. There, she threw herself to her knees and, wringing her arms, cried: "A-Mi-To-Fo!"[1]

Then, lost in ardent prayer, she remained motionless for a long time.

Then, slowly, a rain of lotus-blossoms descended to the ground; from circle to circle, the demons' cries of rage were heard, and the sound of instruments of torture breaking; the damned, delivered from their suffering, intoned songs of joy, the sound of which flew toward the western sky.

Miou-Chen is venerated today in China and Japan, under the name Kouanine or Kouan-Chi-In. She is the Goddess of Mercy.

---

1 "O Great Buddha!" [Author]

THE MAGNETIZED CORPSE

by Jules Janin

WITH regard to good stories, here is one that was told to me by a trustworthy man, who claimed to be the friend of a friend of an eye-witness who played a significant role in the drama that I am about to relate to you briefly, not without making the ardent wish that the story in question might be honored before long by an adaptation for the theater—which is, as everyone knows, the greatest honor that can be desired nowadays.

Not six weeks ago, a young Englishman named Belfort was dying, quite simply from a bad chest and a few crazy years recklessly spent. The young man, although he was nearing the end, did not regret losing his life too much, for he had had his fair share of amours, duels, bad debts, picnics, and even fine sermons—in short, his fair share of all the Parisian joys.

One of his friends, a man of science but a good enough fellow regardless, seeing that Charles Belfort would soon render his last breath, came to say to him, in his softest voice: "If it wouldn't displease you too much, my dear invalid, I'll use my abilities to magnetize you, and I'll choose the moment when you render up your soul; it seems to me that it will be a fine experiment, and that there's nothing about it likely to displease you. What do you say?"

"Not only doesn't your experiment displease me," the other replied, "but it seems to me to be very amusing and interesting, and I thank you for having thought of me for the proof, which will be decisive. Count on me, my dear doctor; you'll be content with my patience, I hope, and I'll be sure to let you know when the moment comes."

With those words, the two friends shook hands and separated, saying that they would see one another again soon. They were both full of hope, and it would have been difficult to decide which of the two was the more content, the moribund or the magnetizer.

Two days went by—two centuries—while the magnetizer waited impatiently for the final agony, which did not seem to want to arrive for good and all. The dying man, for his part, lost patience, and he said to his friend: "Damn it, my dear chap, it's not my fault if death is treating me with such ill-will, but what consoles me is that you won't lose anything by waiting, and I'll be a magnificent subject."

On the night following this conversation, the sick man had a final crisis and fell into a comatose ecstasy; he started sketching fantastic spider-webs with his finger, and yet, in the midst of the most abominable grimaces, he still had the presence of mind to say to his comrade: "You have to lift my head, to hide the light that is hurting my eyes."

The other obeyed. He propped his moribund up in a sitting position, took away every importunate light and set about the operation; which is to say that never, absolutely never, had such beautiful passes and counter-passes—the whole customary apparatus, in short—been performed. The magnetizer was in the swim; but in the end, when he had enveloped the moribund—who lent himself to it with exemplary willingness—with his all-powerful fluid, and saw that his subject had arrived at magnetic perfection, the magnetizer started to interrogate him.

"How are you doing, Belfort? Where are you?"

"My dear friend," the other said, "I'm just dying; you've caught me just at the moment when the breath was leaving my body, and now it depends entirely on you to let me finish the job or to keep me here, suspended between being and non-being, which doesn't seem to me to be a disagreeable state, so far."

"Let's wait," said the magnetizer. "There's no hurry, Belfort, my friend." And with that, the magnetizer went to dinner, without taking the trouble to demagnetize his friend.

The next day the maker of magnetism reappeared in the mortuary chamber; everything was in its place, including the cadaver.

"Belfort," said the scientist, after a few preliminary passes, "what have you been doing since you died?"

"In truth, my dear chap," the dead man replied, "I've been obliged to follow you everywhere you went."

And with that, the dead man told the living one everything that the latter had done the day before: he had dined in a cheap eatery, and from there he had gone to stand on the steps of the Café de Paris; he had been given a ticket to the Vaudeville and he had seen some young women who were pretty enough, but some of whom sang out of tune; finally he had gone back home, and read a little of a novel that he had picked up on the way.

"And if you'll permit me to make an observation," the dead man said, "so long as I'm attached to you by a thread that only you can break, eat better, I beg you, remembering that I'm sharing the experience. You know that I like music, so don't expose me to hearing quavering voices that would spoil the most beautiful faces. All alone here, I'm getting bored, and I wouldn't be sorry if you were to read a good novel from time to time, but at least, for pity's sake, read it all the way through. Finally, if you please, don't go to bed so late; I become irritated not sleeping, because for twenty-four hours, I ought to have been sleeping eternally."

With these words, the man slumped back, and the magnetizer left the room, slightly discomfited by the strange spy that was dogging his heels.

The next day, the living man came back, and found his dead man a trifle numb. He warmed him up with a further dose of magnetic fluid, rendering him, if not life, at least a little color and the ability to speak.

"Ah!" said the dead man, raising himself up. "You're not showing me any charity. What! You go to see such hideous sick people, and I have to hear them coughing, spitting, howling, moaning and all the rest! In the street you follow a horrible woman reeking of musk, a woman in old shoes and a dirty skirt, and I have to keep you company counting the holes and the stains of the filthy creature! Then you go to meet up with some young people, and you tell them about your good luck! You make the streetwalker into a duchess, and a cotton apron into a silk skirt! When you're dead, you know, lying makes you feel ill. And what makes you feel even worse, when you're dead, is stupidity—some quip that would have made me laugh when I was of this world appears to me to be utter nonsense now that I can hear your mind with the ears of my own. So try to talk better my dear chap, and, if it's all the same to you, I'd be obliged if you didn't get drunk on adulterated wine; my throat's been torn apart by the alcohol you've swallowed."

Who do you think pulled a face? It was the living man, who was beginning to think that his dead man was damnable hard to please—because, after all, the previous evening's indulgence hadn't been deserving of such scorn. As for the lady with the worn-out shoes, the living man hadn't noticed the shoe, but only the foot and a little bit of the leg. However, he was fond of his dead man, and he resolved to keep a better eye on himself, in order not to give poor Belfort further reason for discontentment.

When he came back two days later, he found the deceased in a state of incredible excitement. The dead man was sweating copiously, with indignation legible on his distressed face.

First of all, the magnetizer set about trying to calm that anger; he blew his most soothing breath upon those irritated nerves, and appeased that motionless and frozen heart as best he could, which beat in memory.

"What is it, Master Belfort? Who has upset you? And for God's sake, what's the matter with you?"

"What's the matter with me?" replied the cadaver, after a long pause. "What's the matter with me, imbecile that you are? A curse upon the brazen threads that attach me to a fool like you! What's the matter with me! But my dear chap, for two days you've been going from one stupidity to another. The day before yesterday, it's true, you were well-groomed and well-dressed, but you'd fastened your belt too tight and I nearly choked. Your boots—or, rather, our boots—were well-polished, but they were too small, and if I could still walk, I'm sure that I'd be limping with my right foot.

"I've nothing to say about the lovely salon to which you took me; it was pleasant and it was calm; the clothes weren't at all garish; the mature ladies kept to their place, leaving the foreground to the young women; no one played the slightest sonata or read the slightest sonnet; people only spoke in even voices, neither too loud not too quiet, and said the nicest things—trivial but light, benevolent and sonorous. In brief, had it not been for your belt and our footwear, I would have blessed you for having taken me to such a beautiful place. But good heavens! Could you have been any more gauche, maladroit and absurd?

"In a corner of the little room to the left, a more beautiful woman than I ever saw with my mortal eyes was sitting; by dint of attention and will-power, via your terrestrial intermediation. I had attracted the benevolent interest of that amiable lady; already she was looking at me with a certain tenderness, and she was about to smile at me; our two souls were no longer any

135

but one, and we were about to fall in love, when you turned your head like an idiot to greet I don't know what starchy spirit. Then the image of my beautiful lady fled, and if you live for a hundred years you won't find either another face as beautiful or another heart as noble.

"Idiot that you are, having done that, what do you do next? You know that I've left some glaring debts, and that I don't even have a tomb. You haven't a sou yourself; you live from hand to mouth; your rent hasn't been paid and never will be; in brief, you're as poor as a poet and an actor rolled into one—which is to say, abominably poor! Well, you sit down at a card-table, tremulously risk a wretched pistole, and, having won the hand, you pocket the money and run away like a thief!

"Now, do you know what you did there, Monsieur Idiot? You renounced getting your hands on a round sum of four lovely thousand louis d'or, for you'd have won the next thirteen hands, my son! With your four thousand louis you'd have had a carriage and I'd have had a first-class funeral. You'd have had a new suit and I'd have had an embroidered shroud. You'd have gone to seek your supper in the chorus of the Opéra, and I'd have gone to look for Monsieur Gannal.[1]

"Damn your feeble intelligence—you can't make use of what little sense you have, but you amuse your-

1 Jean-Nicolas Gannal (1791-1852) was the pharmacist and inventor who founded and developed the modern techniques of embalming in the early 1830s, winning the Prix Montyon three times by virtue of the benefits thus provided to human society. In 1837 he obtained a patent for his embalming fluid and set up a commercial laboratory in the Rue Saint-Hippolyte.

self dragging another man's intelligence around with you. Go away—you make me sick, wretched living individual that you are!"

When our magnetizer finally understood that whatever he did would surely attract criticism or sarcasm, he fell silent. Now that he felt that he was being followed and observed at close range by some invisible entity that he had retained on the boundary between the two worlds, the scientist dared not take a step in the street; he scarcely dared answer yes or no to the simplest questions that were addressed to him; it was as if he were deaf and dumb. At times he wondered whether he might be the magnetized man and the magnetizer that great motionless—but not speechless—cadaver, the mere sight of which had ended up making him shiver.

An idea, a thought, is such a powerful thing, even independent of life! An idea pursues you, obsesses you, more tenacious than a shadow, as eloquent as remorse or hope, full of starts, excitations and perils!

However, our man went back to his friend Belfort three days later. This time, once again, a great change was evident in his inanimate face; pure and simple scorn had replaced indignation and anger. The half-closed eyes seemed to be saying: "Away with you!" The tight lips were expressing an indescribable disdain. Every muscle, taut from top to bottom, held a contempt suspended from every thread connecting it to the soul.

"What's the matter now, my friend?" cried the living man, "You seem dazed. You can't say this time that I've done or said anything stupid, because I've stayed at home, alone, entirely given over to my thoughts."

"Oh, my dear fellow," the dead man said, "it's the contemplation of your thoughts that's giving me nausea. Motionless as you were, I was forced to look into the depths of that chaos you call your soul. But what kind of animal are you to occupy yourself with so many ignoble, frivolous and shameful things? When I was alive and I called you my friend, everyone said that you were a gallant fellow; you had a reputation for keen, even eloquent wit; you were credited with philosophy, probity and tact.

"For three days, unable to help it, I've been watching you very attentively—but my dear fellow, you're a complete mess! What you know, you know poorly; what you don't know, you replace with words as empty as your head. Your generosity is a certain organic weakness that ends up making your eyes red, and that's all. Your intelligence is represented by a few mechanical cog-wheels that rotate of their own accord like the wheel of a water-mill incessantly repeating the same tick-tock. Your courage—I've seen all the way to its depths, your courage!—is a cardboard mask that frightens children. Your probity—let's talk about your probity!—is written in the margins of the commercial Code and the penal Code.

"Shame upon your vices, those of a badly brought-up child! I wouldn't give four sous for your vices; they make me sick, your wicked shameful vices: they're like a kind of boasting! As for your virtues, they're so worthless I wouldn't even give them to my lackeys; there's something limp and vain about your virtue, which bears some resemblance to a badly-cooked broth. Oh, I advise you not to lay bare the inside of your brain and your heart—it's not a pretty sight, although, on the other hand, it's very sad.

"And what ideas you have about other men! What thwarted ambitions! And I don't envy your work at all, my poor sir! What! You aren't ashamed, even of your castles in Spain, when you amuse yourself rambling on for entire hours in petty daydreams?

"Anyway, Monsieur, let's leave it at that—but I'm damnably sorry that I ever called you my friend!"

It would not have taken much on this occasion for the magnetizer to destroy his work and liberate himself from the unwelcome thought that was obsessing him. He left the mortuary chamber in a very bad mood, and on the way home he said to himself that it was, after all, quite an accomplishment to have stopped Belfort's discontented soul half-way.

Then again, the living man said to himself, sadly, *what good has it done me to have retained that dead man in the edge of his grave? To have myself told such rude home-truths, to hear the story of my everyday life told in such a cruel and grotesque fashion, no longer to be alone with my conscience, my thoughts, my ambitions, my self? If the clairvoyant that sees everything were, at least, to indicate some unknown science to me—a remedy for the gout or some hidden treasure easy to extract—I'd be rewarded for my troubles, but no! For having carried out the most difficult task, the most excellent miracle that magnetism has ever accomplished, here I am dragging behind me a bilious inquisitor who isn't content with anything, and who'll end up making me disgusted with myself.*

Thus the clever man reasoned; he was very annoyed, and firmly resolved to put an end to his dealings with such a miscreant, no matter what it cost.

As he was unable to sleep, the magnetizer went back to Belfort's house that same evening, at midnight.

Belfort watched him come in, and without waiting to be interrogated—for the magnetic fluid becomes, it seems, a habit, and replaces life as a well-lit candle replaces with winter sun—the dead man cried: "I'll tell you what you've just done, amiable doctor! You've quite simply decided to murder me! Yes, you're jealous of this artificial life, you're furious at my revelations, and you've decided to extract me abruptly from magnetic sleep in order to return me to dust and silence!

"That's handsome of you, Monsieur, it's glorious, what you're doing, coming to murder . . . a dead man! Coming to trouble a cadaver in his coffin! Attacking the thought of a man because the man, having become, thanks to you, a part of eternal life, is no longer able, and no longer wants, to flatter you!

"Well, get on with it, then, and turn me to dust— but that dust, when you've cast it to the wind, will summon to its aid another, bolder thought, to follow in your tracks, another gaze, even more clairvoyant, to read the depths of your soul, another avenger, even more implacable: remorse!"

At these threats the magnetizer fled, but, in his distress, he left the door ajar.

The neighbors of both sexes, who had initially kept their distance, took the chance, one after another, and finally all together, of coming to greet and interrogate the dead man, and picked up, here and there, some of those fine verities—I mean a few of those eternal, ever-living truths—that only the dead know how to voice appropriately. Husbands, wives, children, tenants, owners, masters and servants, the rich and the poor, all the way to the porter, each obtained a parcel of justice addressed to them.

The dead man spoke true words and expressed true notions, and what he said was, admittedly, cruel. If you asked him where fortune lay, he would point out a wart on the end of your nose; if you mentioned ambition to him, he would talk to you about modesty, economy and bonhomie. The female neighbors found him so ungallant that they slammed the door violently.

That was all that the late Monsieur Belfort wanted.

A week went by without the magnetized and the magnetizer seeing one another again; they were sulking, but it was obviously not up to the dead man to make the first move. The scientist finally understood that, and came back to his subject's bedside.

"I've thought about everything that has happened," Belfort said to him, "and I'd be glad if you were to carry through the plan you made the other day. You're right: wake me up, so that I can finish dying quietly. It had made such a good beginning, when you came along to disrupt it, that I'd already be devoured by worms and returned via the thousand pores of universal decomposition into the ocean of life and light. Wake me up, then, and I'll die entirely—and joyfully, for, this time, I'll amuse myself by gazing, not at your soul, which isn't beautiful, but at your body, which is very ugly.

"Only the other day—I caught you in that agreeable occupation—you were telling yourself how fortunate you were before, but please, where are these women who can look lovingly at an ape like you? You're badly-formed; you always have one shoulder higher than the other, this one over that one or that one over this one. Your hair started falling out a long time ago, and what's left is hanging on to rotten roots, like last year's thatch after the winter. Your eyes can still see, but I can see some sort of pellicle extending over your line of sight that doesn't augur anything good.

"Oh, if you could see those layers of yellow chalk encrusted in the joints of your fingers, which are corrupting your bones and are going to break them bit by bit, like the boot of torture, but more slowly, more insidiously and with a more obstinate verve!

"Your heart is swollen, my dear chap, and the point is being torn by some viscera or other that is wounded in its turn. Your left lung isn't much better than my right lung. Gradually infiltrating between your skin and your softened tendons I can see layers of thick fat which makes you resemble some sort of sea-cow. Your teeth are already turning yellow; they're loose in their bloody cavities. In your brain I can see veins swollen with apoplectic blood, ready to burst. You're doomed, you see, and—give me your hand—you're dead!"

On hearing those lugubrious words, the magnetizer begs the magnetized for mercy, pity and forgiveness. And, in order to free himself from the vision that is obsessing him, to expel from his mind that voice, which is pursuing him with such bruising stubbornness, in order not to remain exposed to that mockery and those prophecies of misfortune, the magnetizer sets about countermanding the magnetic fluid and destroying that artificial life.

The dead man resists, but in vain; it is necessary that a corpse, which is dead, should yield to a man who is still alive.

Gradually, the voice fades away. It utters one last gasp, and then Belfort, so eloquent a little while before, is no longer more than I don't know what, that which I don't know how to name in any language . . .

It was, in fact, for three weeks already that death had had possession of the cadaver, and now the magnetic breath had ceased, corruption and the worm took hold of their prey again and did not let go.

One shivers at the mere idea that the magnetizer might have died before having demagnetized his friend Belfort. How long eternity would have seemed to the latter then—unless his thought, obedient all the way to the abyss, or to Heaven, had followed the soul of magnetizer.

That would be another trial to attempt!

ASSURED SURVIVAL

by Paul Vibert

I

The soul-ticket. Means of conserving the will.
A psychological colombarium.
A new branch of the science of electricity.

I have already explained here, in detail and peremptorily, that what we call the soul is nothing, in essence, but a fluid akin to electricity, and how it will be possible to do away with travelling in the future, when one will be able to hire the body of an individual for a day or two and install one's own soul—which is to say, one's own individuality—by cable in a foreign carcass, in exchange for a modest remuneration.

Those are givens, and I shall not return to them. Having perfected my system, however, and thus being able to perceive what will happen in the future, I think I can be sure that I have finally resolved the problem of survival, which is so irritating and, at the same time, so flattering—especially for those who have lots of money and are annoyed at having to quit so soon what is only a vale of tears for those who haven't a sou.

All spiritualists and all spiritual people admit that the soul, that imponderable fluid, is immortal and survives our bodies, just like the electrical fluid, which is the very agent of the universe.

Now, this is what I have imagined in order to give pleasure to rich people and the curious, and, fundamentally, what I shall be able to realize scientifically. In the dreams of their profligate imagination, our forefathers desired it before me, for, all things considered, it's nothing more than a new and tangible form of the legend of Faust. As a clientele, I'm certain to have that of all the rich people who are afraid of dying, and all curious individuals who would like to know what will happen on earth in a hundred, two hundred, five hundred years or more—for the soul-fluid is something that can be conserved, and does not decompose in bottles.

So, a great nobleman says to me: "I'd like to come back to the earth in a hundred and fifty-one years"—the exact figure doesn't matter.

I reply: "This is the tariff: a thousand francs a year. First give me a hundred and fifty-one thousand francs."

Then, by an entirely new scientific procedure that I shall leave in my will to the Académie des Sciences, but which I shall be permitted to keep secret for the time being, in order not to deprive me of my means of existence, I shall commence by removing, very gently, without any danger, a portion of his soul-fluid—which will, in any case, renew itself very quickly—and I shall store it, condense it and conserve it, if I might put it thus, in an *ad hoc* flask.

I shall conserve souls thus, as life, voices and movements are literally conserved today by cinematographs, phonographs and thaumatropes.[1]

Needless to say, all this will be done seriously and appropriately, and when a joint stock company has been set up to construct a palatial building, I shall arrange all the souls in a psychological colombarium.[2]

When that is done, I shall give my client a receipt—a futuristic birth-certificate, if you wish—which I shall call a soul-ticket; which, in order that it will not be lost, will be deposited in the office of a notary who will have a special section in his minutes for this kind of operation.

Now it remains for me to explain the purely material side of the operation. It's quite simple.

I shall return to the example of my client, who has deposited his soul-fluid in my psychological columbarium and has given me a hundred and fifty-one thousand francs.

First I keep half for myself and the expenses of the upkeep and supervision of the columbarium. Of the other half, half of that—which is to say, a quarter—will be given to the notary for the conservation of the soul-ticket in his archives. The other quarter is deposited in the Banque de France, with the natural compounding of interest—which will be a tidy sum

---

1 A thaumatrope is an optical instrument for illustrating the persistence of vision, by means of which two rapidly alternating images seem to fuse into one.

2 The substitution of an *o* for the more usual *u* in *columbarium* emphasizes the reference to a dovecot (i.e., a set of pigeon-holes), but the Latin *columbarium* was a metaphorical adaptation of the term to a vault with recesses in which cinerary urns were placed.

in a hundred and fifty-one years. On that day, the titular notary then in charge will easily be able to find parents who will surrender the body of their child for that tidy sum, for they will be enriched in their turn by the procedure, of which I alone know the secret, but which I shall bequeath to the Académie des Sciences. My client's soul-fluid will be decanted into the body of the young child, and my client will return to the world, with his soul and his personality, after a hundred and fifty-one years.

Note that, if he wishes, he will be able to stipulate a preference for being the tenant of a man fifteen, twenty or thirty years of age, in which case the contract will be made directly, the notary offering the sum.

The problem of survival is, therefore, victoriously resolved, in a very simple fashion, very easy to carry out. Understandably, however, it will always be expensive, and only within the range of very rich people, for it will be necessary for my client—still following the same example—to deposit a sum of money in the Banque de France on his own account, at compound interest, which he will be able to access after a hundred and fifty-one years, when he returns to the earth. Someone who only wants to return after a hundred and fifty-one years, though, given the compounding of interest, will not have to lay out a very considerable sum.

I'm aware of the objections. Firstly, of course, it will require new legislation to permit the Banque de France and notaries to engage in operations of this kind; secondly, who can tell whether there might not be upheavals during such a long lapse of time, and whether banks and notaries will still exist? Obviously, that's only human, but with all those *ifs* and *buts* one would never achieve anything great, and would always remained encrusted in routine.

Admit, though, what a joy there would be in being able to return at will to the earth, after a century, or two, or ten, in feeling oneself again. What a joy for the curious, for the scientists who would observe the progress of humankind, what intoxication!

But that's not all, and I shall indicate in the next chapter the fecund consequences that will inevitably stem from my discovery.

II

Different means of transmission. A new honeymoon.
Various schemes within the range of rich people.

I have said that it will require new legislation to authorize notaries and the Banque de France to do what it necessary to fulfil the indispensable formalities; that's understood—but taking responsibility for all this material red-tape cuisine, if I might put it thus, would surely require great establishments analogous to our present-day life-insurance companies, which could offer you the most varied and interesting schemes.

I don't want to cite them all, but, for example, rich men who do not care about the expense, and who are happy at home, could arrange to include their wives in the scheme, in such a manner as to return to earth at exactly the same time, after two or three centuries; and those who are extremely rich will be able to commission the company specifically to have their wife-soul reincarnated in a younger body. Those who fancy a change, by paying a further price for the expenses of the correspondence, would be able to have the ineffable joy of comparing different carnal envelopes and ensuring the survival of their spouse, at a fixed date, in a black, Japanese or Chinese woman.

It goes without saying, of course, that, should the occasion arise, one would be able to offer the same truly regal gallantry to one's mistress, if one had the misfortune still to be a bachelor.

It seems to me that there's no need to go on; the benevolent reader will have understood me without it being spelled out, and there's no doubt that the establishment in question would be able to offer its clientele the choice—if, again, I might put it this way—of schemes infinitely more seductive than those presently imagined even in New York.

It now remains to elucidate a very serious point, with regard to which I humbly confess, in spite of all my research, that I have not yet settled—although I may say, at present, that everything seems to permit me to hope for a happy solution.

The point is, in fact, grave, delicate and interesting. This is what it amounts to: can a man, if he wishes, retain his soul-fluid in his way in order to be reincarnated and live again in a woman's body, and a woman in the body of a man? It's obvious that this would be infinitely more interesting, from points of view as varied as they are different. Suppose momentarily that a man of Zola's stripe were to find himself thus returned in the body of a woman. The great psychologist, having analyzed the sentiments of man, would be able to analyze those of woman—after a certain lapse of time, it's true—with equal sincerity and self-knowledge . . . which is invaluable if one wants to write pages on our poor humanity that are sincere and truly lived.

Once again, however, I repeat, I am continuing my research and I have not despaired in the least of vanquishing this difficulty. It would not generate a true Androgyne, since the phenomenon would only be produced in time, successively not simultaneously, and in the long term—but what a world of marvelous speculations for a thinker, a philosopher, an attentive and resourceful observer. How interesting it would be, for instance, to know from experience to which sex it is more amusing to belong, during the divine moment in which two souls exchange a supreme kiss!

I don't want to deflower the subject; nevertheless, it might be permissible for me to observe that, if I arrive at this superb and definitive result, my discovery will be perfect . . . and when I say that, it's not out of a sentiment of misplaced pride, but simply because I believe, with a very clear and precise consciousness, that in recent years I have taken a huge step forward in this interesting field of the physical and natural sciences concerned with the two mysterious agents, still misunderstood at present, but which rule the universe nevertheless: the material-electrical fluid and the soul-electrical fluid—which is to say, the moral fluid.

That is the future, and I shall be happy and proud if I have been able to cast a little light on the ardent and passionate researches of science in this respect.

THE DEAD MAN'S DREAM

by Gaston Danville

THE orders, which were very strict, were followed to the letter, and in spite of their attempts, journalists, students and curiosity-seekers were unable to gain entry to the autopsy room.

In the four corners, four stone tables are set up, extending their mocking gray mass, corroded by brown ulcers, like antique altars. They are exceedingly old, and the soft friction of the cadavers that have lain upon them has varnished them with a patina, as shiny as that distinguishable in the depths of crypts, on funereal paving-stones on which too many people have knelt down. The middle of the room, the chalk-whitened walls of which only reflect the shady light traversing the narrow, barred windows overlooking a garden, which is ornamented in spring by clumps of periwinkles and hollyhocks, is cheered up by the splashing of a fountain whose droplets form a miniature cascade in a shiny metal bowl.

Only the theater assistant was with me, actively occupied, while smoking a short-stemmed pipe, in making a collection of various calculi, which he had carefully sorted out in a tinplate box. Collecting those little stones was his hobby, which he picked up at hazard from abdomens, in the environment of coiling greasy intestines, as one picks up shiny pebbles or nacreous seashells among wet brown tangles of seaweed. Silently, he arranged them, expelling puffs of blue smoke at regular intervals, the acrid odor of which corrected the indefinable and insipid odor floating in the semi-darkness.

After having consulted my watch, whose hands disappointed me by virtue of their slow movement, I allowed a sharp exclamation to escape, expressive of my impatient annoyance. Then he deigned to quit his macabre task momentarily to say to me, after having inspected the sky covered with a diaphanous mantle of morning mist: "He can't be much longer, Monsieur. They must be making casts, and they'll bring him along shortly."

Then, shaking the ashes out of his mouth-burner, he set to work again, methodically.

The overly long wait was aggravating me, truly, and the contemplation of the tables, and the vulgar fountain, with which I was equally familiar, only offered me a mediocre distraction.

The Imaginary then came to my aid, transfiguring the dismal space and real basement; was I not in some temple consecrated to a grim divinity, which demanded a quotidian tribute of human victims, and was not the hour about to sound for the sacrifice that I, as the high priest, would carry out?

And, in fact, Science, which I was honored to serve in a humble capacity, could easily be represented as that august, mysterious and powerful Idol, since she commands thousands of intellectuals—and not fictitious ones, but people living amid suffering and dolorous labor, shedding blood and tears every day for her, a demanding deity who only delivers her secrets to initiates! How many individuals have prostrated themselves fruitlessly before the Goddess as mute as the sphinx, and died as fervent martyrs for having known her? And as the generations, all ephemeral, have passed away, drunk by the soft sand of Oblivion, she has raised herself up on the fecund alluvia brought by those human waves before they disappeared.

A slight shadow of melancholy was beginning to invade me. I therefore experienced a joyful relief when I heard heavy footsteps approaching and blows shaking the door. I opened it precipitately.

They threw *him* carelessly on to one of the antique blocks, where he rendered a dull thud as he fell, comparable to that produced by a forceful blow with a linen-beater on damp cloth.

He seemed to be very short. The porters stepped back.

"What about the head?" I asked, not seeing it.

"It must be there, Monsieur," replied one of them, untying the bloody sheet.

In fact, it had been placed under his arm.

"Like Saint Denis after the decapitation," said the smiling theater assistant, who was sometimes inclined to be facetious. Becoming serious again, he rolled up his sleeves.

The corpse of the guillotined man had not yet been overtaken by *rigor mortis*. Warm, supple and robust, the muscles causing bulges in the skin—scarcely splashed in places by a red spume that emphasized its vivid flesh-tint—he lay in a calm and confident attitude, with a beautiful purity of lines; one might have thought him an exhausted wrestler, if the atrocious impression caused by the absence of a face and the scarlet furrow sectioning the neck had not recalled the hideous evidence.

Banal, saddening considerations concerned with the fragility of our existence assailed me in spite of my frequent anterior relations with death. It is true that the majority of the corpses on which I had operated had succumbed after the weakening effects of a slow disease or had been overtaken by accidents that had mutilated them. Others, those of old men, shriveled, thin, paltry, debilitated or deformed—all of them, in sum—presented themselves marbled with the red, green and purple patches of putrefaction, already no longer bearing much resemblance to human form, while *he* was only an hour old . . . and an infinitesimal fraction of a minute had sufficed to annihilate his vigorous health, his athletic strength and snuff out his life like a candle-flame.

Now, with the ribs broken in a triangle and chest sliced open, where I rummaged between the faded pink lungs to reach the heart, the invaded carcass only made me think about the skinning of some strange animal in a butchery.

While my assistant slowly extracted the marrow—a difficult operation at which he excelled, bringing it out

154

of the vertebrae delicately, as one extracts the succulent flesh from a lobster's claw, I picked up the head of the executed man.

Completely exsanguinated, it was horribly pale, the violet lips thick and sensual and the eyes open, fixed, the blue-green irises tarnished by a thin mist what opalized their transparency. A silky brown tint circled them. I held it in both hands in order to examine it: the enormous frontal sinuses, the nose with a thin deviation in the middle and the protrusive inferior jaw gave the face a bestial appearance completed by jutting cheekbones; all those characteristics formed, by their combination, an accomplished criminal type.

I took a knife that the assistant handed to me and was getting ready to cut through the hairy scalp, in such a fashion as to lay the skull bare before sawing through the bone to reach the brain, when a bizarre noise, composed of articulate, albeit very faint sounds, a buzz of confused words, stopped me.

Surprised, I looked around; the only animate being accompanying me had his mouth closed, and in any case, the timbre of the voice was unknown to me. It seemed impersonal, extra-human, emanating from the very things that it evoked; it was soft and, I should say, perfumed with terror: that expression almost renders the sentiment I had at the time, for it appeared to me that the voice was caressing me with a sepulchral odor, a mixture of incense and putrescence, and a breath of fear.

I do not frighten easily and have never had hallucinations; at that moment, however, I began to doubt myself and my mental lucidity. I felt a vague dread that made my pulse beat faster and squeezed my throat painfully. Certainly, I confess, I was afraid—a crazy fear, giving rise to a desire to flee—and I almost dropped the murderer's head on the floor in that moment of abrupt terror.

Nevertheless, I mastered that sudden panic and, my mouth dry and my temples burning, feeling my heart hammering tumultuously in my breast, I listened to the voice.

At first, I could not make out anything precise. The syllables flowed, stifled and guttural, without the clear pronunciation that would have permitted meaning to be attached to them. They succeeded one another rapidly, reminiscent of the susurrus of the fast-flowing springs that one sometimes encounters in forests, hidden beneath moss and leaves. At the same time, I thought ironically that it was impossible, utterly impossible, for a head, on the one hand, separated from the larynx, and, on the other, a hand deprived of the blood indispensable to its functioning, to express ideas that it ought no longer to have; and I mocked myself for my credulous attention in trying to grasp some scrap of a sentence more clearly.

However . . . you will certainly have found yourself, sometimes, in the course of a heavy nightmare, suddenly transfixed, as it were, by an abrupt, horrible paralysis preventing any action, which robs you, in the presence of an urgent, immediate danger, of any means of self-defense. It gives rise to an immense breathless anguish, and then a plunge into darkness and an awakening.

For me, the scene happened exactly like that.

The thing that I was holding between my fingers disappeared, or, rather, dissolved in my consciousness along with my own personality. I had the impression—imprecise, to be sure—that I was penetrating into that strange, desert soul, annexing the perceptions, ideas and images abandoned by the other, for whom I substituted myself by means of a sort of taking possession of his former habitat.

Was I *him* or *me*? Perhaps both at the same time, and not doubled; at any rate, I did not ask myself the question. That ambiguous way of being, that equivocal state of mind will doubtless appear to some to be illusory, deceptive and implausible; let it suffice for me to recall that all I am doing now is transcribing, as faithfully as possible, the impressions I had then, without analysis or criticism.

Soon, I sensed an obscure, latent danger threatening, from which I could not run away. My pupils dilated in vain, trying to pierce the darkness, to divine the monstrous peril crouching, lying in wait, protected by the lugubrious opacity that surrounded me, and my lungs inflated extraordinarily in the attempt to relieve the burden of anxiety oppressing them.

A time of transition, empty, for my memory can find nothing therein.

There was, afterwards, the inevitable imminence of the fatal term. I had the intuition that no benevolent, tutelary, charitable force could withdraw me from it.

A square extends, cold and sinister, bordered by leafless trees whose branches establish a network of perforated lace, an extremely fine guipure, beneath the sparkling train of the firmament, dressed with bloody roses and jonquils, brushed by the luminous caress of the breaking dawn. Coral clouds drift over a pearl-gray sky toward golden archipelagos; in the distance, the far distance, tall houses, washed with grayness, with mauve slate roofs, licked by the pale carmine of the rays of the rising star.

On the far side of the empty space, an agitated crowd, noisy and censorious, presses, groaning, behind the lined-up horsemen, sabers held high, speckled with glints; a crowd that I cannot see, but of whose presence the rumor rising from that barrier of guards is sufficient indication.

Why are these human forms dragging me? I don't want to . . . No, but . . . I can't succeed in getting rid of the tight cords that are binding me.

Ha! My gaze collides with a machine that I recognize: two shafts framing a shiny triangle. At the same time I sway, precipitated forwards, and I feel the impediment of a rigid and icy collar around my neck.

The blade is taking a long time—or are these seconds counting double? I'd like to collect myself, to obtain one last lucid, solemn thought before the final moment . . . everything is floating, indecisive, fluid in my head, which is about to fall . . .

However, naïve and candid images now pass by—with an inconceivable rapidity that does not exclude a complete precision of detail—of my actions as a little child, trivial episodes dating from my infancy, their insignificance magnified and retained, young faces and the primitive landscapes forming them.

That revivification of exceedingly ancient memories radiates like a spray of bursting skyrockets, a constellation rapidly eclipsed.

An indefinable sensation of emptiness follows a violent impact on the nape of the neck; I can clearly perceive the absence of my body, and the strangeness of that observation frightens me.

The black splashed with red and the red striped with black beneath my eyelids, palpitating with an irrepressible flutter . . . a remembrance of the most recent impression, the bisection of the cutter slicing through the marrow, drilling me with a shrill dolor . . . all that survives of the final collapse.

Here there is a period of absolute, complete unconsciousness, following which, progressively, I descend once again into myself; a soft warmth, an infinite wellbeing, reanimates me, penetrates me, and I rediscover myself in my laboratory, pouring orange liquid over a brain placed in a crystallizer.

Surprised and frightened, I look around attentively; everything is in its place and there is no possible confusion. That microscope is mine; I made use of those bottles yesterday. How, then, did that incursion into a strange soul, that transfusion in which I must have run through once again the emotional phases preceding his death, not interrupt all my actions?

What has happened?

I have interrogated my assistant. He did not notice anything at all abnormal about me. I persist; he maintains his reply. He has seen me continuing the necropsy, taking the anatomical specimens and return to the building where I now am, in order to place them in the customary solution to harden.

It's true, then! A part of my being applied itself to its occupations, while another relived a terrifying agony.

Well, yes! That funereal phantasmagoria, coexistent with multiple tasks, although not necessitating an intelligent collaboration, is possible; and, after due reflection, I ought not to be so surprised, being aware of cases of that sort, having observed them, and knowing their mechanism.

Even so, an anxious astonishment pursues me; I resemble a man whose knows the geography of a country perfectly, from having read exact topographical descriptions of it, and who finds himself transported to the place itself; I believe that, in spite of his anterior notions, he would nevertheless feel out of place.

And I catch myself doubting that singular dream, searching for fearful and superstitious interpretations.

I shall take a bromide this evening.

DOCTOR Z***'S AUTOPSY

by Édouard Rod

For myself, knowing nothing and holding dreams in doubt,
I believe that after death, when union is achieved,
The soul then recovers clarity of sight,
And that, judging its work with serenity,
Understanding without obstacles and explaining
without difficulty,
Like its sisters in heaven it is powerful and regal,
Measures its true weight, knowing manifestly
That the breath, falsified by the false instrument,
Was neither glorious nor vile, not being free,
That the body alone prevented equilibrium;
And calmly, it resumes, in ideal bliss,
The holy equality of the Lord's spirits.
Alfred de Vigny, "The Flute."[1]

PERHAPS you will still remember the noise made in the scientific world some thirty years ago by the discoveries of Doctor Z***, which suffered the fate of many discoveries and were universally denied. When

---

1 "La Flûte" was first published in 1843.

he finally decided to publish the results of his patient research, Dr. Z*** was living in Bordeaux, where he enjoyed the renown of a good practitioner. The pamphlet for which he bore the expense, *Observations on Some Phenomena of Cerebral Existence*, provoked a general outcry, and he gradually lost his clientele.

It should also be said that the pamphlet in question—an octavo of about a hundred and twenty pages—overturned all received notions, simultaneously threatening by its indirect consequences science, morality and religion.

In effect, the physiologist claimed that the life of the brain is not extinguished at the same time as that of the body; that, on the contrary, it continues for a period that varies between seven and ten days after the last sigh—except, of course, in cases when the brain itself has been directly attacked by a disease, as in meningitis, encephalitis, general paralysis, softening, ataxia, etc.

He went further than that; he affirmed that, while during life the cerebral cells consumed by thought are incessantly reformed, they are irrevocably destroyed after death, with the result that the brain, still intact and fully active when the heart ceases to beat, although already detached from sensation by the wastage or weakness of the inferior nervous centers, gradually declines in that final labor.

A good technologist as well as an excellent chemist, Dr. Z*** constructed an apparatus himself—which, so far as I can remember, bore some resemblance to the instrument invented more recently named the photophone[1]—with which he was able, for four or five days

---

1 The photophone, involving the transmission of speech by means

after death, to track the activity of brains in the process of decomposition.

He destroyed that instrument, as he burned his records, when he saw that no one believed him, that the most indulgent were treating him as a madman and the rest as a charlatan. Nothing, therefore, remains of his great work, and when science has finally deciphered the enigma of death, no one will be able to tell whether the obscure practitioner from Bordeaux was a pioneer or a trickster.

For myself, who knew him, who saw him at work, who listened on many an occasion, in his laboratory, to his conversations full of luminous perceptions, his reasoning, departing from the most scrupulous observations to rise to the heights where thought can finally detach itself from the tyranny of facts, and his deductions, all the links of which were connected by the most rigorous logic, I have always regarded him as one of the beacons that ignorance and human stupidity too frequently take it upon themselves to extinguish, for fear of seeing the darkness of their routine illuminated.

I do not intend to explain Doctor Z***'s theories at length here, not to recount his personal history. That might be instructive, but it is, I think, appropriate to leave it in the obscurity to which fatality has relegated it, and to which he resigned himself without difficulty. But it was given to him once, to read with absolute

---

of a beam of light, was invented by Alexander Graham Bell and Charles Sumner Tainter in 1880; Bell thought it by far his most important invention, but its range was far surpassed by Guglielmo Marconi's wireless transmission system, and it was superseded, although it was the ancestor of modern transmissions via fiber-optic cable.

clarity an instance of that last period of life, which he alone has known, and I want to recall the circumstances of that strange case.

A ship-owner of Bordeaux, Dutch by origin, Monsieur van Gelt, committed suicide in 1854. His family took a great many precautions to hide that catastrophic event, of which malevolent rumor did not take long to circulate in society, where Monsieur van Gelt had been highly esteemed. The secrets of his private life, which had transpired long before, gave that gossip a certain consistency.

The family requested an autopsy, and Dr. Z***, then still in vogue, was given the responsibility. He communicated his surgical observations to the law, but he kept to himself the psychology of the dead man, which he had read as if in a book in the scarcely-drowsy brain.

The ship-owner van Gelt was evidently a man of high intelligence and great heart, so his posthumous ideas presented a character of superiority that Dr. Z*** had never encountered before. He collated his notes lovingly, conserving their personal form. On the day when he communicated them to me, reading his manuscript as an author might read a chapter of his novel, I was amazed: the dead man lived—so to speak—his strange cadaveric existence before me.

I begged my friend to let me have a copy of his notes, and he agreed, on the express condition that I did not publish them before he had published the great work to which his observations were only the preface. I have described the fate of his writings. He is dead now, and I can therefore regard myself as released from my promise and free to deliver this curious document to the public. If I am not mistaken, it will one day cast new light on the presently unfathomed mysteries of eternity. The only element that I shall permit myself to introduce into it, which appears to me to be necessary to the understanding of the script, concerns the ordering of the facts; I have brought together in the early pages details relating to the circumstances of the suicide, which are dispersed in the notes as if at the hazard of memory.

. . . I have exhausted what it is appropriate to call the calyx of suffering; for some time catastrophes, superposed upon me like heavy stones on a man being walled up alive, and misfortunes have been pursuing me with a tenacity almost incredible in the force of its ferocity.

First of all, it was my only son, twenty-six years old, who fled with some creature after having robbed me in the manner of a treacherous accountant. Then my daughter died of typhoid fever at the moment when I was about to marry her to a young man she loved.

Soon afterwards, I discovered that my second wife—whom I had married without a dowry, for love, foolish old man!—was deceiving me with one of my nephews, to whom I had given a position in my business, and whom I regarded, alas, as a second son. Rendered cowardly by that love, almost senile and almost ridiculous, the roots of which stifled my courage, I accepted with interior tortures my role as a deceived husband, begging the wretch for the refuse of her tenderness, striving to conceal a wound that was getting larger every day.

Worn out by so much emotion, I became ill. I consulted a physician; he recognized that my morbid state was caused by the first symptoms of a cancerous infection of the stomach. Finally, after a disaster that coincided fatally with a financial crisis in Lyon, I saw the moment arriving when I would no longer be able to meet my obligations. At sixty-two years of age, at the end of an honorable career, having worked hard and done good, I thus found myself surrounded by dishonest affections, cuckolded, ill and poor.

Among the few ideas that could still germinate within my brain, raked as if by the claws of birds of prey, a comparison was insinuated between my fate and that of Job. And I found myself even more unhappy than the patriarch: he had God, while I, throughout my overworked existence, had paid no heed to supernatural matters, which inspired an insurmountable mistrust in me, and even a little of the disgust that men of action have for the reveries of the contemplative.

At that moment, removed from all activity, forced into bitter contemplation of myself, meditative for perhaps the first time in my life, I began to desire faith, which the unfortunate regard as the supreme panacea. To acquire it, however, would have required time; and even then, would I ever succeed in vanquishing my deep-rooted skepticism? Would not my innate need for truth always triumph of the suggestions of my sentimentality? Certainly, in spite of my efforts, doubts would subsist in me, poisoning the consolations of the priest.

That refuge was thus refused to me. There remained one other, more reliable: death. I accepted it.

The fear of bankruptcy vanquished my last hesitations. At another time, I would have tightened my muscles, stiffened my will and struggled until the final defeat, but I felt paralyzed by a definitive lassitude, like a shipwreck victim whose limbs have become heavy, who loses consciousness and abandons himself. I did not even wait for the certainty of my disaster to be absolute; the probability was sufficient for me, and I bought an American revolver.

. . . I went home; I locked myself in my study and there, while parading my eyes over the files filled with papers in which my entire activity was stagnating, over the curiously-wrought old furniture with which I liked to surround myself, and the few valuable paintings hanging on the walls, I slipped into a long reverie. My life passed before me in images whose colors sang with strange symphonies; I started going back over the course of time, stopping at unforgettable dates.

I arrived at the distant years of youth when I had battled furiously to live, my heart swollen with immeasurable ambitions, tormented by insatiable appetites; and I lingered there with delight while certain charming details gradually emerged from the monotonous tint of the past, like holes of light in a fog.

One memory, above all, pursued me for some time and made me smile. It was in the month of May; I had left the obscure mansard in the Rue de Jeûners to which I went home after my long days of work; I went for a walk in the woods of Meudon with my first mistress, a blonde milliner, slim and cheerful, who loved me as I loved her, without any hidden agenda, without any thought for the morrow, just for the pleasure that we gave one another. We had a little money and we drank warm milk at a farm. Suddenly, she started, the milk spilled over her beautiful Sunday dress. She was distressed. We were hidden by a bushy arbor; I kissed her for a long time, and she forgot her chagrin. Her name was Marguerite. There were flowers everywhere . . .

. . . The clock, chiming midnight, extracted me from my reverie. The intervals between each of the strokes seemed long to me; the chime, metallic and sonorous, was lugubrious. I understood that the hour in question really does have something solemn about it; on hearing it fall into the heavy silence of my last night, I understood why it is designated for crime. And I told myself that it was necessary to finish it. In any case, I had nothing more to do: no testament, since my succession would probably be swallowed up by a deficit; no letters, since those I loved did not love me and would learn of my death with dry eyes.

I only wrote, on a piece of paper that I left in a prominent place: *Today, 26 June 1854, I have killed myself*. I signed it. As midnight had just sounded, I had hesitated slightly before writing the date.

[That piece of paper, which had initially gone astray, was found by the judiciary investigation *several days after Dr. Z*** had communicated his notes to me*, and removed all doubts concerning Monsieur van Gelt's demise.]

My decision was firmly made. I retained all my calmness, but it seemed to me that I was acting in a dream, that nothing that was happening was definitive, that I might suddenly wake up with new horizons before me, as in a splendid dawn—and without having to do anything for that.

Then I sank back in my armchair, my eyes glued to the weapon, the barrel of which was gleaming in the lamplight, hypnotizing me. A great torpor invaded me. Increasingly vague visions floated before me, occasionally making me smile. I would have liked to stay like that eternally, letting time go by without losing consciousness of its duration and yet without feeling any more without thinking any more . . .

Then, suddenly, the memory of the resolution I had to carry out returned to me; reality reasserted itself. I shook myself, like a man about to go to sleep who suddenly remembers something he has forgotten to do and makes an effort to chase sleep away.

It was almost mechanically that I opened my jacket, my waistcoat and my shirt. I sought the location of the heart, which started beating violently under my hand, as if to affirm by its precipitate beats the strength of its life. At the same time I felt a glacial chill running through my veins; I believe that my teeth were chattering, although my brow was inundated with sweat. I made gestures of anguish; I was suffering like a patient on whom some painful operation is about to be carried out, who is afraid but desires to proceed even so, and who is pushing away the surgeon while crying to him: "Do it, then!"

Will-power triumphed over the last revolts of instinct, however, in a supreme contest, so rapid and passionate that it seemed to me to be a spasm; I was able to take the revolver, the ivory butt of which was burning my hand. I placed the mouth slightly above the place where my heart was bounding, taking care to leave a little space between my flesh and the barrel of the weapon, which was trembling so much that I was obliged to steady it with my left hand. Finally, in a shudder of my entire being, dominated by a frightful terror of the unknown that loomed up before me, suddenly gripped by a desire to live as poignant as remorse and by regrets sharper than any pain, I pressed the trigger.

Truly, I believe that my will-power, at that precise moment, was annihilated, consumed it had been by its final effort: the abandoned nerves simply carried out of their own accord and movement commenced.

I felt an atrocious pain, but I did not lose consciousness; undoubtedly, I had only broken a rib; I had to start again. But I was seized by a kind of delirium: mechanically, I pressed the trigger twice more, without hearing the sound of the detonations. The last shot struck home, for I felt my heart stop beating, my blood pause in my veins, and a great rigidity stretch my limbs, like the hand of an invisible giant . . .

. . . I'm dead, there's no doubt about it. By what miracle, then, are Thought and Sensation obstinate in persisting within me? My eyes can no longer see, but I have a marvelously precise vision of what surrounds me; my ears can no longer hear, but the slightest sounds—the fluttering of a moth trapped in the room, the distant murmurs from outside, the sputtering of the lamp on the brink of going out—seemed to me to be reverberating within me by virtue of a crystal clear echo; my limbs are already stiff but I feel, scarcely muffled by a thick carpet, the hardness of the parquet on to which I've slid; I can even perceive the odor of powder that fills the room.

I analyze my situation with a lucidity superior to any I've ever deployed before. "Undoubtedly," I say to myself, "this state won't last long; my thoughts will gradually stop, as my limbs are becoming cold and stiff"—that double sensation of cold and stiffness is excessively painful to me—"and my entire being will fall asleep in benevolent final repose."

Even the memory returns to me—for my faculties continue to operate as they did a little while before, perhaps better—of having heard in a lecture an account of the effects of curare poisoning, and I think that a phenomenon of the same kind is taking place in me, that I'm not dying at a stroke, that it's necessary to be patient . . .

. . . But no! No appreciable diminution in my physical suffering, not the slightest disturbance in my reasoning; and that cold, the terrible cold that chills me to the marrow without my being able to shiver as I once could, when I was young and went to bed in a room without a fire!

And now those dolors are becoming more precise, as a poignant anxiety is added to them: what if this is the immortality of the soul that people talk about? What if it's necessary to remain like this throughout the cycle of the eternal ages, simultaneously dead and alive, Thought persisting in a stiff, cold body that is decaying? Who can tell? Perhaps God exists; perhaps this is the last torture that he inflicts on us; perhaps he punishes in this fashion those who have been unable to glimpse his infinity or who have transgressed his mysterious laws? Are there prayers that might touch him . . . ?

. . . The minutes and the hours elapse with an in-describable slowness. I start thinking about cataleptics who are buried alive, who wake up in the grave with howls stifled by the earth, gnawing their firsts, and convulsed by the pangs of asphyxia. What if, by virtue of some strange lesion that has never been produced before, of which surgery has no suspicions, I'm only in a state of catalepsy? What if I wake up in three or four days, or a week, convulsively, with an immutable weight on my chest . . . ?

But no, it's impossible. I'm dead; I'm really dead. The human body is submissive to precise laws; it has been dismantled piece by piece, like a machine whose smallest mechanism is familiar. I felt the bullet pass through my heart; hence, I have nothing more to fear; my ideas will gradually calm down, silence will fall within me. My present state is logical; doubtless all the dead experience it, all of them have experienced that same anguish—and all of them have calmed down, as I shall calm down . . .

. . . Meanwhile, daybreak is beginning, in wan gleams that are trailing over me. There are noises out-side in the street, reaching me as if through a thick wall. A few more minutes and my manservant, accustomed to waking me up early, will knock on the door, and, receiving no reply, will come in. He's a worthy man, who has served me for ten years. I've been good to him, in several circumstances; perhaps he'll miss me . . .

Then my wife will enter in her turn, and my neph-ew . . .

And I feel a frisson pass through me at the idea that I'll soon be able to measure their affection irre-vocably . . .

Someone knocks on the door; for ten years, the same raps have been struck every morning, and it was my voice that replied. As no response is forthcoming, the knocking is repeated, more loudly.

The door opens.

Jean goes as pale as I must be, stifles a cry, makes a movement to go out, hesitates on the threshold, comes in and closes the door *carefully* . . .

He comes over to me, puts his hand over my heart, listens . . .

He carries me to my bed. Why is he looking at me with such a fearful expression? Why is he turning me to face the wall? I can see regardless, since my faculties are in some way disengaged from my senses, since I'm living a superior and independent life, since my vision is vaster in spite of the fixity of my eyes . . .

What is he going to do?

He goes to my writing-desk, to which I've given him a key. He opens it. He rummages in the drawers, striving to release a secret drawer whose mechanism he doesn't know, where the money is kept. I hear the dry click of gold coins in his hand . . .

And, the theft accomplished, although his legs are unsteady, although his teeth are still chattering with fear, utterly distressed, he runs out of the room shouting for help. People will say: "The domestic was very fond of his master, very faithful; one doesn't find his like any more today . . ."

After all, he's a poor man. He would never have had the courage to steal from me while I was alive, and perhaps never had any such idea—and yet, the sight of my cadaver frightened him more than the law, to which he gave no thought. He must, therefore, be driven by a very powerful motive; undoubtedly he has immediately deduced the causes of my suicide, he has been struck by the sudden and clear awareness of his situation; he's no longer young, he counted on remaining in my service for as long as I could provide him with a small income, or, if I died before him, that he'd be provided for in my testament. Instead of that, the hazard of seeking employment is recommencing, all of the placed arrangement of his life has been disturbed . . .

Then again, who knows what school he has passed through previously; who knows what circumstances have rendered him sinful or defiant? Perhaps days devoid of bread have developed appetites in him stronger than his conscience, which would have bent him sooner or later to their irresistible domination. He has lived with me for ten years without my ever asking him about his life; perhaps he was abandoned as a child, or his father beat him without a reason, or his mother didn't love him . . .

And then, after all, I have no further need of the money that he's taken. It requires an effort of memory for me to recall that I've worked all my life to earn it, that I've killed myself because I was able to lack it, that others kill themselves for the same reason and live as I have lived . . .

Two days ago, if I'd found the slightest irregularity in Jean's conduct, I'd have sacked him without hesitation; for the slightest misdemeanor, I'd have dragged him pitilessly before the courts, because I was rigid, one of those who regarded it as a duty for honest men to pursue the guilty. Now, I'd like to be able to get up in order to tell the man, whose conscience is doubtless in torment, that I forgive him.

It's doubtless the beginning of detachment, or perhaps things are appearing to me in a different light?

My wife comes into the room, and says: "Leave me alone."

Now we're face to face, the torturer and her victim, and death has inverted the roles: she's the one who's suffering now. I can see the traces of her emotions and her remorse passing over her face; it's me who is placid and tranquil now.

She approaches me slowly, as if fascinated; she closes my eyes, whose fixity doubtless makes her feel uncomfortable; then she steps back . . .

I'll never know what she's thinking.

Perhaps I, who wanted her to be happy, made her unhappy. I remember how sad she was before the marriage, and that it didn't worry me; I said to myself: "It's the unknown of her new life that's troubling her . . ." Her parents forced her into it, I'm sure. Perhaps she was in love with someone else, with the omnipotent chastity of first love, and I doubtless wounded her virginal delicacies as I overturned her young woman's dreams. She must have cursed me . . .

She draws closer to me, very pale. She touches my hand. She recoils again with a movement of dread, as if that icy hand had burned her . . .

I don't reproach her at all, though, because I acted like other men: egotism blinded me; I thought I'd make her happy by taking her; it's a common illusion. She suffered because of me; what does it matter? Nothing remains of her tears, any more than anything will remain of her regrets. I too have wept for her; already I can scarcely remember . . . and who knows . . . ?

The door opens again; it's my nephew.

He stops a few paces away from her; then he comes closer. They're both grave. I've never calculated their struggles, never thought that their sin has doubtless cost them dear, that they loved one another, and took account of what they called their infamy, but that love conquers all, in accordance with the law of nature; that the things that the living find monstrous would appear quite natural to them if the passions of the moment didn't blind them . . .

Meanwhile, she rests her head on his shoulder with the gracious movement of a woman soliciting protection; and, her throat full of sobs, she says "He was very good, though!"

Was I good? I don't believe so. I only applied, no more and no less, whatever the circumstances, the rule that measured my actions against the common standard. I gave to beggars and I let the poor starve; according to the caprice of circumstances, I felt my heart ready to melt with pity, or as hard as stone; I respected the law, but I also made use of it for the defense of my interests; between two courses of action, I always chose the one to which I was more forcefully driven by the motives tyrannizing my will.

In sum, now that I can judge my life in its entirety, I don't regret any of what I've done and wouldn't want to have done anything different—and yet, my activity seems to me to have been limited, futile and fatal.

After a silence, he replies: "He was a true father to me."

I was mistaken on his account, therefore. I thought him ungrateful; he was unhappy.

She continues: "My God, how guilty we are!"

And they stand before me, ashamed.

Then she throws herself into his arms, weeping . . .

Oh, I wish I could get up and say to them: "Love one another! Love one another! Certainly not for the enjoyment of love, which isn't worth the pain, but because it isn't worth the pain, either, of struggling against one's desires!" They're young, they're handsome, the blood is seething in their veins; what right do I have, an old man who has already had my share of joys, to want to separate them . . . ?

. . . The hours go by. It seems to me that a modification has taken place in my condition; I no longer feel any physical discomfort; the sensation of cold has disappeared; I even think that I'm enjoying lying down, as if after heavy fatigue, and the ideas that continue to pass through me no longer trouble me.

People come: old friends who mourn me. One of them, my oldest friend, stayed by my bedside for a long time without saying anything, shaking his head from time to time, doubtless thinking that it would soon be his turn, and dreading it. The indifferent have composed themselves at the door as they rang the bell, putting on distressed expressions as they took off their hats. The employees of the company have filed past one by one, buttoned up in worn frock-coats and poorly gloved. They've been told that it was an apoplectic fit; they seemed anxious.

Candles are burning; a nun is mumbling prayers by my bedside, which she interrupts with a sulky expression every time someone arrives . . .

I remember that once, when I was out walking, I sometimes saw swarm of gnats swirling, flying in all directions like specks of dust, and didn't know whether they were following a common goal or whether chance alone determined the sum of their movements. Truly, it's the same for so many comings and goings, for those contradictory anxieties that I read on all the faces, for the warmth of the hands that touch mine fearfully and leave me with a vague impression of fever.

The human face no longer strikes me as anything but a distant memory; the people who pass around me seem like shadows moving in a mist. When I compare their agitation to my immobility, the sound of their footfalls, which they stifle, as if they were afraid of waking me up, and the murmur of their voices, with my silence, and the animation of their eyes with the fixity of mine beneath my permanently lowered lids, I wonder where the reality of existence is. Between their condition and mine, between being and non-being, is there really such an imperceptible nuance?

I contemplate life as a traveler who has just passed over a mountain casts a glance behind him; he has been walking for a long time, his feet have been bruised by sharp stones, he has hesitated before many obstacles; but now, the torrents that barred his path are only thin white lines beneath his feet, the rocks that loomed up before him are black dots, he can no longer see the precipices into which he nearly fell, and the distance traveled seemed to him to be such a little matter that he thinks he could touch the nearby peak with his finger.

Then, the shadows of evening rise up, everything is drowned and disappears into a uniform shade; space no longer exists.

Night falls. My wife has decided to keep vigil with the nun. They've both fallen asleep. In the efforts of their respiration, I hear painful thoughts, poorly allayed, or heavy dreams pursuing them. The idea of their actions, which they're judging sinful in their imperfect consciences, is still troubling them, and also concern for things that they believe to be important.

In my slumber, which is better than theirs and devoid of nightmares, nothing similar is happening. Of forgotten cares nothing remains to me but indifference, and I understand irresponsibility . . .

. . . At times, my brain stops: I'm no longer thinking . . .

. . . The second day begins. My vision of the things surrounding me is not as clear; the golden dots of the candle-flames are paling. Noises are muffled; and the sensation of blindness and deafness that is invading me, instead of being painful, is full of charm.

My son has arrived. He has fallen into a chair at the foot of my bed, without speaking. I don't know where he has come from, or how the news of my death reached him; perhaps he learned about it from a newspaper in some café. Anyway, I have no curiosity in his regard, although I judge him differently as well. Instead of letting his youth develop, I compressed it, wanting him to work as I had worked, without taking account of the difference in our situations, "on principle," as I put it. I opposed him in his inclinations, to the extent of preventing him from pursuing the career of his preference. From childhood, I measured out his pleasures parsimoniously, under the pretext of showing him the miserliness of life's joys. Was it astonishing that his youth burst forth?

He had, all things considered, no reason to love me, but he's mourning me; his conduct was the fatal result of circumstances for which he was not culpable, but he's deploring it; it's the illogicality of every thought that life crushes. While vain remorse torments him, I understand him and I absolve him—to tell the truth, without afflicting myself with his affliction, without sympathizing with his undeserved anguish, without my quiescence being in any way troubled by his grief, for afflictions are frozen along with the blood.

With the supreme intelligence of things that I feel within me, I also feel a supreme indifference. In the same way that I have escaped all the laws of human morality, as I finally understand relativity, I have fled the tyranny of the heart. I have no more hatred for those who made me suffer than gratitude for those who have loved me. The good and bad hours that I owe to the commerce of human beings are now too distant for me to be able to make any distinction between them.

Every day, in life, does one not experience agreeable or painful sensations of which one does not retain any memory? No one, for example, thinks for days on end about the pleasure he had experienced in a scented bath, or a good meal, or entering into a warm room after having suffered from cold, any more than the pain caused by a pinprick or bumping into a door. Well, my great joys and my great pains, those that caused me to wander the streets with my breast on the point of explosion, those which made me weep as an adult as a child weeps, all of that is as distant, as faded, as depleted as the thousand fugitive impressions that every day bears away and replaces. How, then, can the slightest rancor against those who have afflicted me subsist in me, since the pain has gone? And how can the slightest affection, since the memory of individuals no longer awakens anything within me . . . ?

. . . My son and my wife have always detested one another. This morning, a few hours before the burial, they seemed to be reconciled by their common mourning and remorse; they wept together. But the crisis of despair passed; they started talking about ordinary things, about me, and suddenly, in response to something my wife said, an argument burst forth. They blamed one another reciprocally for my death.

"You're the one that killed him!"

And I learned, thus, new details regarding both of them. While I was alive, by virtue of a kind of tacit complicity, they closed their eyes to their respective faults, helping one another if necessary, in spite of the fact that their intimacy was less powerful than their self-interest. Now the common enemy is no longer there; they can tear one another apart at their ease. They display before me their improper actions: how the adulterous affairs began; by what methods of dissimulation they kept them hidden for a long time.

"Your chambermaid knew everything; at what price did you buy her silence?"

I learn that my son's theft was not the only one he committed in my employ; that when he started on that path, he was driven by a long series of dishonorable faults.

"Wasn't it me who paid for your first mistake? You didn't ask me then where I got the money?"

I also learn about my own defects: I was too demanding for everyday life; I complained needlessly about unimportant things; I had ridiculous manias, the manias of an old man of which my wife made fun; I frightened everyone around me with my severity . . . what do I know now?

Perhaps all that was true—but what does it matter?

The quarrel continues, although the time is approaching when they will come to fetch my body. I know them better now than I ever did, better than I knew myself. I see that, even just now, I was entertaining illusions on their account; their tears deceived me; perhaps they were false; perhaps they were putting on an act before themselves and juggling their sentiments in order to fool themselves.

And yet, I persist in my judgment: they're neither better nor worse than anyone else; human beings are malleable dough, which things fashion and soil at their whim; they're passive mirrors in which images leave their reflection, sometimes pleasant to behold and sometimes repulsive; the bed of an eternal stream over which filth and flowers flow. It's life that forms them; life alone is guilty and dirty.

Questions of money come up incessantly in their dispute. Suddenly, my wife goes pale, struck by a sudden idea: she has been wrong to irritate my son.

"My God!" she cries. "What will become of me if he hasn't made a will?"

My son replies: "What good is a will? He's ruined." And he adds: "It's your expenses—you, who came into the house like a beggar . . ."

She interrupts him, standing up in front of him: "Didn't you leave it like a thief?"

They're white with anger, both trembling; their sadness and their remorse have disappeared.

He moves toward her, his arm raised. She doesn't recoil.

"Oh, hit me! Hit me! You're cowardly enough for that. But be careful! I'll defend myself!"

She picks up a knife that happened to be close at hand. Are they going to fight, here and now, without waiting for me to be taken away?

My son retreats slowly. He stops on the threshold and says: "Hurry up and marry one of your lovers, so that we can be rid of you!"

He says that very loudly; if any servants are passing in the corridor, they would have been able to hear it. My wife has drawn closer to me, as if to ask for protection . . .

. . . It seemed to me that I could hear, very distantly, a storm. The same rumbling that might perhaps make passengers on a ship howl in terror, lulled me like a gentle murmur. The wind, which was tearing sails and breaking masts out there, was a fresh breeze brushing my face like a beloved breath. Because of the distance, the sea seemed to me to be scarcely rippled, and I took the vessels, tossed and twisted, overturned, for motionless dots. The anguish of the unfortunates struggling desperately found no echo in me, so replete was I in the sentiment of my security . . .

. . . I am no longer paying any heed to the miserable quarrels in which I once took part, and it will not be long before I'm separated forever from human beings by the earth heaped on top of me . . .

. . . That desired moment is approaching; the supreme ceremony is beginning.

I can hear the sound of sobbing; anger has given way once again to tears, more appropriately. There are whispers. People are there.

The lid of my coffin is lowered. I can no longer see anything. I can scarcely perceive the noises in the room. The nailing begins; at the first blow of the hammer all the voices have falling silent, as if frightened by that harsh sound, which is imprisoning me in the supreme solitude. Then, that task finished, footsteps resume, a dull agitation. How many times I have waited, in bereaved houses, for the signal to follow the coffin, in the crowd of relatives and guests; and almost always, thoughts of matters other than death followed me . . .

. . . I am hoisted on to the hearse, slightly astonished not to feel any shock; it appears that I am separated from material sensation, without having lost all consciousness of what is happening around me. The procession sets off; the noise of horses' hooves, wheels and footfalls is only a muted buzz for me. It requires a mental effort for me to imagine myself being transported from one place to another; the notion of movement no longer exists. All of space seems to me to be constituted by this tiny corner that I occupy, in which everything is without anything moving. If I did not have memories and experience, I could easily believe that the world is rotating, and that while it rotates, specific objects remain eternally in place . . .

. . . Prayers for the dead are chanted, which the organ accompanies with its purring. From time to time, the halberd of a Swiss Guard sounds a dry click on the paving-stones, or the hand-bell instructs the assembly to kneel down . . .

When I was alive, I had fits of atheism in which I wanted to overthrow the Church. I detested its religious ceremonies, which I found puerile to the point of derision. Well, I judge them differently now; I don't feel any need for God, of course; I have no more idea than before whether he exists or not, in Heaven or elsewhere. It seems to me, however, that those monotonous chants might soothe and appease the dolor of the living, that they might engender vague hopes—deceptive but consoling—in hearts still full of doubt. As for the dead, that last echo of human voices that reach them, those genuflections that they represent in memory, the movements of the costumed priests . . . all of that summarizes admirably the nullity of their lives, and all life; if any regret for the things left behind still subsists, it will fade away completely into that supreme solemnity.

I am carried away, and we walk for a long time. My thoughts still wander over religious questions. I can't make up my mind whether God is a useful or a harmful invention; undoubtedly, he doesn't matter, like everything else that humans have found.

I am lowered into the ground; the spadefuls of earth that are thrown down rattle on my coffin. This is the moment when all the affection that there is in living human hearts for the dead feels stirred to the depths by the dry thud that a slightly larger pebble sometimes renders sonorous. Among the murmur of those desolations, the priest resumes his prayers . . . I know that, although I cannot hear them; I can no longer hear anything. The separation from the living is accomplished; I can no longer even perceive the noise that the people I loved are making as they leave; I have no knowledge of the final tears that are being shed for me . . .

. . . Time has moved on, but nothing can any longer allow me to distinguish the minutes or the hours, the seasons or the years. I shall not know when the flowers bloom whose roots will soon plunge into my being. I shall not feel the warmth of the summer sun; I shall not be cold when the snow extends over the dead grass like another shroud; in spring, I shall not hear the chirping of the birds in my cypress, in which the sap is rising. And I experience a kind of voluptuousness in thinking about the confusion of everything into which I am disappearing. There was a time when, although I remained motionless and awake, the minutes seemed long to me; now, the minutes melt into one another to form eternity, as drops of water do to make a river, and they draw me gently into their flow . . .

. . . Gradually, my memories dissolve. I can scarcely recall my life. It seems to me that I can see a long way, and very high. I am no longer merely the traveler whom the mirages of arrival deceive as to the distance covered; I am the aeronaut suspended in space, at heights that humans have never reached. He no longer sees the cities, the mountains seem to him to be imperceptible pimples, the seas puddles, and of all the noise that creatures make, no murmur reaches him; above the drifting and disintegrating clouds illuminated by strange light, he floats as if in a new element.

The events of which my life was formed are gradually erased: my poor childhood, my youth full of struggles, my years of prosperity, the dolors of my latter days, all draw away and melt into a uniform hue. I forget the differences between pleasure and pain. I no longer know that I once loved; no memory, of any kind whatsoever, can trouble my thoughts, which continue to flow nevertheless, but slowly and with an exceeding limpidity, like a body to which nothing can form an obstacle.

One last concern remains in me—or rather, one problem whose solution still interests me: I seek to know by what series of successive impulsions my will had determined that suicide, which required so much effort.

I rediscover the motives, by an effort of memory, but I no longer understand how the dread of ruination, regret for a dead woman, fear of malady, the dolor of being deceived—all those abstractions—were able to change into a brutal fact, to provoke a positive resolution and a real suffering.

Certainly, I don't regret having killed myself; in the space where I am, there is no room for regret; but I can't explain to myself how the motives for my action were able to emerge from the indifferent monotony of things and act upon me to the point of making me exchange one condition for another. The acuity of the dolor, the force of affections, the tenacity of anguish—those are as many notions that escape me. The veil that, at a time that I can no longer measure, already enveloped and hid my memories of time past, has thickened. Everything that once happened to me appears as material objects appear, in an increasingly profound darkness. Vague forms move heavily in my thoughts; I imagine that during the long nights of the Arctic regions, the blocks of ice move in the same way . . .

. . . At times, I amuse myself with efforts to recover the details of my life or the faces of those I loved, and the very futility of those evocations satisfies me. When I was alive, it sufficed for me to close my eyes immediately to see faces that have long disappeared, and so clearly that I could have believed myself to be beside them. At present, in this obscurity in which my eyes are always closed, I seek in vain; the images are no longer designed; and it's without the slightest regret that I observe the flight of those shades, however dear.

Thus, everything fades away, as if Time, which marches on without my hearing it, were destroying gently, one by one, the impressions engraved within me . . .

Indeed, I remember that a few hours ago—or a few minutes, or a few days; I no longer know—certain events of my past became exact to me again, preoccupying me. At present, I can no longer locate them; I am, therefore, escaping myself; the sentiment of my own personality is fleeing me, like the memories, like all fatiguing impressions. I no longer know exactly what my *self* is; it seems to me that I'm melting into millions of beings, that I'm disappearing into things, that I'm no longer anything but one with a formidable unity . . .

If humans succeed in imagining that which cannot be seen, cannot be heard and cannot be felt; if, above all, they have a presentiment that one only arrives by a slow gradation at the conditions of which I'm on the brink, disaccustoming the self to past habits . . . they would no longer fear Death. That king of terrors, as their sages call it, would bring them an unalterable peace, the delights of a slumber whose duration is unmarked, on a bed so soft that it cannot be felt. In the great silence and the great obscurity of the tomb, nothing exists but soothing sensuality, which becomes ever more gentle, like fading gleams, like dwindling harmonies.

I sense that my brain is still alive—but my thoughts are deliciously asleep . . .

THE GOLDEN CLARION AND THE EBONY OLIFANT

by Catulle Mendès

IT is a question always controversial among scholars as to whether, in Paradise, days and nights are submissive, as on our earth, to changing hours, or whether the celestial abode is incessantly resplendent with the beauty of light. Fortunately, it is one of the functions of poets—the others are rhyming rondeaux or ballads and making, with the wives of the bourgeois of the city, children as beautiful as the morning, who will, in their turn, rhyme poems and make children with loving bourgeois wives—to reveal what all other men do not know, and, without wasting any more time, I will tell you in honest faith that a sun in the sky up above, like that in the sky down here, rises and climbs, and descends and sets. But how much more radiant it is than the obscure sun, adapted by a clement God to suit the weakness of human eyes!

Perhaps you feel some curiosity to learn by whom I am so well-informed. Know that it was by an angel. Oh? What species of angel? A guardian angel. Very well, the guardian of whom? Not me, certainly. Who, then, if you please? My friend Alcyonne—you know, the one who travels the roads saying to good-looking young men: "I'll never finish unfastening my girdle if you don't help me."

That's a fine occupation for an angel, to be the guardian of a person like that! So, having once been her guardian, he wasn't any longer, and if he came in the evenings to lean with folded wings over the white little bed where she gave the impression of a bunch of jasmines on a bed of lilies, it was uniquely for the pleasure of seeing her in a chemise.

So, to return to my subject, there really are days and nights in the divine abode; it is even the custom for an archangel, chosen from among the most handsome, to sound a golden clarion to announce the dawn, and to sound an ebony olifant to announce the dusk, while a very old saint summons the Elect of both sexes.

Now, in a pathway in a cloud, in which eglantines flourish that are tiny stars, one of the Elect recently arrived from earth said to one of the Blessed who had been celestial for a long time: "My sister, I confess that I can to longer stand it here. It's absolutely necessary that I go back down there, at least for a few hours."

"Oh, my sister! What temptation is troubling you in the paradisal enchantment?"

"My God! My sister, I don't want to speak ill of the pleasures that are offered to us in this place of eternal recompense; I grant that the choirs of harps have a peerless sweetness, and that there is a real satisfaction in wandering, the toes brushing pink mists, amid the infinite forbearance and caress of the skies. Perhaps when

I've been in Paradise for thousands of years like you, I won't be able to conceive of any other joy than that of listening to your music and strolling along the Milky Way, which is undoubtedly a pleasant promenade; but I'm not yet entirely liberated from the regret of human delights, and I've resolved to escape today."

"Mercy! Think of the danger that threatens you. If anyone learns that you've fled the heavens, you'll be precipitated into the worst Gehennas of the fuliginous Inferno."

"Yes, but no one will find out, thanks to you, dear sister. As soon as the ebony olifant has sounded, as soon as I've responded to the evening roll-call, I'll pretend to reenter, as usual, the azure dormitory where billions of little clouds serve us as beds, and slyly, adroitly, I'll take flight toward the earth—it's an imprudence to give wings to the newly Elect—but I'll be careful not to linger for too long. I'll return before the golden clarion sounds the awakening call, and as you'll take care to leave the door of diamond encrusted with chrysoprase ajar, I'll regain my bed without anyone having perceived my absence. As soon as the morning appeal sounds, you'll see me rubbing my eyes and yawning, giving a perfect impression of a little soul who has slept sagely on my dark blue and starry pillow."

"Wretch, what are you asking of me? Although I love you tenderly, I could never resolve to be the accomplice of such a grave escapade. Fie, my sister! You're in Heaven and you want to play truant!"

"I tried it more than once, on earth, and never had reason to repent of it. In any case, all your objections will only make me more determined, and if you won't consent to leave the door to the dormitory open, well, someone will catch sight of my return and I'll be precipitated into Hell, that's all."

The Blessed, a long time celestial, was so good that she did not want to expose her companion to such a terrible adventure. She did what she was asked to do; and after the evening appeal, the young Elect slipped away toward the terrestrial abode.

Where, then, was she going? I am not far from thinking that she remembered some tender bed of which, when alive, she had not had to complain; and, like a moonbeam insinuating itself between the curtains, perhaps she caressed with immortal lips amorous eyes that were weeping for her. Perhaps even, in the arms of the slumbering lover, she became—for amour is omnipotent—the real lover that she had once been; what her kiss had of the paradisal would not have astonished the mouth of the sleeper, so divine had it already been before.

What is certain is that she was not bored on earth, for she remained there much longer than ought to have been necessary, and up above, in the celestial dormitory, the Blessed who had left the diamond door encrusted with chrysoprases ajar was alarmed to see day about to break. Alas, what would happen if the absentee delayed any longer in reappearing?

It was not to be feared that the dawn would awaken the Elect; dreams are so beautiful in Paradise that slumber is prolonged there willingly; but the Archangel who sounds the ebony olifant in the evening and the golden clarion in the morning was very faithful to his duty; he usually slept with one eye open in order to catch the first light of dawn. Surely, he was about to sit up on his couch, seize the clarion and fill the twilight with a violent fanfare. Everyone would get up, there would be a roll-call, the disappearance of the new Elect would be observed, and nothing would be able to save her from the eternal punishment.

The charitable Blessed gazed with anguish at the shadow, still starry but soon matinal, through which the imprudent voyager had not returned. Oh, my God, what could she do? How could she prevent the announcer from sounding the awakening?

Bewildered, she quit the dormitory, ran toward the Archangel's tent and parted the curtains. Fortunately, he was still asleep, with both eyes closed. She considered him, full of fear and also admiration. How handsome he was, lying there in his silver armor! But the light was already penetrating the tent.

Oh, it was terrible! He was about to raise his eyelids and put the clarion to his mouth. Instinctively, she put herself between the light and him. A futile precaution: he awoke. But as she had deployed her wings in order to intercept the daylight, it was not the dawn that he saw but an adorable body, of a saint, certainly, but a woman, and that body, so lilial, was completely naked, for the Blessed have no other garment than their wings.

He extended his arms, ecstatically. Alas, how she was trembling, how she feared being obliged—oh, in Heaven!—to a sin that would be all the more fright-ful for being so sweet! Undoubtedly, she could have fled, but if she had stood aside, he would have seen the daylight. It was necessary that he did not see it. She had to give the absentee the time to return from the base world, to regain her couchette of azure and starry cloud. She had to have the magnanimity, in order to save her companion, to expose herself to the worst of perils.

He put his arms around her; she did not pull away, and even, resigned and heroic, kissed him, on his eyelids, in order that he would not perceive the dawn.

For a long, long time she consented to that sublime sacrifice, so long that the clarion finally sounded, shaking the entire sky.

But who, then, had sounded the awakening call? It was not the Archangel, whose lips, at that moment scarcely cared about the mouthpiece of a clarion.

It was the young Elect herself, finally returned from earth, and between the clear blasts, she giggled, saying: "Oh, if I had known in what fashion I was awaited in Heaven, I would have refrained, my sister, from coming back up so soon!"

LOVE AMONG THE STARS

by Camille Flammarion

"WHAT up with you this morning?" I exclaimed, on seeing André arrive in my study, with a disconcerted and desolate expression. His face was very pale, his eyes haggard his hair unkempt and his step weary, as if he had come back from a long-distance run. "You obviously haven't spent the night stargazing, although the sky was as clear as I've seen it for a long time."

"On the contrary—yes, I spent a long time observing the sky last night; but I'm emerging from an unparalleled astonishment, and I certainly haven't slept a wink this morning. I'm still flabbergasted. But what you mistake for terror was only an agreeable and charming surprise, followed by a boundless regret—a surprise so great that I haven't recovered from it."

"Have you discovered a new star with a fantastic spectrum, a nebula of extravagant form, a comet with hectic tresses? Is it only the insomnia that succeeds a vivid excitement?"

"It's an adventure more extraordinary than any you could imagine. I dreamed about Dora—yes, Dora, my deceased beloved."

"Oh, your imagination! What tricks it plays on you! You've become the victim of hallucinations—you, whose mind is so calm and ponderous. Don't trust yourself! I've already told you that. It's a dangerous slope. You're too much a poet. I prefer mathematics—it's safer."

"I'm not arguing. Hallucination, dream, whatever you like; but I'm still overwhelmed by what I've seen and heard—and that's not unreasonable at all."

"Well, tell me your story. I don't doubt that it will be very interesting."

My friend André was a young man of twenty-five, an excellent observer of the sky, describing with great exactitude the planetary aspects of Mars, Jupiter or Saturn—to which his studies were preferentially devoted—but a trifle dreamy and mystical. A great and unforgettable distress had struck him, and since that time, which was still quite recent, he had been plunged into a constant melancholy.

He had fallen in love with a delightfully beautiful young woman, as dreamy as himself, ardent and passionate, whom he had suddenly lost after three months of adoration. And during the two years since the blow had struck him, he had thought of nothing but her, scarcely succeeding in forgetting her for a few moments in the scientific work that absorbed all his strength and energy.

Life without her was sad and colorless, and he had often wanted to die. He hoped to die soon, and in fact, his health, once so flourishing, was deteriorating insensibly. He believed in the survival of the soul and wondered incessantly where his beloved might be. Several times, he had told me that he thought he had sensed her presence nearby, and heard some kind of internal voice speaking to his soul. I had tried to deflect him away from these ideas, which seemed to me to be dangerous to his mental health, and I had believed that he was no longer thinking about them when he arrived that morning, so troubled and agitated by his vision.

He explained that at about two o'clock in the morning, while he was examining through his telescope a region of the Milky Way very rich in stars, he had, so to speak, swept the beautiful constellation of Cygnus with his instrument, and had paused on the admirable double star Albireo, composed of two suns, one golden yellow and the other sapphire.

While he trained a very powerful ocular lens on the blue star, and was preparing to observe it with a spectroscope in order to make a special study of its curious light, he had experienced a sort of dazzling in his eye, which he had initially attributed to the bright glare of the star, and had also felt a slight electric shock on his shoulder. He continued the observation nevertheless and fitted the spectroscope to the telescope. Either in consequence of the fatigue of the night's observation, however, or simply a to rest momentarily, he had sat down in the large armchair in which, occasionally, after long observations, we had the habit of stretching ourselves out and going to sleep briefly.

The rays of moonlight entering through the cupola, forming a light streak of blue-tinted light, were caressing the apparatus, the globes and the maps. He tried to get up to carry out his spectroscopic observation, but very close to him, he had seen, with his naked eyes, the adored form of his beloved standing in the moonlight, and had simultaneously felt nailed to the armchair by a superior magnetic force.

I shall, however, leave it to André to tell the story, for what follows is exactly what he told me.

Dora was standing there before me. Above her shone Albireo. My beloved was even more beautiful than before, idealized and as if made translucent by a celestial clarity.

My first impression was amazement. I was not in the least afraid, and yet I felt a glacial frisson run from my feet to my head and I began to tremble. I remained sprawled in my armchair, as if my body were made of lead. She didn't come closer to me, and it seemed to me at first that I didn't want to approach her.

She looked at me tenderly with her large azure eyes, which always seemed to be opening on some new astonishment, and said to me eagerly: "Why haven't you come? I'm waiting for you. We haven't yet known love!"

The tone of her voice was the same as before, and as soon as I heard it, the apparition lost its strange character and became—for want of a better word—natural.

At that mild reproach, that regret and that avowal, all our hours of happiness reappeared before me, animatedly: our passionate intoxications, our delightful ecstasies, our endless kisses—and the very extravagance of our sensuality, all those enchanting scenes suddenly resuscitated in my brain, went through me like a lightning-flash of radiant joy.

I couldn't help replying: "What! We haven't known love?"

"Certainly not," she replied. "We've only had its gross sensations."

"Oh, how exquisite!"

"Yes, for the Earth. But how different it is here!"

"Where's here?"

"In the system of Albireo's azure star."

And she told me that she lived there, in the midst of a sort of angelic population. While I listened, I seemed to be living that new life with her. It was no longer death; it was life. I found myself with her again, as before.

"Yes," she added, "what a difference there is between the love one knows here and that which we tasted on Earth!"

I confess that I experienced a disagreeable expression on hearing that confession.

"How do you know that?" I cried, piqued by a sudden bizarre resurgence of the thorn of jealousy.

"Foolish! Still foolish!" she replied, with her adorable smile. "Jealous of a dead woman!"

"But you're not dead, since you're talking to me about love, and claiming to experience joys unknown on Earth. No, I'm not jealous—but I still love you. Well, I'm capable of being reasonable. Explain yourself."

"On Earth, we only have five senses: sight, hearing, smell and touch each play a role in our sensations, although true love resides essentially in the attraction of souls toward one another. We only have five senses, or even four."

"How many more have you today, then?"

"Seventeen. And I repeat, I'm waiting for you. And of those seventeen, there's one that surpasses all others, worth as much as the rest put together, which on its own might be called the sense of love."

"Which is?"

"It's the electrical sense. In love, electricity plays a preponderant role, even in terrestrial organisms, which are so gross and obtuse. The human soul is a substantial entity, electrical in nature, which radiates far beyond our visible material body. That electricity emits invisible waves, which are very different from those of light."

"Yes, I know," I replied, my mathematical mind taking over. "Luminous waves are three ten-thousandths of a millimetre in length, while electrical waves are thirty centimetres."

"I didn't know that."

"I understand perfectly well what you're saying to me, therefore—that there's a radical difference between the magnitude of the vibrations that give birth to electrical or luminous effects."

"None of the five senses of the terrestrial body can perceive electrical waves. Among us, by contrast, it's the first of our seventeen senses. It's much more important than sight itself. Why does one love? Why does one experience sympathies and antipathies? Why does one remain different? That's a mystery unknown to you, although it's very simple for us, who perceive it so directly by means of a special sense.

"The soul, which is an electrical substance, emits into its surroundings electrical waves invisible to you but perceptible to us. You might compare these waves to the sound waves that emanate from the vibrating string of a violin, a harp or a piano. If these sonorous waves encounter in their passage another string able to vibrate harmonically with the first, the second string will emit a sound without anyone having touched it. It's an experiment that you can make at any time.

"If two souls vibrate in unison; or sometimes, better still, in harmonic accord, their mutual waves, one encountering one another, associate and fuse, and the two beings are united with one another by a chain more solid than iron. It's not only their gazes that are knotted, it's their entire being. All that one might do to oppose that union would be wasted effort. It will be accomplished, if necessary, after death.

"If a cacophony results from the encounter of the vibrations, antipathy is the result, and the most beautiful reasoning can do nothing about it. That man is antipathetic to me; that woman gets on my nerves. Don't seek to correct the first impression; it will be wasted effort.

"Well, on Albireo, we see these vibrations of the soul, these etheric undulations, as you see by means of light; we perceive them by means of our electric sense, while they remain foreign to you. These electrical vibrations, which are like the very atmosphere of love, are unknown to you on Earth. You experience love much as the deaf experience music."

"Oh!" I said. "How ungrateful you are!"

"No, my adored one, I remember everything. But remember that love is the intimate union of two beings. In terrestrial amours, there is no entire melting into one another. But here, where the electric sense is entirely developed, our etheric bodies are like two electric charges that annihilate one another in lightning. The combination is so intense that of two beings who embrace, only one remains—like oxygen and hydrogen, which, in combining, lose their individuality to form a droop of water, a limpid pearl that contains the entire rainbow and summarizes the universe."

"But what happens afterwards?"

"Well, afterwards, one can recover oneself! I don't know how it happens, but one is resuscitated."

"That's not impossible. Electricity can dissociate a drop of water and separate once again the oxygen and hydrogen whose union formed it."

"You know how to explain everything scientifically."

"So," I added, "one goes as far as losing consciousness of one's existence—really dying—and being reborn?"

"Do you understand now that our seventeen senses, governed by the first among them, provide sensations compared with which the most vivid joys experienced on Earth are merely the coarse impressions of mollusks? And what light inundates us! What flowers! What perfumes! It's like a perpetual ecstasy. Of, if you came, if you were here!"

"Can't you take me?" I exclaimed, launching myself toward her.

"Come!"

I seized her in my arms, stuck my lips to hers, and suddenly saw, in the heart of a very soft and tender blue light, that Dora was bearing me away on immense wings. I was clinging to her body, lost in delight. Numerous beings, drifting like us in the atmosphere, had the form of dragonflies, with antennae, palps and aerial organs, which doubtless represented the new senses that she had mentioned to me.

I understood that I had been suddenly transported on to one of the planets of Albireo's azure sun. Cascades of blue water fell from the rocks and ran through an immense garden carpeted by brilliant flowers. Birds with bright plumage, seemingly luminous in themselves, filled their air with their songs.

"Let's go through this light," she said, "toward the evening horizon and descend into the palaces of night."

Having moved out of the illuminated hemisphere, we arrived in semi-darkness. All the rocks, all the vegetation and all the animals shone with a blue, green or roseate light, phosphorescent or fluorescent. The rocks undoubtedly possessed properties analogous to those of phosphates and sulfates of barytes, which store solar light received during the day and radiate it during the night. The flying creatures were similarly luminous, in the fashion of fireflies. Darkness, on this world, is never complete, firstly because of that curious phosphorescence of every body, secondly because of Albireo's second, golden sun, the distant light of which is almost never absent, and also because of a ring analogous to that of Saturn, which, lit by these half-suns of different colors, is sometimes blue, sometimes yellow and sometimes green, and distributes the strangest gleams through the semi-darkness.

How small a thing is our poor and minuscule terrestrial world, which we imagine to be everything, by comparison with those ultra-terrestrial marvels!

My beautiful and beloved Dora carried me lovingly between her wings, and we descended toward the shores of a lake, beneath an immense arborescent foliage, the vast leaves of which extended like a cradle of verdure over a carpet of moss strewn with a thousand little flowers.

"This is where I live," she said. "Let's rest."

In my delight and ecstasy, I wanted to seize her in my arms and savor on her lips the exquisite happiness of being loved by her—but scarcely had she touched the ground than her terrestrial form was instantly transformed into another, similar to the beings that we had encountered flying in the atmosphere. She was no longer my Dora. She was, however, even more beautiful and more radiant, and compared with her, I felt like an earthworm.

"To love me still, to love me forever," she said, "it's sufficient to die! Quit the Earth. Here, you will be mine."

"Have I not quit the Earth, then?" I replied, astonished.

"No—look."

She touched my lightly on the forehead with the tip of an antenna and I felt a sharp electric shock. I opened my eyes and found myself alone, sitting in the large armchair. My beloved had disappeared.

I no longer have any doubt that she really is living on that star in Cygnus. She is calling me there and I shall soon recover her. I love her more than ever!

＊

Such was André's story. That apparition had had such a powerful impact on him that, from that day onwards, his mind appeared to be wandering far from the Earth. His poor health declined rapidly, but he lived happily in his dream, with the desire, the obsession to see it realized.

I was not surprised when, a few months after the adventure that has just been reported, I was told of the sudden death of my dear comrade.

On a beautiful summer night, perhaps haunted by the same vision, he had stretched himself out in the same armchair, next to the great equatorial telescope, aimed at Albireo, and, in the morning, he was thought to have fallen asleep there—but his cadaver was completely cold.

To his right, a little bottle containing hydrocyanic acid—one drop of which is sufficient to dissolve the bonds attaching the soul to the body—had fallen on to the floor.

MINUTES

by Maurice Renard

A T the hour of the night when Thomas Reaper arrived at a certain point on the Thames Docks, there was absolutely no one outside, because of the cold. Thick snow covered everything. It had fallen in great abundance, but it was no longer falling now and the stars were shining harshly in the sky.

"Damnably cold! Damnably cold!" said Thomas Reaper, walking with great difficulty. His feet were sinking into the snow, which creaked as it yielded with a silky mildness.

A little later, Thomas Reaper added: "Because I'm so tired. So, so tired."

He was a small, rotund and thickset man. His whole body rolled as he went along, and he was covered in snow, clad in a light white crust of which he had no thought of ridding himself in any fashion.

"So tired . . ." he said, again, faintly but not plaintively, in a curiously neutral voice.

He stopped, and nothing could be heard any longer except the murmur of the icy water of the river behind heaps of wood and pyramids of barrels.

He stopped, and did not move for several minutes. Yes, in truth: several minutes. He had the air of a little man considerably preoccupied with what he had come to do on the bank of the Thames so late at night, doubtless after having walked a long way, to be so, so tired.

The snow came half way up his calves. It was as if he were planted there, lost and bewildered.

There were houses to the left. They could be seen outlined. They were, it seemed, private houses. Heuh? Heuh? Were they really private houses? Yes, certainly: those cottages with a garden and a fence, which Thomas Reaper found so pretty and desirable, having only ever lived in very modest redoubts, personally.

Was there not a light in one of those cottages? Was the window above the door not illuminated? Or was it a reflection?

Suddenly, Thomas Reaper saw that light become much brighter; and the door opened. And in the luminous frame, the silhouette appeared of a tall, svelte young man. The fellow seemed to be interrogating the night. Leaning forward, he was looking in the direction of London.

And Thomas Reaper suddenly exclaimed: "Why, it's John, of course! Truly, why am I as tired as this? I'd had completely forgotten, completely. That's a bit much! Hey, John! Here I am, son! Here I am! Oh, good! I'm jolly content to have arrived!"

"Father! But what are you doing there? Come in! Come in, then! We were despairing of you."

How cheerful he is, that John! And handsome! And well-dressed . . .

"Oh, but I say, boy, here you are decked out like a lord! What elegance!"

John has a charming, slightly conceited smile.

"Business is going quite well, Father."

And without making a fuss about anything, neither his father's fatigue nor all the snow that is covering him, John pushes him gently into the beautiful illuminated house, where there is furniture such as Thomas Reaper had dreamed all his life.

"Ah! Business is good?" repeats the little fellow, taking off his overcoat on the threshold so that the snow won't wet the carpet. But let's see, business . . . is it . . . ?"

Thomas Reaper frowns, and tries to make a fleeting memory precise, which draws away and dissipates entirely.

"Everything's going very well, Father. There's good fortune here! Come in; Mary and Mama are waiting for you, with little Bob and little Jane."

This time, Thomas Reaper is overcome and delighted.

"Oh, John! Mama is here! My God, I've been saying since this morning that she must be with you. And truly, she's here . . . ? But Mary . . . tell me, what Mary?"

John starts to laugh quietly. "Mary Smith, naturally. Mary, my beloved wife. In sum, Father, have you forgotten everything?"

It's too much. What? John has married Mary Smith? Thomas Reaper's most ardent wish has been granted. He cannot explain why that marvelous event has escaped his memory. He has all the joy of repeating: "Mary is the dear wife of my dear John! And Mama is here! But who is Bob? And who is Jane?"

The door at the back of the vestibule has opened both battens. Mary, so gracious, launches herself in front of Thomas Reaper and throws her arms around his neck in order to kiss him very tenderly.

"Hello, Papa! Dear little cherished Papa!"

And behind her advances good Mama Reaper, always mild and gray, self-effacing, but so happy at the arrival of Thomas Reaper that her eyes have something in common with the stars.

Good Mama Reaper is carrying two admirable babies, one on each arm. They are, in truth, true exhibition babies, plump and rosy, who are laughing in bursts and holding out plump little arms toward Grandpapa.

"Splendid! Splendid!" says Thomas Reaper, who wants to embrace all of them at once. This is Bob, I think! And this is Jane! Oh, John, you, established, married, the father of a family!"

John continues to smile delightfully. He contemplates, with a discreet joy, the family scene formed by Thomas Reaper, Mary, Mama and the children, all enveloped by happiness.

There is, in the depths of Thomas Reaper's soul, a certain obstinate astonishment. It's something rather confused. But he is in great haste no longer to think about it, to forget that his memory is so extraordinarily lacking. He wants to enjoy such felicity, which fulfils all his wishes, with a full heart.

"Now," says John, "perhaps we can go to supper?"

Scarcely has he spoken than another door opens, and the table appears in the dining room. It is florid with roses; and the soup is fuming lightly above the lid of the tureen.

"Sit down here, Father," says Mary, "between John and me, facing Mama . . ."

"But first," said John, "let's thank the Lord."

Is it possible? John, now, says the prayer.

And it is Mary who plunges the ladle into the soup tureen, saying charming things that Thomas Reaper dos not hear, because, in spite of his immense happiness, he is so, so tired . . . that he goes to sleep on dear John's shoulder, with one hand in Mary's hand and the other in that of good Mama Reaper.

At dawn:

"Oh," said the first policeman. "There's a man dead in the snow.

"Stiff," said the second. "Oh! Hang on, I know that man; he lodges in the same house as me. Do you know who he is, Perry? Poor chap! Well, his name is Reaper. His wife died last year, and his son John . . ."

"The one who was hanged yesterday?"

"Exactly. A true bandit. His father had done everything for him. Poor father! Yesterday's blow must have felled him. One might think that he'd been wandering all day, and then he came to fall down here, of congestion. Look at the snow, Perry. No footprints around the body."

"What I can't explain," said the other, marveling, "is that he looks so happy. That's not ordinary."

THE PHANTOM IN THE ROSE

by Lucie Delarue-Mardrus

WHEN the orphaned young man recovered his senses, he simply believed that he had undergone a second operation after his six months of illness.

If he was still deafened by a kind of ringing sound and his skin was crawling, was it not a residue of the effects of chloroform?

When, lungs full of that stupefying sweetness, one begins to lose consciousness in anesthesia, it seems that one's being is dispersed like a vapor throughout the world, and that the first effort one makes on recovering consciousness so, so to speak, an effort of reassembly.

The young man could not discern things yet, but he was sure that when he opened his eyes, he would find himself lying in his bed. The beautiful face of his fiancée, his only family, would be leaning over him anxiously, and around that beloved face he would distinguish the décor of the room where he was suffering, a strict, tidy room, fitted out in accordance with the customs of sanitaria. The nurse would also be there, who would take his pulse, and then the intern, and then a few faces of friends . . .

However, he was in no hurry to recover his sight. He felt that he was plunged in an ineffable wellbeing. No more illness, no more fever. An interior smile beatified him entirely. For a long time, his tenderness was exhaled thus, mute, blind and motionless, sweeter than incense, toward the fiancée whose presence he sensed, close by. Then, his consciousness becoming increasingly determinate within him, he ended up extending his will, and finally emerged victoriously from the limbo of slumber.

Had he truly opened his eyes?

With stupor, instead of rediscovering his habitual pillows, his bedroom, and his servants, he observed that he was standing up, plunged in the obscure corner of a room that he recognized as the drawing room of the Château d'Aspille, where, every year, his fiancée's family came to spend the beautiful season.

The day was declining. A sunset bloodied the autumn entering like a tide through the ancient window-panes. Shadows were gathering in the curtains; the lamp was not yet lit. The young man saw his fiancée sitting in an armchair beside the large fireplace, in which the flames were dying. She was leaning on her elbow, her chin in her hand, staring fixedly at his eyes.

His astonishment was such that he did not even think of asking her a question. He stayed there, without speaking, without moving, his eyes looking into his fiancée's, and little by little, with an immeasurable terror, by various evident and imperceptible signs, he understood *that she did not know what she was looking at.*

He wanted to cry out, to call her by her name. His will formulated: "Mathilde?" but no sound was audible. Had he become mute, then?

However, the young woman had shuddered. Her hypnotized gaze became animated, her hands fell back. She murmured, as if in response to the young man's appeal: "Jean."

With all his soul, he precipitated himself toward her; but as he commenced the gesture of extending his arms, he perceived that he could not see those arms.

He had no arms; he had no body; he no longer had anything. He was invisible.

A flood of maddening thoughts unfurled in the young man's mind.

I am, however, awake . . . I am, however, reassembled. I can see, I can hear, I can feel . . . I exist! And yet . . . my fiancée is sitting there; she is looking at me and cannot see me . . . Is it because . . .

And suddenly, the truth, the implausible Truth fell upon him like the blow of a sledgehammer. He had just perceived a petty detail: his fiancée was dressed in mourning.

Then, his voice, which could no longer be heard, pronounced, slowly:

"I'm dead . . ."

How long did he remain absorbed in the horror of that discovery? How long did he strive, without being able to succeed, to remember the circumstances of his demise?

Now, with a sad curiosity, he examined the situation. *This, then, is death,* he said to himself. *One retains alive the senses and understanding, but their envelope is no longer here. It's elsewhere, in the ground. Why am I not above my tomb? I don't even know where it is. Why have I recovered consciousness here? For I'm conscious; but it's only passive senses that remain to me This is it: one can see; one can hear; one can feel; but one no longer has anything active, for example, talking, or grasping. It isn't the will that is lacking, but one is like a man who has had his legs amputated, who feels that his feet are cold . . .*

He looked sadly at the darkening window panes, and mused:

The park of Aspille is there, with its yellow trees buzzing with wasps, its autumnal valleys, its meadows, so green, where the month of October is beginning to scatter red and russet heaps. We walked there, Mathilde and I, for an entire season. How ingenuous and affectionate we were! Nothing was more innocent than the deep gaze of my little promise; and I, in spite of my desire and the frequent opportunities that were offered, respected her with a sort of embarrassment. What is there more redoubtable than an innocent gaze? Today, when I'm delivered from my maladies, cured of life, I feel so light, so healthy! How I would love to walk with her again! I haven't retained any memory of the tortures of my illness. Nothing remains to me but an extreme tenderness for the woman who cared for me, a sort of emotional weakness, of candid chastity, an entire poetry that perhaps wasn't in my character. Alas! Alas! It would be so good to live . . . !

Night had fallen completely around the young man; an opaque starless autumnal night. Suddenly, a shrill exclamation of joy and terror brought him back to himself.

"Maman! Maman!" cried the insensate voice of Mathilde. "Maman, I can see Jean, I can see Jean! He's there in the corner. I can see him! It's him! He's come back . . . ! Maman . . . !"

A noise of overturned chairs. The young woman has stood up in the dark. A door opens, a lantern blinds the darkness. The mother, very pale, has precipitated into the drawing room

"Still all alone and without a light!" she reproaches, sharply. Then her voice softens. "My poor child . . . you'll end up making yourself ill . . ."

She hugs the distressed child against her, whose teeth are chattering.

"Maman," Mathilde stammers, "he was there . . . in the corner . . . I assure you! It's your lamp that has effaced him . . ."

The mother looks at her child fearfully. She is doubtless thinking: *The child is going mad!*

And for a long time, holding her against her shoulder, she speaks. Jean listens avidly. How he is regretted! He learns in what fashion he was extinguished. He has been dead for a week. Only today has all the distress of the funeral begun to calm down. His last words were a request to be buried in the park at Aspille. The body was transported there. That is why these ladies are here.

An incalculable gratitude for Mathilde fills his soul. He tells himself that it is doubtless the strong sentiment that he has for her that is maintaining him alive like this, in spite of death. Then, drawn by his desire to be nearer to the sobbing child, he has been displaced.

His vacillating being, which no envelope any longer maintains, is floating hither and yon in the room, as uncertain as a child's balloon. That is perhaps why phantoms prefer to fix themselves in corners. At length, he will learn the practicalities of his new condition.

After much groping, he contrives to remain almost tranquil beside his darling. At that moment, her head buried in the maternal lap, shecollapses and abandons herself to a bitter spasm of grief. As the phantom, subtler than a breath, has brushed the nape of her white neck, the young woman turns around, and for a second time, without being aware of it she plunges her streaming gaze into that of her fiancé.

The next day, at dawn, the young man found himself at the foot of the bed of his inconsolable friend. Had he slept? He had woken up at the same time as her, and as she was about to commence her toilette, by virtue of a charming sentiment of delicacy, he turned to the wall again.

Once her toilette was finished, he followed her downstairs, witnessed her breakfast, listened to the day's conversations, visited his own tomb by the side of the child in mourning, and returned to the château. When night fell he went to sleep, as he had the previous day, to wake up the following day at the foot of the bed.

At length, the days succeeding one another monotonously, the phantom became bored. One morning, while he was gazing with indifference at the pretty demoiselle, who was having a bath, he started to reflect.

Fixed regarding his new destiny, was he not beginning to envisage things in a slightly different manner? He was certainly no longer in the same phase of emotion as before. The poeticizing effect of the illness seemed to be considerably attenuated. As a phantom, he found himself similar again to what he had been in the human condition as a healthy man, neither more sublime nor more demonic. Was he not, save for the flesh, composed of the same elements?

Gradually, his egotism regained the upper hand. He found that life as a revenant could be quite agreeable: no hunger, thirst or desire; no needs; an extraordinary lucidity. Death was a total castration. It rid the self, once and for all, of the demanding and, in sum, rather uncomfortable, flesh. Now that he no longer had a body, the young man revaluated things. In truth, three quarters of his tenderness for Mathilde had evaporated with his sexual apparatus. Who would ever have suspected such a thing? What a revelation regarding the so-called sentiments of the heart! Fortunately, he had died before marrying. After six months of honeymoon, he would have been very unhappy.

Had he not already had enough of this family life in which one wept all the time? Ideas of independence came to him. He would travel the world. He would see everything, he would hear everything, and remain invisible. What an amusing and risk-free existence! What liberty!

Adieu, my darling! he thought, with some irony. Sure that it was not his tenderness, as he had imagined at first, that was maintaining him in a conscious state, since he had just perceived that he no longer loved his fiancée, he could leave. He therefore saluted the young woman mentally and, traversing the closed window, he found himself outside.

But a new surprise awaited him.

After having spun for a few moments with two or three leaves detached from the large chestnut tree, he felt himself, in spite of his will, imperiously caught by an inexplicable magnetism. He was like an animal on a leash pulled back by an abrupt gesture. Violently, he traversed the window again, but found himself back in the room.

Stupefied, he tried to emerge for a second time, and was brought back to his place for a second time.

Am I free? he said to himself, with anguish and revolt.

But Mathilde's large eyes, while she dressed herself mechanically, gazed into the distance with an expression so lamentable that the phantom fiancé divined that she was thinking of him with adoration.

Conceit consoled him slightly; then, in consequence, his mind, singularly apt in argument, was suddenly enlightened; but the new proposition that he found made him shudder terribly.

If it isn't my tenderness, he reasoned, *that enables me to remain, in spite of everything, living in close proximity to that young woman, it must be hers, her posthumous tenderness—let's say her regret—that has reconstituted me entirely near to her. I'm a part of her, as her own sentiment is a part of her. I am therefore linked to her in a fashion narrower than her shadow. It's because her chagrin evokes me that I return; it's because her eyes still seek out mine that I can see; it's because her voice speaks to me that I can hear; it's because her heart appeals to me that I can feel. The experiment presents me with the proof. I believed myself disengaged from all attachments, as light and fantastic as a fay, but I felt the leash harshly as soon as the first efforts to escape. I'm very humiliated. Already I was planning to abandon my fiancée in an ugly fashion, and I discover that I depend on her. I'm not my own master . . .*

He concluded gravely, brought back to the austere reality:

Are the regrets of the living, then, the only veritable revenants, and the only oblivion of the dead forgetfulness in the hearts of humans? Unless one remains immortal by means of some work that reminds the living of them incessantly, it's necessary that the deceased are forgotten some day. One inscribes on tombs in vain the fallacious assertion of eternal regrets! Sooner or later, the phantom disaggregates; that temporary condensation, due to the warmth of regret, is dispersed again. And it's then that the dead die . . .

He gazed at his fiancée, so pale in the black dress that she had just put on. And like a child requesting protection, frightened, ashamed and submissive, he begged: "Mathilde, Mathilde, never forget me! Mathilde, don't allow me to disaggregate! Mathilde, regret me forever!"

At those mute words, the young woman, believing that she was opening her arms to emptiness, began passionately to embrace the spirit that was speaking to her, and with the voice that made her mother anxious, she sobbed all alone in her room, in the midst of the charming disorder of her toilette: "Jean, my Jean! No, no! I'll never forget you, I swear to you! I swear to you . . . !"

220

※

Seasons passed. For three years, the mourning child and her mother had not quit the château, but, for nearly eight months, the phantom had felt less evident from day to day.

Doubtless, the magnetic thought of the young woman, which resuscitated him, which sometimes went as far as enabling him to appear, in glorious bodily form, was slackening. For, after having, for interminable months, followed his fiancée step by step, witnessed the cares that she lavished on his sepulcher, heard his name cried in her sobs, the unfortunate young man saw her posthumous flirtation cooling in a disquieting fashion. Every morning, time seemed to chip away a piece of the poor glorious body. Hearing and sight were becoming vague; understanding was weakening. Little by little, the specter was no longer anything but a thin vapor confounded with the morning and evening mists. He was dispersing in the general melancholy of the autumn that was once again tinting the beautiful park of Aspille crimson.

He did not suffer from that state of affairs, for his consciousness was almost obliterated. He sensed himself simply living in the fashion of trees, clouds, water and the air of the weather. He had forgotten his name, forgotten his lover, forgotten his past condition of an organized being. And doubtless, enveloped in the great formless soul of things, he would have been extinguished in that fashion if, on one beautiful afternoon of the after-season, a little ray of sunlight had not woken him up once again with a start from the annihilation into which he was sinking. This time, he found himself endowed again with human intelligence, buried and as if incorporated in a rose flowering above his own tombstone.

"What's happening to me?" his mind formulated, at first.

Then the memory of his life and his death returned to him abruptly.

"Ah! Mathilde, Mathilde!" he sighed. "So it's you, now then, who are abandoning me? See the condition to which you've reduced me! And why, now, having resumed the rhythm of thought, am I plunged like a bee in the hollow of this mortuary rose swaying next to my sad cross? Doubtless you've just thought about me forcefully; doubtless your heart has just identified me with this rose . . . ?"

He was not mistaken, for, an instant later, he saw the young woman, very sprightly in her blue dress, advancing toward the rose and toward him. A young man was following her, a living man, nicely turned out, probably her new fiancé.

"You see," she said. "I told you so. This is the last rose of the season, and it's on his tomb that it has grown. Poor Jean!"

A few tears appeared in her eyes. The phantom in the rose was overwhelmed. Never had he felt closer to life. The petals in which he was buried lent him a new flesh, odorous and fresh. And now he felt tortured by a sudden and violent jealousy because of the young living man who was accompanying Mathilde. With all his borrowed perfume he exhaled himself toward her, in a breath so provocative that she appeared to understand, and, almost fainting:

"This rose is so strong," she said, with coquetry. "I want to kiss it. There's a little of Jean in it . . ."

Then she advanced the lips that Jean had never taken.

Then, under that passionate mouth, quivering entirely with a carnal passion, the phantom who had become perfume was engulfed with a supreme surge into the breast of the young woman. Thus, he was the first to possess her. For an instant more, conscious, intoxicated by pride, he saw the eyes of his little promise, which capsized, and he heard her moaning sigh.

But the new fiancé had also seen and heard. That is why, imperious and gentle, he leaned toward her as she sighed and applied his peremptory kiss to the mouth swooning on the lips of the rose.

Traversed, as if by a sword, by that first amorous embrace, Mathilde tottered. The past, the present and the future were abolished at the same time for her. Jean, completely forgotten, sensed that he was finally annihilated in the universal breath of life. Killed by the kiss of the living, his phantom swirled for a second, disaggregated and vanished. . . .

Death had just died.

IN THE AFTERLIFE

by André Couvreur

I

I had just died.

My miserable mortal remains were there, collapsed on the parquet of my study, under the indifferent gaze of my books, my manuscripts, my engravings and my trinkets—all the precious décor of my mind when I abandoned the pen. My right hand was still clutching my revolver, held as an officer in the reserves, a weapon that I had certainly not thought destined to kill me on the day when it was confided to me. A red trickle was escaping from my perforated temple and, as if by irony, fragments of my brain, traversed all the way through, had gone to splash the wall, describing a little geographical design there, similar in its contours to the homeland I was quitting for some as yet unknown region.

Around my inert body complete silence persisted. Naturally, I had not informed anyone of my resolution. I had chosen, in order to be undisturbed, the afternoon of a beautiful Sunday on which our staff, Mélanie the cook and Anna the chambermaid, had been given leave, and when my Floriane was spending the day in the country with her parents, while I was presumed to be visiting our friends the Rouvions—whom my wife could not abide—in the vicinity of Marlotte.

Such was the ultimate perception that I carried away from my sojourn in this base world. It is claimed that violent deaths determine a sudden flux of thoughts in which the capital events of the completed existence are retraced in next to no time; there was nothing of the kind in my case. In the brief passage from life to death I really experienced nothing but the despair of being separated from Floriane, in circumstances that will be revealed in due course, and also a sort of buoyancy provoked by the relief of being suddenly rid of an organism with which I had been obliged to preoccupy myself for thirty-eight years. As for what would become of my soul, liberated from matter—the only interesting thing—that curiosity did not even enter my head.

Yes, what would become of me in my immaterial condition?

I shall refrain from debating here what the philosophies of all lands have had the pretention of establishing with regard to being after no-longer-being. For some, it is total abolition, a fall into the black gulf of nothingness, and that is all. For others, the spiritual entity, the soul, immediately finds a new substance, in which it incorporates, suddenly to recommence submission to a parcel of eternity, and so on. For yet others, without materially transmigrating, it nevertheless persists in this base world, floating there around the living, invisible, like the waves that science utilizes to harm people more than to serve them. Finally, for a number of religious believers, it escapes into a still-imprecise world beyond, where its terrestrial past is judged with a view to a supreme recompense or punishment.

That is what people think, but I had always abstained from applying my brain to it, in order to take sides, as it embarked upon the merrier skiff of literature. I also preferred devoting myself to material realities, that being much more in accord with my natural indolence. Then again, even at the moment when prudence might have commanded me to envisage that great problem, other concerns intervened, which, one way or another, had turned me away from metaphysical speculations. They will be revealed in due course.

In fact, my first impression belied the doctrine of nothingness, since my body was there, inert on the floor, inaccessible to sensations, devoid of any breath or palpitation, and yet, I continued thinking. It was the case, therefore, that something remained of me, something independent of my substance. It was the case, therefore, that my mind was not exclusively tributary to my body. It was the case, therefore, that my soul persisted. But what surprised me even more was that the soul in question, disengaged from matter, nevertheless retained a material image—to put it another way, that it conserved a visible appearance, and that the appearance was exactly that of my body.

I was no longer anything but a fraction of the association of the carnal and the spiritual that I had been for thirty-eight years, and yet the spiritual, the sole subsisting fraction, had not lost the representation of the carnal. Explain that as you may; I shall restrict myself to reporting it.

Another proof was given to me, in any case, immediately after my last sigh. It was the arrival, to either side of me, of two other spirits, as imponderable as me, but nevertheless similarly provided with a physiognomy, without my being able to imagine how they had got in, all the doors being locked.

I was dazzled by their appearance. Floriane excepted, I had never seen effigies so seductive. I am obliged, out of obedience to the rules of the French language, to give those spirits the masculine gender, but my admiration, always impressed by the feminine esthetic, would willingly have ranged them on the side of the fair sex. Let us say that they were the most tender, the sweetest and the purest expression of beauty. Their abundant hair—one was blond, the other brunet—was deployed over the shoulders. A vaporous tissue, harmoniously pleated and tightened at the waist, hung down to their bare feet, confusing its immaculate whiteness with two wings sprouting from their back, furled for the moment.

I would gladly spend longer describing the seduction of their features, the perfect oval of their faces, the candor of their long-lashed eyes, the velvet of their complexion, but I think enough has been said for the classical image before which I had piously joined my hands as a little child to be recognized in them.

"Angels!" I exclaimed, without being astonished at still being able to emit words, although the words in question were undoubtedly nothing but an exchange of thoughts.

"We've been delegated to bring you," said the blond.

"Where?"

"To Heaven," the brunet confirmed, smiling.

"But my poor angels, you'll never succeed in lifting my seventy-eight kilos!"

"Yes, of course—you no longer weigh anything."

"Let yourself go."

It was then that the paradox was confirmed that, although I was immaterial, I was nevertheless still tangible. It sufficed for them to lift me up by a fingertip for me to come to my feet. Then they each put a hand under my armpit. I heard a slight flutter produced by their wings, and all three of us flew through the window, in spite of it being closed.

My house, the neighborhood, the entire city, the green countryside, and then the sea, overflown in less time than it takes to write, disappeared from my sight. The stratosphere was no more than an instantaneous passage. Then there was space, devoid of compass, without appreciable direction. We were floating in the world beyond.

II

Did our fantastic voyage in the heavens last for a second, a minute or an hour? I would have had difficulty in establishing that. I had lost the notion of the human value that the English assimilate to currency when they proclaim that "time is money." I had similarly lost the notion of space, since I was now unable to measure the distance that we were traveling.

All that I remember of my celestial journey is the noise produced by the wings of my equipage. That could not result from the beating of the air, since air is material and we were abstracted from matter, but even so, their palpitation produced a very soft musical symphony, which reminded me of "The Ride of the Valkyries." That was my particular favorite, and the music delighted me.

I also remember that the angels, whose function as porters did not leave them on the same plane as me, turned their heads several times in order to smile at me. Was that to reassure me? Was it to hide their pity? No matter.

I was to be far more astonished when more powerful harmonies resounded, at the moment when we were cleaving through a sea of clouds to run abruptly into a wall, behind which something had to exist. I say a wall, but it was in reality more of an immense fortress, with crenellations, machicolations, a drawbridge and ditches disposed to drown aggressors: in brief, an entire powerful defensive system, contrary to the idea I had formed of penetrating into an essentially pacific realm.

Are souls also condemned, then, I wondered, *to protect themselves on high against the evil that reigns on earth?* I realized later that the formidable fortress was only raised in order to give new arrivals, still haunted by human wickedness, an impression of strength, which a welcome in a frame of simple clouds would not have inspired in them, and that the tragic representation was fictitious and illusory: a simple projection of images on vapor, much as the earthly cinema reproduces photographs on canvas to provide an illusion of reality.

When we reached it, terrestrial protocol was still observed. The drawbridge was lowered automatically, and a small door opened in the monumental portal. We passed under a vault that would have been dark had it not been lighted by the flaming swords of a double row of guardian angels, as delightfully lovely as those who had conveyed me. Then we went into a vast uneven courtyard circumscribed by arcades, at the other side of which was outlined a monument in the purest Gothic style, in which the inscription *Supreme Tribunal* was inscribed in letters of fire.

The angels had left me to move by myself. I could walk as if I were still alive. My reflections were also those of a living person, in the sense that, expecting the novel, the surprising and unusual splendors. I was astonished to come across a monument that, in spite of its considerable dimensions, resembled some provincial Palais de Justice. Had it not been for the angelic guard watching over the barriers, the distant music that had greeted us and as still persisting, and also a view through a gap in the wall that revealed, a long way away, the light of a fire embracing infinity, I could have believed that I was still on our miserable earth.

Having gone up the steps of the Supreme Tribunal, we were received by an angel who was not carrying a sword but was equipped, like our ushers, with a chain falling over the front of his torso. After a welcoming smile, he exchanged a few remarks with my transporters, who confided me to him.

I followed my new guide through dimly-lit corridors. I was able to perceive, when doors were opened therein, a succession of vast offices in which, under unreal lighting, multitudinous angels were working, some bent over papers, others running their pretty fingers over typewriters, exactly as in a place of business. Their occupation intrigued me less when I learned, subsequently, that they were employed in drawing up the identity documents of newcomers, compiling the accounts of their virtues and their sins, which must have necessitated an incredible amount of work, if other worlds are as populous as ours and if, by virtue of a universal equilibrium of conscience, morality is as relaxed there as it is on our world.

I could not help pitying those delightful bureaucrats, in thinking about their work, but my pity was attenuated by the reflection that the work must be their happiness, and that they were surely endowed with a cerebral facility not sheltered by the baldness of the paper-pushers whose mild indolence the State hires in France.

Finally, my introducer halted before a small door indentified by the simple label: *St. Peter's Office*. He knocked on it.

A fine baritone voice from within, such as one hears on the Canebière, but without any distinguishable accent, gave permission to enter. I obeyed, tremulously, at the sign that the angel gave me to advance.

I was before the master of my fate—of all fates.

And yet, the saint in question—the most powerful of all the saints—offered no particularity calculated to frighten me. I will even say that I had never encountered anyone who seemed, at first sight, to be so spontaneously likeable. Ensconced in a copious leather armchair, at a table laden with papers, with a telephone within arm's reach, he presented, in his capacity as chief saint, the worthiest face of the worthiest man one could imagine. Had it not been for his sacred toga and the luminous aureole circling the thicket of his hair— scarcely grayed by the millennia—one might have taken him for the benevolent father of one of those French families whose situation is prosperous, who eat well, drink well and sleep well, leaving their affairs to run on the tracks laid down by their ancestors. His candid blue eyes, his rather prominent nose and the abundant beard spreading over his breast completed that reassuring impression.

He also encouraged me with a sign. "Come closer . . . don't be afraid . . . I won't eat you . . . not today, anyway . . ."

When I had taken a few steps toward him he addressed the angel: "Do you have his form, my child?"

"Here it is, St. Peter."

After a genuflection, the angel withdrew. St. Peter read the account that had just been handed to him attentively. His bushy eyebrows reflected the various impressions of his reading, during which I was astonished again that he was obliged to have recourse to the form to recognize me. Why did he need it? Ought he not to know everything about me by virtue of his special privilege? Was a simple cast of the cerebral probe into my past not sufficient for him, then? But again, I realized that all these stratagems were simply to impress the client.

Now, I shall reproduce our conversation exactly. I ought, however, to warn my readers not to be offended by the manner in which he proceeded as soon as we were alone. Although they might expect, as I expected myself, only to hear benign language emerging from the mouth of St. Peter, and all the devout compunction to which we inhabitant of earth attribute to the delegates of the divinity, he employed, on the contrary, a liberty of expression sometimes spiced with cheerful slang expressions, of the kind that the relaxed manners of our epoch tolerate. Doubtless he wanted to put me more at ease, in order that I would more easily yield to him the secret of my soul. Artists are fond of spices, it must also be said.

After that preliminary, off we go.

Still consulting the form, he began: "You're Jacques Louis Paul Perdunier, known as Giky to his friends?"

"Yes, St. Peter."

"You were born in Seclin, in the Nord, and you're thirty-eight years old?"

"Yes, St. Peter."

"Your youth was uneventful. After brilliant studies at Lille, you obtained a first prize in philosophy in the general competition, in consequence of which you were about to undertake studies in law—license and doctorate—in order to enter the Bar, when the Great War broke out. Moved by a laudable patriotic sentiment, you anticipated the call-up, and at the end of the abominable world conflict you emerged as a lieutenant, with four citations and three wounds?"

"Not serious ones, St. Peter."

"No matter . . . you had given proof of courage and shed your blood. Not everyone can say as much. I recall the indignation of *poilus* with regard to ambushes when, in that epoch, we were receiving them in droves—which, in parentheses, caused us a lot of trouble. Poor fellows, they arrived in a real state! Yes, I know, there were also drunkards, jailbirds and rogues among them, but their ordeals inclined me to indulgence. The lice of the trenches alone equilibrated a considerable number of sins, so far as I was concerned."

"The lice are, in fact, my worst memory of the war . . . permit me to ask you not to forget them in my case."

He ignored my appeal to his generosity, however. "It's incredible that humans, so adept at killing one another, cannot organize themselves against lice! Oh, your science, your genius . . . !" He shrugged his shoulders, and continued: "To get back to you, the war revealed you by virtue of a successful novel: *Forward march!*, awarded a prize by the Académie Margoulin. Then, renouncing the Bar, you devoted yourself entirely to literature. You obtained more success with *The Underside of Those Women, The Good-Time Girls of the Five-to-Sevens* . . . alluring titles . . . and a third one which, on the basis of the title, I was curious enough to open: *Vice and Virtue.* I thought I might find a little morality therein. *It's high time*, I thought, *that novelists gave us a little help* . . . I was singularly deceived, alas! In the first few pages I discovered that your virtue is the resistance of a wife to her husband, in order to reserve herself exclusively to a third party! Very respectable! Before finishing the first chapter I had thrown the book on the dung-heap . . ."

I felt a trifle resentful of his intransigence, but dared not manifest it. To be sure, my novel was of the bedroom variety. It dealt with conjugal deceit, the eternal subject of literature—but how much more discreetly than the fare that readers ordinarily employ to tickle their curiosity! And how much better written!

The great administrator of justice continued: "You'll have observed my disappointment; let's not talk about it any more. You then ventured into the theater with a little secretion, *A Kiss in the Dark*, which obtained a considerable financial success. Is that correct?"

"Quite correct, St. Peter."

"Good. These various successes led you to look in the direction of the Cupola. And in truth, that's excusable, for it's tempting to garnish oneself with laurels, like a stewed rabbit, to buckle the sword of literature about one's waist, and, parodying Henri IV, to recommend oneself to the crowd with a white plume. A very human ambition . . ."

He was scarcely respectful of our institutions, the good Saint. I would have liked to see him on earth, pen in hand . . .

"So, you were preparing for the Académie," he continued, "with an artful and progressive conquest of your future electors, by a complete evolution of your romantic subjects, which became edifying, and for which I would congratulate you if the motive were not ambition. I cite among others your trilogy *Probity!*, *Courage!* and *Kindness!*—works that diminished your print runs but augmented your chances. Still accurate?"

"I agree, St, Peter."

"Perfect. Let's pass on now to your marriage. I can concentrate on that, since it's the origin of your appearance before me. I'll leave aside the various petty amours of your youth, simple peccadilloes. The Almighty has provided humans with the primal instinct; we excuse those who succumb to it . . ."

He paused momentarily. Then, this time without the aid of the form—which confirmed that it was only an artifice—in one breath, as if he were reciting, he continued.

"You had been cared for, toward the end of the war—after your third wound, contracted on the Front at the Somme, which caused you to be evacuated to Amiens and committed to a temporary hospital known as the Hôpital Lavalard—by a nurse, Mademoiselle Floriane Pastel, a very young woman recently recruited to that admirable society for the aid of wounded soldiers, the Red Cross.

"Mademoiselle Pastel's beauty was not belied by the eloquence of her surname. You fell in love with all the impetuousness of a heart that has only been beating for twenty-two years. Her youth and inexperience not permitting her to be entrusted with the dressing of wounds, she had been assigned to the pharmacy, and it was her who furnished the wounded, every morning and evening, with the potions prescribed by the surgeon.

"She was particularly generous to you since, on her own initiative, she diluted the medicaments into numerous bottles, which necessitated her returning several times a day to bring them to your bed. How you swallowed those little doses! And every time, there were long conversations, which had nothing to do with Floriane's duties, but extended over your families, your relatives, your plans and your tastes—a marked preference on both parts for literature. She furnished you with her books, still closely akin to the Bibliothèque Rose,[1] and you submitted to her in exchange the notes that were going to permit you to write your first novel.

"Can you still see her, so fresh in her white smock marked with a red cross, leaning over the edge of your bed, discussing enthusiastically the latest book by the ancient and solemn Comtesse who still found virginal accents in her old meninges? You were scarcely listening, so captivated were your thoughts by that animated pastel . . .

"All in all, a delightful idyll, perfumed with carbolic acid, which captivated you more and more every day, making you regret that your wound was not more serious, and consequently in more enduring need of the assistance of the little bottles. But didn't you obtain permission from the chief physician to replace the normal convalescence leave with a longer sojourn in the hospital? And that while your family was waiting for you anxiously?"

I bowed my head. "You know, St. Peter, when love possesses you . . ."

"Yes, I know . . . I know . . . you did, moreover, make amends for your ingratitude toward your parents later, when Mademoiselle Floriane Pastel became Madame Jacques Perdunier, by confiding her to them for a longer period during a journey of reportage with which you were charged by the great daily newspaper for which

1 A series of children's books launched by Hachette in 1856, inaugurated by the works of the Comtesse de Ségur, following up an earlier series of illustrated children's books with uniformly pink covers. It still exists, its name having long since become a common term for juvenile literature in general.

you worked. She was mortally bored throughout the time that she spent with them, in the country, in that gloomy property in the Nord . . .

"In penetrating the depths of your determination, however, was it really familial sentiment that guided you? Were you not rather obedient to the fear of leaving Floriane alone in Paris, delivered to all the temptations and all the tributes that a pretty woman receives?"

"Perhaps . . ."

"Certainly!"

"Love is not devoid of a little jealousy, St. Peter."

"Jealousy—that's the word I was waiting for! You are in every respect one of the best-favored of men. Nobility of character, generosity, altruism, devotion—as many characteristics that animate you. You even immolated yourself on the altar of the fatherland. That's perfect! But those exceptional gifts—which, if I go back to the curriculum of your form, have been manifest throughout your life in seemly actions, and score you a lot of points in favor of virtue—you have always counterbalanced by a failing that passes among humans as a mere flaw, but which I place, personally, on the level of the worst vices: jealousy . . .

"Jealousy: a base sentiment, an animator of crime; an inept sentiment, moreover, unworthy of your intelligence, which was, in sum, the origin of the act of despair that had brought you before me."

"I had my reasons, St. Peter."

"None! Everything you thought regarding the relationship between your wife and your friend Georges Ferval was pure unhealthy imagination."

"I have difficulty believing you . . ."

"You're in the holy place of Truth here! Know that I have never told a lie in my eternity! What reason would I have? Do you think that I wield the stick to that extent?"

His indignant attitude corroborated his words. Nevertheless, I exploded.

"I don't believe in pure friendship between man and woman. By all his actions, Georges manifested to me that the attraction he experienced toward Floriane surpassed friendship. Would he have come so often to Paris from Toulon, where he was assigned? Would he have arrived to plant himself constantly upon us, sprightly and spick and span in his naval officer's uniform, bearing his gifts, his futilities . . . extending to a ring, the last time?"

"Pardon me, but it was an old ring of no value, of the kind with which junk shops teem."

"It doesn't matter—he dared to give it to her. And Floriane immediately put it on!"

"Simple politeness."

"No! Jewelry that seals! Everyone knows what the gift and the delighted acceptance of a ring signifies! Anyway, all their behavior was significant. They looked at one another at length, smiled at one another, joked at my expense with a common accord. And yesterday, last night, at the Élysée ball, did she not refuse the majority of cavaliers to reserve her dances for him?"

"Of course! Everyone knows the cavaliers of the Republic! What a breed! And as you don't dance yourself, well, it was necessary . . ."

"And when the ball finished, at four o'clock in the morning, and we were getting into the carriage, if you'd seen the way she said goodbye to him, holding on to his hand for so long . . . and she . . ."

"A petty familiarity quite comprehensible when one has visited the buffet several times."

"One only drinks piquette at the Élysée buffet! No, no, champagne can't excuse them. Anyway, they only had orangeade, except once, one glass!"

"You were watching them, then?"

"Indeed!"

"Jealousy . . . jealousy that deforms everything that is normal!" Suddenly bursting into laughter, St. Peter said: "None of that proves that you've been cuckolded, does it?" Immediately becoming grave again, however, he added: "Nevertheless, your suicide, explicable as it is by your nervous state, is a sin that merits punishment."

"Hell?" I shivered.

"Oh no . . . that would be excessive. On earth, you know, people have a false idea of our severity. What? We've been sanctified by our virtues, and we don't obey the first among them, which is charity? Don't believe everything that's said about where the seven capital sins lead. I know that terror has been used to maintain morality, that it's a brake on evil instincts, and from that point of view, the eternal furnace is a salutary legend—but think about it: who hasn't committed a capital sin in the course of a life? Paradise would be a desert, damn it!"

Immediately, he bit his lip. "Did I say *damn it*? Forgive me, it was a slip of the tongue. I commit a few of them, being too intoxicated by your eccentric language . . . a language that, by the way, has so much phraseological clarity, power and harmony that I've made it my diplomatic language. I simply wanted to emphasize my protestation with an energetic interjection . . . and a blasphemy passed my lips! Forget it, and only remember our indulgence. Look, I'll give you an example, by telling you a story that presents a certain analogy with yours."

He collected himself momentarily, stroking his beard.

"Yes, only the day before yesterday, an individual was brought to me who had gone *bang! bang!* in the head, but after first having killed his wife. Ordinarily, such cases, being rather banal, aren't submitted to me. Our services know, in accordance with the standard ready-reckoner, what course to take. It's ruled like paper for musical notation and they proceed on its authority. But this time they were dealing with a worthy laborer, a ditch-digger by trade, whose case lent itself to hesitation. He had had the bad luck, that honest citizen, to marry an inveterate drunkard, abominable to his children, whom she beat. That evening, returning home drunk, as usual, she plunged a red-hot iron into the arm of her new-born, who was crying with hunger. On seeing that, the ditch-digger leapt at her throat and squeezed it until she lost the taste for rotgut. Well, I chatted to that criminal for a long time, as with you. I understood his perpetual ordeal in being so badly matched. I consulted his form, which was extraordinary in its honesty, rectitude and civic courage, for a rustic . . ."

"And what did you do, St. Peter?"

"With the woman? I didn't have to occupy myself with her, of course—the grill, automatically."

"But the ditch-digger?"

"Over the ditch-digger, I hesitated somewhat . . . but he was such a good citizen that I sent him the other way."

"Which is to say?"

"To HIM."

"HIM?"

"In capital letters, my friend."

"Pardon me, St. Peter . . ."

I ought not to have forgotten the notion of the Sovereignty of that supreme refuge, but I was entirely focused on the attitude of the saint. He accompanied the confession of his forbearance with a gesture of the right arm. Limply raised, letting the hand hang down, significant of a momentary renunciation of his mission as an administrator of justice. His aureole appeared to me to be even more luminous. He radiated generosity.

I was inspired by that to dare to raise an objection. "I can only applaud your decision, but the woman? The drunken woman—was she really responsible? Did she merit such a cruel fate?"

"She only had to refrain from drinking."

"Drinking . . . I'm not speaking for myself, who only drink water . . ."

"That's an error, my son!" said the Saint. "Wine is an intestinal antiseptic. Wine is a salutary beverage, and you have admirable vintages in France. I remember, in the course of an inspection I carried out on earth, when I was obliged to submit to all the corporeal exigencies of humans, having drunk a certain little claret from Touraine, which was to kneel before! Whereas alcohol is a disastrous poison!"

"That's understood—but would that woman have drunk the ethyl if the State hadn't favored its sale? And are you not, fundamentally, responsible for that calamity in allowing the State to do it?"

"There, we're of the same opinion," the Saint put in. "But what can we do? Alcohol has other objectives than poisoning the race. And then, we have to leave humans a certain initiative. They abuse it, as with all the liberties we grant them. They elect the purveyors of bistros that parliamentarians are. So, believe that I don't spare them, those henchmen of the zinc, when they fall under my paw. I've even given orders for their coefficient to be recalibrated. A politician automatically loses a quarter of his virtue points. Perhaps that would make them hesitate to solicit votes, if they knew it?"

We were in such accord on that point that I summoned up the courage to make a personal request. "Dare I beg you, O Master of my destiny, to have the same indulgence for me as for that poor ditch-digger?"

"Send you to Paradise? You can't think so! Your case isn't the same thing at all. You haven't passed through the same ordeals as that worthy man! All your sufferings were the creation of your own imagination."

"Floriane is guilty!"

"I tell you that she isn't!" He reinforced his negation by clicking his thumbnail on his teeth. "Floriane hasn't done that, or anything else, that legitimates your suicide! I don't know what will become of her later . . . with women, it's necessary to expect anything . . . but for the present . . ."

"I have the regret, St. Peter, of wondering why you persist in exculpating her thus, when in the depths of my reason . . ."

"You don't believe me?"

"No, I don't, St. Peter."

"That's good. I'll take advantage of your incredulity to attempt an experiment that I've been thinking about for a long time, and which will convince you subsequently . . . So, I'll postpone my decision in your regard." As he observed my emotion, he added: "Don't worry. I'm going to employ you in the fashion of a psychic guinea-pig; but as you're an elite subject, I think you won't have cause to regret it."

He pressed the call button of the telephone. Someone responded instantly at the other end of the line. Perhaps, once again, it was only a simulacrum and the communication was quite simply established by an exchange of thought. At any rate, as soon as he had pronounced the words: "Come, my children," the two angels that had abstracted me from my planet reappeared in the room. They took hold of me by the armpits, as if to depart.

"You'll come back to see me from time to time and we'll chat," St. Peter said to me by way of farewell.

Lifted off the ground, I went along the enfilade of administrative services again. Many of the celestial bureaucrats had stopped work to watch us pass by. They were still smiling, but it seemed to me that there was a hint of irony on their lips.

Then, once again, there were the great wing-beats of my transporters, first through the clouds and then infinite space: space strewn with a shiny dust, the homage of the stars.

III

The miserable world from which I had been removed a short while before soon reappeared, in a vision of I don't know how many trillions an hour, initially confused by distance, but which then became more precise. I suspected it by virtue of the fact that we were plunging through rarefied air, which I was not breathing, but which I was certain was the air of the stratosphere.

Then we traversed the clouds emitted by the terrestrial crust, eventually to fly over the sea, the countryside sown with foliage, towns and villages, and finally Paris, which I identified by means of Monsieur Eiffel's ladder.

Finally, here comes my street, my building, through the walls of which we pass. Here comes the landing of my third floor, on to which the only door of my apartment opens.

At that terminal point, where the angels deposited me and immediately vanished, I had the entirely physical impression that I had instantaneously rematerialized, but in an extraordinarily reduced volume.

Only too true!

There is a large full-length mirror on that landing, an admirable attention of my landlord, which permits us—Floriane and me—to stop before it when we leave for the theater or a soirée to check the correction of our costumes. It's necessary that no awkward crease or stray lock of hair spoil the impression of elegance that we're about to produce. Floriane adds a little powder to her face there; I adjust the rectitude of my cravat.

Well, there, in that mirror, what is it that I see?

I see a dog.

A little dog of the breed known as English terriers, black with short hair, with fiery patches above the gilded eyes, an elongated body with slender legs and a sleek paunch, sufficiently plump without being fat. A handsome little dog, in truth.

And I had the conviction, at the same time, that the dog was me, that it was inhabited by my intelligence, by my soul, the possessor of my past, disposed for my future, endowed with my instincts—destined, in fact, to continue Jacques Perdunier in the substance of an animal that was not yet baptized.

Oh, son of a bitch! One can make fun of a penitent, but not to this extent! Me, a celebrated writer, designated for the green coat, decked out thus! Buried in the skin of a beast! Saint Peter had played a damnable trick on me, if he hadn't sent me to damnation.

And I looked at myself in the mirror, expressing my amazement with a hateful crispation of my chops, exposing the glare of my teeth, ready to bite.

However, as I contemplated myself, reflection diminished my rage. With what aim had my judge decided to have recourse in my case to a metempsychosis forbidden in his realm? Did not divine law and holy morality formally proscribe the transportation of a spiritual entity into a new incarnation? I believed so, at least. Doubtless, I must be the first person to which that incredible adventure had happened. Yes, the first, since St. Peter had let it slip in my presence that he was going to attempt an experiment he had been thinking about for a long time, that he was going to make me his "psychic guinea-pig."

So, as I reflected with all the faculties of my intelligence grafted on to another carcass, my anger dissipated and my jowls relaxed. Soon, a joyful agitation of my tail was concordant with the complete evolution of my humor.

Let's see, I said to myself, *I could be up there, purging in I don't know what manner my self-murder, but St. Peter has decided that I ought to be sent back to Floriane's proximity. I'm therefore going to live again in her atmosphere, be nourished by her—instead of nourishing her—and perhaps receive abundantly the caresses that she measured out under the conjugal regime. And I'm complaining? Doubtless I'll torture myself again with what I'm going to discover regarding her relationship with that traitor Georges Ferval, but will my jealousy conserve, under my metamorphosis, the acuity of a masculine rivalry?*

Come on, let's recover a little common sense.

Calm down, calm down. And let's see, first, how I can set foot inside my home again. Floriane is away for the day. She'll come back from her parents' place after dinner, at the time I indicated to her as being before that of my return from our friends—which is to say, bedtime. Now, I killed myself well after the departure of the servants, at about four o'clock. My celestial journey was instantaneous. My appearance before St. Peter lasted . . . let's say thirty or forty minutes. The angels brought me back as quickly as they took me away. All things considered, therefore, it ought to be about five o'clock. The orientation of the sun through the window of the stairwell confirms that. It thus remains for me to wait for a good five hours outside my door. Let's try to make the most of it.

I spent a long moment then studying myself in the mirror. Only then did I perceive that I had not changed sex. Is it credible that that had not been my first curiosity? It was, however, an important matter. That went without saying. I was a male, since it is necessary for me to use that gross term. The observation was a comfort to me. The inconveniences of the female condition are well known—the frenzy that unleashes them at the times when procreation demands it.

I was a male and, let it be said without vanity, a male who appeared to me to be as seductive as possible. Details of my new being, which amazement had prevented me noticing when I first made my acquaintance, persuaded me that I had, in esthetic terms, everything I might desire. I could not help admiring my anatomy, which exemplified my breed in all its purity, with the two gold patches above the eyes, the slenderness of the muzzle, the sleekness of the neck, the aristocracy of the feet, the luster of the hair and, above all, the eloquence of the ears, partly suppressed and tapering to a point, which pricked up at the slightest external sound and the slightest internal emotion—for it is well-known that dogs speak with their ears and their tail, and mine, cut short, in accordance with a fashion that, in this instance, did not make it ridiculous, expressed by a rapid vibration my contentment in being home again.

Yes, all those details made me a rare animal. Human snobbery, that enormous stupidity, now disdains the breed of English terrier that I represented so magnificently, after having been so enthusiastic about it. We are no longer fashionable. With us, it is much the same as it is with music and old dances. Dance-halls no longer admit anything but the cacophony of negro music and savage contortions. It is the same with the adopting of long-haired dogs—lapdogs, barbets, Pomeranians, King Charles spaniels—as many sullen uglinesses with lice in their fur, and consequently propagators of epidemics, and perpetually scratching. As for me, a sweep with a sponge, and I remain a paragon of neatness and hygiene. I don't want to malign my new brothers and sisters, but I granted myself an indisputable superiority on that score. Such was, at any rate, my opinion when I was a man.

I was appreciating myself thus at my full value, before the mirror, when the sound of the elevator door closing down below warned me that someone was about to come up. *Look out!* I said to myself. *Let's not be noticed.*

I had the presence of mind to go and hide behind one of the benches that exist on the landings of well-to-do houses, which had been waiting there unsuccessfully for years to accommodate the seats of people fearful of mechanical devices and fatigued by climbing up on foot. Invisible in that refuge, I saw the old gentleman who loved on the fourth floor pass by, with whom I had had altercations because of his passion for deafening wireless broadcasts, to which he gave free rein late into the night in order to soothe his insomnia, which provoked ours. I had severely taken him to task for it one day, and since then we no longer spoke to one another. He passed by humming like a brass band. I had the prudence not to reply by barking.

Some time afterwards the elevator vibrated again. I went back to my hiding place and saw a young telegraphist appear, who stopped on my floor. What! The concierge had not sent him up in the service elevator? I would take him to task for that. Oh, but no—I no longer had the voice for that.

The telegraphist rang the doorbell, for form's sake. He waited without conviction, and then bent down to slide a telegram under the door, which he had just taken from his bag.

A telegram at this hour? Was it for me? Was it for Floriane?

My jealousy, suddenly flaring up again, stronger than prudence, precipitated me toward the delivery boy in order to read the address before the missive disappeared. Too late, alas! A kick in the side greeted my curiosity.

When the telegraphist had gone, I perceived that the tip of the envelope, insufficiently pushed through, was still visible at the bottom of the door. By virtue of a delicate mutual convention, Floriane and I each refrained, unless the correspondence concerned us both, of taking cognizance of the mail that the other received. As a dog, however, I no longer had to encumber myself with civilized scruples.

I tried, therefore, to pull the telegram out with my claws. I only succeeded in pushing it a little further in. Then I put my muzzle to it for a long time, sniffing hard. My sense of smell, singularly enhanced, allowed me to recognize an ambergris perfume dear to Georges Ferval. There was no more doubt about it; the telegram was from my rival. It could only be destined for Floriane.

Proof already, I thought . . . and sadness over-whelmed me.

After which I rooted around to the right and the left, a little on the ascendant stairs, and a little on the descending ones, collecting dust and posing in front of the mirror, but always to return to the revelatory odor, to the stub of the telegram that mocked me.

The sun was totally eclipsed by the window. The electricity did not take long to replace it. A religious silence reigned. Kitchen odors reminded me that I had not eaten since the day before. People were dining everywhere, in the peace of their hearths.

And I was alone!

Patience has its limit, even for dogs. I was beginning to grumble when the elevator advertised once again that someone was about to come up.

It was her.

Oh my splendor! Never, on seeing her emerge from the elevator cage, so sprightly in her summer dress, tinted pink by the day's warm air, with the smile that never left her, pricking her cheeks with two dimples, had I marveled so much, never had I been so convinced that she was my sole reason for living. And I had just stupidly acted out the tragedy of separation.

She moved a bunch of tea-roses from one hand to the other, in order to take her keys from her handbag. She prepared to open the door. I could hold still no longer. I quit my hiding-place and bounded toward her, putting my paws on her skirt and whimpering with pleasure.

But she shoved me away.

"What's that dog doing here? Have you finished soiling my dress?"

My emotion must have been communicated to her, however, perhaps by one of those psychic exchanges that exist between humans, and which might just as well—why not?—pass from animals to the successors of Adam and Eve, for she left the key in the lock to consider me at length.

Softened, she murmured: "But it's adorable, the little mongrel! Who can it belong to? That slut on the fifth? A gift from her gigolo . . . which he'll have stolen somewhere?"

A supposition that dispelled *a priori* the possibility that she might take any interest in me. Indeed, after a caress on the head that made me quiver she dismissed me.

"Go away, dog. You're on the wrong floor. Go look somewhere else. Go."

She closed the door in my muzzle. On the other side, she bent down to pick up the telegram. I saw the fragment on which I had worked so hard disappear. I would know nothing, then.

I was most annoyed at having been left outside. I waited for a moment, and then appealed, with a plaint that would have softened the heart of a gangster. A futile supplication. She must not have heard me, in her bedroom, situated at the back of the apartment. Or was she absorbed by her telegram? Then my plea mutated into an irritated barking, as only a tenant fortified by his right to enter his domicile could have uttered. At the same time I scratched the closed door frantically.

She reappeared. She still had her hat on her head. It was, therefore, the telegram that had occupied her attention.

"What, you again!"

But I did not wait for her to decide to let me in. I irrupted into the apartment and made straight for the drawing room, where I leapt up on the Louis XVI sofa—and there, henceforth sure of being able to dispose her in my favor, I struck the irresistible pose of a dog that, to use the common expression, sits up and begs.

"Oh, but he's so sweet! You have no master then, doggie? You have nowhere to sleep, so you're introducing yourself by force into my home?"

She remained meditative and uncertain, admiring my pose, gripped by the languorous little whimpers that I was emitting without interruption.

At that moment, Maria, our chambermaid appeared. Her afternoon of liberty concluded, she was coming, as a faithful servant, to ask whether Madame needed anything.

"Do you know this dog, Maria?"

"No, Madame."

"It doesn't belong to anyone in the house?"

"There's only one dog in the house, and that's the Pekinese on the fifth."

"Can you imagine that this one came in without me calling him, and that it doesn't want to go?"

"It divines that Madame is so good," Maria flattered, smarmily.

"What are we going to do with it?"

"Madame can always keep it overnight . . . I can prepare a basket in the kitchen for it to sleep in . . . and think about it in the morning."

"You're right. It would be inhuman to put it out on the street this evening."

Inhuman—never had that word, applied to a dog, been so apposite.

"And tomorrow we'll interrogate the local concierges. Go on, Maria. Give it something to eat—the little thing is probably hungry. You'll be able to find a drop of milk. When Monsieur comes in later, I'll send him to the kitchen to see if it's being good. As a precaution, tie it up with a cord. Go on. Bonsoir Maria—I don't need you any longer."

A supreme felicity: I was staying in the apartment! I would be sleeping in the kitchen with a cord around my neck, but I had been admitted. Tomorrow, they would keep me.

Maria had already taken me in her arms to carry me away. She smelled good. She emanated the same perfume as Floriane, and for good reason . . . But I could not tell her. In any case, she took it upon herself to make me forget her odor by emitting a supposition before going out that spoiled my joy.

"I've just thought, Madame: might it not be Monsieur Georges' dog, who has come to see Madame, and who, not finding Madame, might have left it at the door to await her return?"

The wretch! She plunged my back into my drama.

So, an understanding, a complicity, existed between mistress and maidservant, since the latter called the *other* by his forename, and supposed that he might have visited her in my absence . . .

I detested that girl. I could have sunk my teeth into the breast against which she was clutching me!

However, her reflection did not trouble Floriane.

"No, Maria, Monsieur Ferval has no dog. How could a naval officer have a dog? In any case, he wouldn't have brought it from Toulon. Good night, Maria. Go to bed now. Tomorrow, breakfast at eight-thirty, as usual."

Maria took me away. In the kitchen, while grumbling, she put a wicker bread-basket on the floor for me, without even adding a dish-cloth that would have served me as a mattress. I was thus obliged to spend the night on straw, which, without being the damp straw of a dungeon, offered me no less discomfort.

Furthermore, Maria knotted a piece of string around my neck, the other end of which she attached to the leg of a table. She also omitted to give me the nourishment prescribed by her mistress. All those circumstances revealed that she was in a hurry. I understood her haste when, once she had gone out, I heard her running down the service stairway instead of going up to her bedroom.

My night . . . oh, my first night at home, captive and hungry, weeping all the tears of my heart! My night, a few meters away from Floriane! I imagined her giving the final cares to her sumptuous flesh, not waiting for my return to lie down languidly in our beautiful all-white bed. Her eyes were closed, her pretty blonde head framed by her left arm—the position she adopted to go to sleep. She was smiling in a dream at a naval officer. And I, the amorous spouse, the master, was subjected to St. Peter's experiment in the basket of a psychic guinea-pig, in the neighborhood of saucepans, dish-cloths and the kitchen sink.

I do not want to insist on the sadness of that night. It will be understandable that it kept me awake until four o'clock in the morning. I ended up, however, yielding to the heavy fatigue of my celestial journey and the emotions that had followed it.

IV

The next morning, at eight o'clock, the key grating in the lock of the service entrance woke me up. It was Maria. What a sight! A face exhausted by the nocturnal excursion, red eyes framed by livid circles, residues of wine, dancing and that which had followed.

She collapsed into a chair. "And to think that it'll be necessary to run around all day for the bosses! There's no justice in the world!"

She spotted me then. "And that dirty beast! That's all I need!"

I had made up my mind about that joker long before. I would sack her without delay.

Sack her? What was I thinking? As If I were still her "boss," as if I could dismiss her . . .

She busied herself before a mirror repairing her face with the aid of ingredients she hid in an improvised make-up box, a stew-pan that was never used.

Mélanie, the cook, came in at that point. She was a conscientious old spinster, integrally honest, who had been in our service since our marriage. She had a just pride in the succulence of her cuisine. At any rate, she placed herself in the same level as Alexandre Dumas *père*, who cooked as well as he wrote. I anticipated that she would cherish me.

"A dog!" she exclaimed.

"Don't worry. Well, throw it back into the street."

"No you won't! He's lovely!"

"It's obvious that you're not the one who'll have to look after it."

"Mademoiselle hasn't given up her idleness."

"Go on . . . hurry up with the chocolate."

I savored that repartee, significant of two natures. When the breakfast was ready, Maria liberated me from my leash and took me away with her tray. We went into the bedroom where Floriane was still sleep. She only woke up when the large curtains were drawn, bringing her the gift of a radiant daylight.

"Why, Monsieur hasn't come back."

"Monsieur will have been retained by his friends," suggested Maria, perfidiously.

Monsieur is me, I would have barked, *and Monsieur takes note that his absence is observed without provoking any emotion.* It is true that Floriane held out her arms to me and covered me with the caresses that Monsieur merited, with an enthusiasm of which the true Monsieur would doubtless have taken advantage.

"Did he have a good night?"

"Very good, Madame. I stayed up late with him, continuing the pajama suit that Madame asked me to sew for Juan-les-Pins. He was very good."

"You had some milk?"

"Yes, Madame, there was some left. He drank it to the last drop?"

"Have you taken him downstairs?"

"He did what he had to in the kitchen, the big and the small."

"Take him down anyway—and ask the concierge who he belongs to. If he isn't anyone's, I'll keep him myself. He's a lovely dog, isn't he, Maria?"

"Oh, yes, Madame . . . But before keeping him, ought Madame not take him to the police station?"

"So that he can be sent to the pound? Oh, no. He deserves better than that."

"Madame is perhaps taking a risk."

"Go on, Maria, do as you're told. And keep an eye on him, to make sure that he doesn't run away."

She started her breakfast, set down within arm's reach. Monsieur's absence did not prevent her perfect teeth from chewing the toast merrily. She even offered me a piece, which I swallowed voraciously.

"He's poorly-trained . . ." she reflected.

Once in the street, in all honesty, I have to confess that my first act was to render to nature the tribute that a sentiment of propriety, persistent in spite of everything, had prevented me from delivering to the tiled floor of the kitchen. But I limited myself to that sole relief. I did not repeat it ten times over, at every emanation of another, as the irreverence of my brethren drives them to do. I say irreverence, but perhaps, after all, it is merely a matter of politeness, which my novelty under the pelt had not yet signaled to me as a testimony of canine civility. I would have been ashamed for my species.

My reserve astonished Maria. She pointed it out to the concierge as soon as she had introduced me into the lodge to make enquiries on my account.

When she had been informed she said: "Might as well be this one as another. He's clean—you won't have to clean up after him as much."

"Cleaning up after dogs isn't my job," declared the concierge categorically. "That's your business."

"He'll have to behave himself, then!" Maria threatened.

It was thus, in the liberty of my being, that I was returned to Floriane. She had just finished her chocolate. On the tray, my legitimate cup remained full beside her empty one. She poured it out in order for me to drink it. I lapped it up all the more avidly because I was, after all, reclaiming my own wealth. The sentiment of property is as dominant in dogs as it is in humans.

When I was replete, Floriane took me in her arms, brought me into the bed and cradled me there with the most tender words. Her husband's belatedness did not seem, for the moment, to have caused her any anxiety.

"Come and be cosseted," she murmured to me. "You're an exquisite doggie. I'll do everything I can to see that you don't leave me; I sense that I'm going to love you madly." Words that she had never said when I was in her arms before and she had claimed to love me—and the *tu*s she addressed to me, so unlike the refrigerating *vous* that we employed, entered into my heart like music.

Alas, I could only reply by uttering joyful little yaps and licking her plump arm. Our declaration of mutual love lasted a good quarter of an hour, after which she left me on the pillow in order to go into the dressing-room.

"Stay there, doggie. I'll come back."

She had never allowed me to watch her dress, out of a sentiment of modesty that I thought fundamentally laudable, while deploring it. I also think that she did not want me to know about the artifices with which she perfected her beauty. But this was an opportunity too good to miss; I had no reason not to take advantage of the privilege of dogs. I therefore quit the pillow to which she had consigned me, and followed her.

"Little rogue, you want to know everything about me?"

She did not know how right she was.

I thus obtained the secret of her esthetic procedures. Stripped of all veils, she examined herself before her three-paneled mirror, from head to toe, front and back. With tweezers in hand, she undertook a careful gardening, uprooting with heroic traction hairs that had strayed from the normal flower-beds, even pruning lawns that she thought too bushy. Then she greased her face with an ointment that cost ten francs a gram, insisting on the places where her excess of thirty years was designing the infancy of wrinkles. She massaged them pitilessly.

"Autumn soon!" she sighed.

But no, you're still in spring. I shall always see you . . . I replied, internally.

But why these scrupulous cares? For whom? Was it not to be able, when I returned, to offer me the homage of her peeled beauty?

After a quarter of an hour of fervent make-up, she was finally ready to slip into her beautiful mauve silk undergarments and, on top of them, the organdie dress that I had recently paid for, melancholically, without letting her suspect that I thought the price in excess of our budget.

While she finished getting dressed, another anxiety possessed me: to know what the telegram contained.

It was abandoned on the dressing-table, close enough to the bed for it to be possible for me to leap up there, over the night-stand. I accomplished that acrobatic feat creditably—but what frustration; the accursed paper only displayed the address, the rest of the assumed writing remaining on the underside. I then had the idea of tipping it on to the ground, in the hope that it might flip over to reveal its contents. I was about to succeed in that, my paws having drawn it toward me, when Floriane arrived. She picked it up, reread it, then tore it up into little pieces, which she threw into the toilet bucket. I had been cheated yet again.

Just then, the sound of the doorbell caused me to anticipate that I was about to find out why Floriane had made herself so beautiful. Of course! It could only be him!

"Monsieur Ferval is in the drawing room," Maria announced, in fact.

"I'm coming."

I feared for a moment that I might not be able to witness their conversation. Floriane moved to the door hastily, without giving any further thought to me. Before going out, however, she called: "Come on, Coco."

And it was in her arms that I confronted the thief of my honor. He was standing in ecstasy before the portrait of Floriane by André Devambez,[1] a magisterial work that represented her lying on a sofa, her eyes dreamy, one hand turning the page of a book whose

---

1 The painter and illustrator André Devambez (1867-1944) was a friend of Couvreur's; he illustrated the serial version of the novel *Un Invasion de macrobes*.

thought she was meditating: an attitude typical of her, perfectly rendered by the great artist.

Georges had not heard us come in. He remained riveted to the beautiful image for some time, while Floriane, also prolonging her silence contemplated for her part, *in anima vili*, with equal admiration, the sportive silhouette of her visitor. Oh, he knew what he was doing, that friend, dressed in his seductive naval officer's uniform, which is not usually worn when on leave.

Was I about to know everything?

He finally sensed her presence. He turned round, and expressed his joy by kissing her hand for a long time.

"To what do I owe our presence at such an early hour?" Floriane asked, with a hint of mockery.

"Bad news, *mon amie*."

Mon amie. Before me, he called her "*ma chère amie*," Was not the suppression of the adjective, the emphasis on the masculine possessive pronoun already an indication of property?

"You're frightening me. Is it about Jacques?"

"Jacques? Why Jacques?"

"Can you imagine that he hasn't come back from the Rouvions, where, as you know, he spent yesterday?"

"Bah! He'll have missed the train. No need for you to be alarmed by that."

"I'm not alarmed—but all the same, I'd like to know whether he did miss the train, and the real reason for his lateness."

"What makes you think there's another?"

"Oh, nothing . . ."

That "nothing," revelatory of the interest that they had in me, fell upon my heart like a funeral oration over an insignificant tomb. I was not even worth a suspicion of anxiety. The bad news concerning Georges was much more important.

"I've just received orders to return."

"You're going back to Toulon without finishing your leave?"

"Yes."

"What's the reason for this abrupt recall?"

"I don't know. I haven't yet had time to call in at the Ministry to find out whether it's a matter of a cruiser in the squadron."

"They can order you to embark just like that, without warning?"

"They can when international difficulties crop up—but I don't think that's the reason this time. On that side, at least, things are quiet for the moment."

"When are you going?"

"Tomorrow evening. So I came to confirm my telegram, to apologize again for having to let you down the day after tomorrow."

Finally, the revelation! They had a rendezvous arranged for the day after tomorrow.

The day after tomorrow, those wretches had decided to find some infamous refuge, perhaps even Georges' hotel. Their confession went through me like a drill.

Alas, I was obliged to recognize that Floriane was the more impatient.

"Can't we do it today?"

"Unfortunately, no. Today I have to go to Le Havre to see the notary who's settling the inheritance, as you know. That will take me all day."

"Tomorrow, then?"

"Tomorrow, I have to make another trip, to see Maman, as you also know."

She knew many things that I did not. But what escaped me even more, and which confused me, was the sudden change of direction their dialogue took, devoted exclusively to the fashions of the coming winter. Were they fearful of indiscreet ears? Not mine, at any rate. Ardent as I was to penetrate their secret, they could not suspect it. Or were they making use of conventional language to signify other things? At any rate, they talked about fabrics, he with a competence that confirmed his futility so far as I was concerned, while rendering him more agreeable to Floriane; she had a frenzy or coquetry of which I was well aware.

"I only want to wear silk crêpe," she declared.

"You're right. It's more becoming."

Crêpe—the apparel of widows . . . as if they suspected an imminent mourning.

"In sum, you can't see any means this time?"

"None—but I suspect that it won't be long before I return to Paris."

"It's very annoying nevertheless. Will I be able to wait?"

"Yes, yes . . ." Georges calmed her. It was only then that he noticed me. "What! So you've got a pooch?"

"Since yesterday evening. He arrived instead of my husband. Pretty, isn't he?"

"Yes, he's delightful." He put out a hand to stroke me. I replied by showing my teeth.

"Aha! He doesn't seem friendly. Is he jealous of you already?" Without suspecting how truly he spoke he added: "I can understand that." Then he asked: "What's he called?"

"I don't know."

"Call him Zizi, then. That's a charming name for a dog."

"You're forgetting that Jacques, in intimacy . . ."

"Giky, Zizi—that's true. But my God, you won't get them mixed up, even so!"

"Zizi it is."

"And I request the favor of offering him a collar."

Baptized by my rival! Garroted by my rival! That was too much. I manifested my resentment more ferociously. He judged it prudent not to insist. Besides which, the time of his train was approaching.

"I'll go. I'll come back tomorrow morning, at about ten o'clock, to say my goodbyes."

"I'll see you then, my friend."

She left me to escort him to the door. I don't know what they said to one another in the antechamber.

V

The separation from Georges Ferval in the antechamber lasted for some time, unless Floriane was distracted by some household occupation. I was beginning to think that I had been forgotten when she returned to the drawing room.

She looked at the old clock on the mantelpiece, whose face was dominated by a Venus on a Roman chariot, guiding two mares with long reins. For my part, I thought it singularly appropriate to the circumstances.

"Eleven o'clock and he isn't here yet. It's incomprehensible . . ."

She sat down at the telephone in the bedroom and asked for the long-distance operator.

"No. 117 at Bourbon-Marlotte, if you please." The number of the friends with whom I was supposed to have spent the previous day.

When she had Madame Rouvion on the other end of the line she enquired after me prudently. Nestled on her knees, I heard the reply.

"But we waited for him in vain . . . ," said the lady, nasally.

"What! You haven't seen him?"

"All day. That was very annoying for us, because I'd ordered the chicken with olives that he adores especially for him, and we were obliged to eat it overcooked— hard, dry and detestable. One doesn't do things like that! I had to console our poor cook as best I could; she was in tears. She has her self-respect, the girl, which is understandable . . . but I swore that next time, we'll replace the chicken with something grilled . . ."

Then the distant voice became pitying. "He let you down as well last night, then, my poor dear?"

"He has business affairs and obligations to travel at the moment, which disrupt all his plans."

"Men's affairs . . . we know what that means. I'm sincerely sorry for you, my dear friend. But a piece of advice . . ."

Floriane did not wait for the advice. She hung up, abruptly. When, three minutes later, the ringing of the bell caused her to pick up the receiver again, she hung up once more on hearing the voice of the obstinate counselor again.

I complimented her on my behalf. That Rouvion woman was a venomous parrot. I only tolerated her out of sympathy for her husband. The business reason that Floriane had given her to excuse my absence also testified a respect for our conjugal façade on my ex-wife's part, of which I approved no less.

She waited a little longer. Then, sure that Marlotte would not bother her any more, she recommenced her investigation. A little more nervous at each rotation of the dial, mistaking numbers, demanding the correction of errors of her own making, she made enquiries of my parents, my brother Jean, my sister Marie-Thérèse, our cousins Pigeois and my bank.

Might not an accident have taken me to a hospital? She questioned the Assistance Publique, then our doctor, and then, successively, all the railway lines. From public transport she passed on to my editor, the newspapers for which I wrote and, as a last resort, consulted the Morgue.

At every negation she became more annoyed. "Oh, what does this mean? Might that viper Rouvion have been right?"

I saw her finger sketch out the number of Mademoiselle Rose Vilon, the principal interpreter of my last play. The actress had been the cause of a small jealous scene the year before—oh, very slight, and the only one that Floriane had caused throughout our marriage—when Madame Rouvion, still under the guise of looking out for our marital harmony, had confided gossip, the pure product of her imagination, which alleged that I was the artiste's protector. I had had no difficulty demolishing that perfidious invention, but it was not surprising that Floriane remembered it. This time, however, as soon as she heard the voice dear to the public, the fear of ridicule made her hang up before even exchanging a bonjour.

She did not eat lunch. She replaced her organdie dress with a somber outfit—already!—and left the apartment, confiding me to Maria.

"I don't know why the boss has a fire up her backside," Maria reflected to the cook. "Can it be because of Monsieur?"

I did not see Floriane again all afternoon. She must have been continuing her search. I could not fault her obstinacy. Was a residue of tenderness its only stimulant? Was she not also obedient to anxiety regarding a material situation of which my disappearance threatened the loss? Not that she was particularly self-interested. She was even endowed with a natural generosity that drove her to treat others with a largesse for which I had sometimes reproached her. But ultimately, she appreciated above all, for herself, the good living, the comfort, the impeccable service, the automobile, the teas in which delicacies were unspared, the oft-renewed wardrobe and the ostentatious gesture of putting twenty sous into the hand of a professional beggar—so many petty follies which, in the current financial climate, were disconcerting for a husband. Now, her dowry was modest, as was the ease of her parents, to whom my disappearance would force her to return, while waiting for a new marriage at the reduced pay of a naval lieutenant. In that regard, I won a considerable triumph of banknotes. That would be my vengeance.

Her absence weighed upon me. In order to be patient, I undertook several investigations in the direction of my cadaver. To think that I was there, behind that locked door, and Floriane had not even thought of opening it! I found that negligence inconceivable. I put more courage into it than she had. I pointed my muzzle at the interstices, noisily breathed in the tragic air. No odor yet; my meat was too fresh. As long as they did not take too long to discover me! As long as I did not become, after my death, an object of repulsion!

At about seven o'clock, Floriane came back. She was accompanied by a notary of our acquaintance. He stayed for a long time conversing in the drawing room. I was not admitted to their conference, but I heard its conclusion in the antechamber, while Floriane was showing her counselor out.

"No, believe me, my dear Madame, there's certainly no monetary question that might have determined Monsieur Perdunier to . . . absent himself. All his financial affairs, of which I have the care, are perfectly healthy. I can guarantee that. It's necessary to look elsewhere."

"Where?"

He did not offer an opinion—but I understood by a casual gesture that he was corroborating the opinion of Madame Rouvion. Floriane interpreted it in the same way, for she said: "You're mistaken, Monsieur. Of him, it's not possible."

The lawyer made a further gesture, which signified: *Oh, men . . . !* and he withdrew.

I don't know what happened afterwards. Floriane abandoned me completely. I was banished to the kitchen, where I became reacquainted with my improvised bed and the string binding me to the table. I saw the meal taken to Madame come back in its entirety, lacking only a bunch of grapes.

"Perhaps she's ill," said Mélanie compassionately.

"More likely she's overstuffed," Maria corrected.

I was the one who benefited from the leftovers; Mélanie did not spare them. And in truth, I didn't shirk the pâté with which she'd filled a deep plate. Unlike Floriane, I had no reason to lack appetite. I knew how things stood on my account.

✳

My night was similar to the one before.

At about nine o'clock in the morning I had just come back from my little tour of the street when Floriane came into the kitchen to give instructions for lunch. Ordinarily, she issued them from her bed. She was wearing a mauve peignoir and seemed to be in a tranquil mood, but the circles around her eyes revealed her insomnia. She picked me up and caressed me limply, wondering whether I had accomplished my matinal canine duties, which Maria confirmed.

Immediately, though, the hussy enquired: "Should I set the table for two, Madame?"

"Certainly," Floriane replied simply—only to retract it immediately: "Unless Monsieur is still traveling."

"Ah! Monsieur in traveling?"

"Where do you think he is?"

"One never knows . . . with men . . ."

Always the same sly criticism of my former sex, proffered by that ancillary slut, as by Madame Rouvion and the notary. I don't believe, however, that we were interpreted so very unjustly."

"And then," Maria persisted, with false pity, "Madame seems so tormented."

"What makes you think that, Maria?"

"Everything, Madame . . . Madame didn't eat anything yesterday evening . . . Madame hasn't slept . . ."

"Not slept?"

"Madame only has to look at herself."

"I did sleep badly, in fact, Maria, but for another reason. I was battling all night with a flea. You'll search for it, won't you?"

"And there it was! Those eloquent circles around my beloved's eyes, which I attributed to the anxiety of my hypothetical escapade, derived uniquely from the fact that I had been replaced in the conjugal bed by a minuscule insect!

I owed to that insect, of which I might have been the carrier, my immediate replacement in my basket and that of the cord around my neck. That was about to prevent me from witnessing the imminent farewell visit promised to my wife by Georges for that very morning: a visit in the course of which I was sure to be definitely enlightened. Exasperated, I had the idea of appealing to the good heart of Mélanie. I started running madly around the table leg to which my tether was fixed, so that it diminished progressively, to the point that my neck was soon tight against the item of furniture.

"But he's going to strangle himself! It's not permissible to keep the poor beast tied up like that!" cried the candid cook, liberating me.

Now free to wander as I pleased, I decided that it was time to put an end to the ignorance of my entourage as to what had become of me. I was the only one able to put them on the right track, since no one had thought of the study where I was nursing my last slumber. I went in that direction and started leaping up furiously at the door, howling mortally.

They did not understand at first. Maria fetched me back to the kitchen twice, smacking me, and twice I returned to the same howls of distress. On my third trip, Floriane shouted from her bed, where she had gone to lie down again: "Why is he barking like that? Come here, Zizi!"

I did not obey, but continued my performance. Then she got up, came into the corridor, and remarked: "What's in there, to put him in that state?"

She tried to go in.

"Why, it's locked."

She put her eye to the keyhole. The key was on the other side, and she could not see anything.

"It's locked from inside! Oh, what a bother!"

She went into the drawing room, where there was a door communicating with the study. She repeated her attempt to open it, in vain. Then a presentiment gripped her, which caused her to suspect, certainly not that I was lying inanimate behind those doors, but that she might find, there where I worked, the key to the enigma. Even if one no longer loves one's husband sufficiently to have been excessively upset by his absence, and one has only suffered insomnia because of an avid flea, marital negligence nevertheless demands to be clarified.

"Quickly, a locksmith!" she went into the kitchen to order.

It was Mélanie who brought back a portly practitioner, the bearer of a goatee, a bunch of keys and a lock-pick. The door ended up yielding.

And then . . .

Then, if I had been able to believe in Floriane's love, I would have had striking evidence of it. On perceiving my cadaver, still holding the murderous weapon in the right hand, she stood still at first, dazed, rooted to the spot, her eyes widened by terror, her entire body agitated by a tremor, while scarcely comprehensible words collided in her throat.

"Him! . . . Him, here! . . . He's killed himself! . . . Is it credible? Am I mad? . . . It's not possible! . . . Why has he done it? My Jacques! . . . My Jacques! . . ."

She threw herself on my body, calling to me desperately, begging me to come back to life, not to leave her here alone, henceforth without any reason to live. Her hand, not frightened by the dried blood, caressed my face. Her mouth inclined toward mine, utterly icy. Incapable of weeping, she finally suffered a crisis of nerves, which extended her by my side.

Around her, the spectators reacted differently. Mélanie made the sign of the cross. Maria imagined her picture in the newspapers. The locksmith caressed his goatee, like a man undisturbed by a corpse, who has seen many others during the war, while clearing the trenches, and also as a proletarian, summoned too frequently to ceremonies of the same nature, and who is able to be paid for his disturbance.

And me, in the meantime?

Perched on an armchair in order to enjoy a good view of the spectacle, I was no more emotional than the locksmith.

Enough play-acting! I growled. *I admit the initial surprise, but not the dolor and the attack that succeeded it. Showing off. I don't believe it.*

As it was necessary for me to participate in the event, however, I started barking. My howls were addressed neither to Floriane nor to her entourage, but to the rigid imbecile lying on the ground, my ex-individual. A comprehensible psychology, at the memory of all that I had given to that woman of my confidence, my generosity and my labor, and the fashion in which she had thanked me.

Mélanie's pity brought the scene to an end. Aided by the locksmith, she transported Floriane into her bedroom, in order that she could complete her spasmodic performance there. I did not feel the urge to go and console her with a little lick. I was waiting for my rival. He was missing the ceremony. He had promised his farewells for ten o'clock, and the clock was already marking eleven minutes past.

The sound of the doorbell made me think that it was him. I ran into the antechamber; but it was only the Commissaire of Police. Alerted by Maria, he arrived in a very good humor, his face replete, smoking a cigar like a Grand Duke before Bolshevism. He was accompanied by his dog—I mean the Commissaire's dog, not one comparable to me: a little man, pale and thin. He barely took off his hat in the presence of my remains. He had the discovery explained to him by Maria. She narrated it to him with a prolixity that denoted her delight at being mixed up in the story.

"The reason for the suicide? The marriage wasn't going well?"

"I daren't say—but you know, Monsieur, with men . . ."

"No, I don't know," the Commissaire cut in. Then, in a low voice, to his secretary: "We'll find out later." By way of a conclusion, he added: "Cuckolds overreact, decidedly. One might think that the police were made for them!"

After which he went away, without asking to see the lady of the house.

Georges did not arrive until midday.

By his contrite air, I could see that he had already been brought up to date, doubtless by the gossip of the concierge. The event authorized him to cross the sacred threshold, and it was to Floriane's bedroom that he went. I followed him there.

They remained silent at first, contenting themselves with a long pressure of the hands.

He spoke first: "What got into him?"

"I'm still wondering."

"His business affairs were going well, though?"

"Very well. His feuilleton was a success. He was well paid . . . for a novel that isn't a policier, it was reasonable. In addition, Monseigneur Bellême, the day after Claude Alaire's funeral, had told him that the moment had come to offer himself for his armchair. He even added, jokingly, that he'd soon be wearing a green coat. And now he's shot himself! Isn't it stupid?"

"You, personally . . . you haven't given him any reason . . . ?"

"You know very well that I haven't, Georges. Nothing that could have made him anxious . . . not that!"

"Then it's incomprehensible."

"Let's go see him," she said, resolutely.

I retained from that curt dialogue that she called Georges by his forename and that she had conducted herself in such a fashion that I could not suspect anything.

I expected, however, still more confirmation of their common salvation by the death—but their visit did not shore up my conviction, and that was my fault. When I saw, instead of the greeting that any visitors might have given me, Floriane content herself with a cold gesture, and Georges only respond with a shrug of the shoulders, a sudden, cold, invincible anger precipitated me at him in order to bite him.

If only I had had the solid jaw of a wolf that grabs a thigh and feasts upon it! If only I had possessed, in my gums, the virus of rabies before Monsieur Pasteur!

Unfortunately, my lap-dog jaws only succeeded in ripping the trousers of my rival's beautiful uniform—which resulted in my being taken back to the kitchen by Maria, and receiving there one of those corrections that a dog remembers, and then being locked in a cupboard where I purged my tongue without being fed, without being taken downstairs, without breathing any other air than my own—a captivity that lasted for three days.

With the result that I knew nothing more of that happened subsequently: whether Georges returned to Toulon immediately; whether my coffin was comfortable; whether my wife had the requisite attitude of grief; nor whether my funeral was embellished by the presidential rhetoric of the various literary societies to which I belonged.

The only thing of which I was perfectly sure *a priori* was that Floriane would wear a ravishing outfit, and that her mourning would render her even more desirable.

VI

It was decided, immediately after my burial, that Floriane would go to spend the first phase of her widowhood at Les Bolois, her parents' property in the Eure.

I loved that corner of nature, where the old folk let their years flow gently by, by courtesy of a modest but secure income. My father-in-law, Monsieur Firmin Pastel, initially rented it in order to send his family there for vacations. Later, he bought it, once he had handed over his cement business to his principal employee.

It was a large estate of a hundred hectares, cultivable land and woods favorable distributed for exploitation and hunting. A stream, emerging from the flank of the nearby hill, wound sinuously through it, also permitting battles of wits with trout. Here and there, the green-tinted roof of a farmhouse inhabited by agricultural workers protruded. Meadows extended around it in which abundant variegated livestock idled somnolently. Incapable of idleness, Monsieur Pastel spent his sixties running his estate personally.

The most cheerful location, however, was still the one where the main dwelling stood. Constructed in the style of the Second Empire, it was discreet in its importance. High enough to dominate the landscape, it was nevertheless invisible from the distant national highway, to which an avenue of magnificent poplars led. In front of it was a vast lawn, caressed by a tranquil expanse of water, which extended as far as the foliage of a centuries-old park.

It was for that refuge that Floriane embarked, the day after the funeral, in company with her family: her father, her mother and her brother Louis, still a bachelor. They occupied the four corners of a first-class compartment. A small coat dressed me in black, like everyone else. They had also bought me, for the occasion, one of those little wicker cases which spare dogs from traveling in a special kennel in the luggage wagon. It also served to by-pass the orders of the employees, as well as the train conductor, who, when he came to punch the tickets, had the indulgence not to notice me on the knees of the Mother. I was part of the family.

I want to stress the exquisite generosity of dear Madame Pastel, who treated me subsequently as if she had an intuition that I was something other than a banal dog. She still bore under her gray hair the residues of a beauty that must have been resplendent when she was twenty—a beauty so faithfully transmitted to her daughter that I could imagine what Floriane would look like at the same advance age. Only their eyes, although they were the same color, were dissimilar. The candid blue of the one was sharpened in the other by a cheerful malice, to which I had been subjected since the first day, but for whose seduction I now deemed that I had paid dearly.

The mother and I had always got on well, even before I became her daughter's fiancé. She had brought forth arguments in favor of our marriage that had vanquished Papa's hesitations. She had not changed her mind because of the abrupt denouement of a marriage she had always believed to be perfectly solid. Being unable to admit that Floriane had strayed from a conjugal dignity of which she had provided the example, she wanted to attribute my cooling to a sudden crisis of madness provoked by an excess of intellectual labor. What was astonishing, she said in my defense, in the cerebral mechanism breaking down by dint of incessantly searching for words, sentences and stories?

My father-in-law's character was in complete contrast to his wife's. Noble, serious, categorical in business, endowed with a practical sense that had brought success in all his enterprises, he only departed in family life from his principal qualities as a head of industry; then he gladly became jovial, and even humorous. He turned all the minor events of his hearth into jokes. One would never have thought he was the same man, seeing him in his office and at his dining table—for he liked good food and, without excess and as a dilettante, as much for others as for himself, vintage wines. His cellar was a temple. He donned a smock to put his wine in bottles. I loved to see his benevolent face radiant when he entertained friends. Once he had raised his glass to their health he would plunge his nose therein to breathe in the incense. As when hunting, his grumbling was satisfied when he saw his prey fall.

His Epicureanism did not prevent him worrying about his children. He had sent his son to the École Polytechnique, and then into civil engineering. For his daughter he had wanted a husband who was totally secure, so he had resisted Floriane's inclination toward me. She had told me about their first conversation in my regard, on the day when, with an abandon that he was able to inspire in her, she had declared our intention to unite our lives.

"You're mad."

"Yes, Papa, I'm mad about him."

"A journalist!"

"The most beautiful of professions. But Jacques, although he writes articles for the newspapers, isn't only a journalist. He's already a reputed man of letters. His first novel was awarded a prize by the Académie Margoulin."

"He writes novels! That's even worse! I refuse."

That bourgeois suspicion was attenuated when he learned that my pen already assured me material security, and that the inheritance of a little family wealth permitted me, as he put it, "to butter the parsnips." His resistance collapsed completely on the day when Madame Pastel revealed to him the tidy emoluments that had honored my voyage to Italy in order to conduct an enquiry into the social evolution of that country.

"He's a fellow with a future. And Floflo's losing weight."

"She's losing weight?"

"You haven't noticed? Five kilos in three months!" She was exaggerating the three.

"I accept!" the worthy man said, fearfully.

Subsequently, he became prouder of me than of his son. He came to see all my plays. Eyebrows wide, he announced that I was headed for the shore of the Pont des Arts.

280

My sudden suicide bewildered him as much as his wife. He did not put the blame on the excess of my labor. He applied the principle of *cherchez la femme*. Poor Floriane had lost weight again. It could only be that. Decidedly, these novelists, what a breed!

I judged the state of mind of the family quartet—since I no longer counted for the quintet—by their various attitudes while the train carried us away. But it was Floriane that I observed most of all. Believe it or not, she was reading the latest work of one of those creators of nonsense now held in such low esteem by her father. And her thoughts might have been absorbed by it!

Sometimes, however, a return to decency extracted her from her reading. Then she directed at the fleeting landscape a gaze charged with melancholy, which my disillusionment pushed as far as Toulon, rather than arresting it in the corner of Montparnasse cemetery where I had been buried the day before. I could only interpret her feigned sadness, in accord with her costume, as the apparel of a new seduction.

She had thrown back her mourning veils. Her face was as carefully made up, her blonde hair as coquettishly distributed. Her ungloved hands were not devoid of the crimson nail-varnish that I deplored. Delightful black deerskin brodequins espoused her dainty feet. From what high-class manufacturers, from what luxury boutiques, had those artifacts emerged? My consolation was that I would no longer see the bills.

We arrived at Evreux at about six o'clock in the evening. Mélanie, whom Floriane had kept on after letting Maria go with a generous severance payment, quit her second-class compartment, next to ours, to help with the luggage. I noticed her red eyes and weary gait. She carried me to the antique limousine that was waiting outside the station. The luggage was loaded on to the kind of gallery that automobiles no longer have, and we set off for Les Bolois. Floriane had replaced her mourning veils. Monsieur Pastel, who was well known in the locality, ordered the gardener, who was also the chauffeur, to make a detour.

"We've become curious beasts," he grumbled.

Indeed, when we arrived at the estate, the people of the village, assembled by the roadside to lie in wait for us, watched us pass by with a commiseration that irritated my father-in-law. Ordinarily cordial with those humble folk, he scarcely acknowledged their salutations.

He was more kindly disposed toward the frantic welcome of Castor, his hunting dog. I shall have occasion to return to that animal, which St. Peter gave me as a principal companion. He was sympathetic to me from the start, manifesting no annoyance at my intrusion. It's true that I was such a little thing by comparison with him . . .

Floriane went up to her bedroom immediately. I knew the way well enough to have preceded her there. A young woman's bedroom that had become our conjugal nest, it was filled with memories of our love, principally photographs, which were scattered almost everywhere, on the walls, the mantelpiece and the nightstand.

I saw us there in the nudity of a sunlit beach, in our wedding outfits, emerging from the church, and also among the guests at a literary banquet where the magnesium flash had taken her by surprise while she was showing her teeth, which rendered her provocative. Dear evocations of our concluded tenderness, what would become of you? Would you now be relegated to an album, in order for Georges to triumph officially in my stead?

Floriane took me in her arms and, holding me in front of the photograph of the church, said: "Look, Zizi, that was him. How genteel he was then."

She unpacked with a hereditary care. She took from her trunk newly-acquired dresses, presaging her eventual abandonment of her mourning. She redid her hair and make-up, and then we went down for dinner.

They chatted about everything at that meal, in which they ate, I remember, trout *meunière* and partridges. They talked about everything except me. It was necessary, to bring back my shade, for the wireless to intervene. The chambermaid had switched on the apparatus, as she did every evening during the meal, while the Eiffel Tower was broadcasting the daily current affairs item. Well, immanent justice determined that the waves should be occupied with me at that moment. The sympathetic voice of a speaker, which I knew well, was commenting on my death, reporting on my funeral.

"Switch it off! Switch it off!" cried Floriane.

"No!" protested Monsieur Pastel. "On the contrary, we need to know what people are saying."

The dead are quickly gone, and very little would have been said, but for the abrupt fashion in which I had quit the world. The reporters had found pasture therein. An interview with Maria, who attributed my final act to a gallant neurasthenia, nourished newspapers avid for petty scandals in that slack season.

The speaker therefore insisted more than decency permitted on my dramatic end. He then handed the microphone over to a literary critic for a ten-minute lecture on my works. I expected that dear colleague, a novelist himself who caressed the same green ambition as me, to renew a malevolence that he had scarcely hidden in his previous articles. To my surprise, he covered me with flowers. He deplored the loss of a great servant of art. He demonstrated the repercussion, so favorable to French renown, on my trilogy, *Probity, Courage* and *Charity*, being careful to pass over the frivolities that had preceded it. He focused on my dramatic work in the second place. Certainly, I imagined that the satisfaction of no longer having me as a competitor had encouraged such eulogies, but I was flattered nevertheless. So were those around me.

"Look how the pooch is listening," Monsieur Pastel observed. "One might think that he understands."

"Here, Zizi," said Floriane, offering me a slice of the partridge that she was savoring in the manner of a widow whose appetite has not been diminished by grief.

I neglected her offering on hearing a third speaker, returning to the subject of my funeral, say that the Minister of National Education, after having inclined over my grave, had kissed Floriane's hand. A minister's kiss is of no great value nowadays, but Floriane must have been proud of it even so. I, on the other hand, refused to take the meat from that hand at that moment. A minister's kiss . . . that could hardly be of any interest to the nation!

I relate all these details, which will doubtless be thought unimportant, in order that my confidants will not judge me a somber Othello, obsessively carried away by his jealousy without appreciable reasons. It is an ensemble that, without being such striking proof as having surprised Floriane in the arms of a handsome naval officer, constituted a symptomology on which I had the right to base my suspicions.

As far as I was concerned, the following days at Les Bolois rolled by in indolence. Everyone resumed their petty lives. Monsieur Pastel went back to hunting, Madame Pastel occupied herself with household matters. By the third day, my brother-in-law Louis had gone back to work. Mélanie replaced the cook, who was on the point of giving birth. And I played continually with an apathetic Floriane who, for the moment, in the sullenness of a rainy September, relieved the tedium of her retreat with an increasing affection for her little Zizi.

I brought her diversion, movement and tenderness. She had to worry about my nourishment, and my cleanliness in every regard. For her, I was like a baby. Her attentive cares made my regret once again that we had not had children. A child is a pledge of feminine fidelity . . .

The first night, she confided me to Mélanie. The second night, she let me sleep next to her bed, on a cushion. Further progress on the third night: she allowed me after much insistence on my part and endless scratchings, under the covers at her feet. Thus I resumed my place in the conjugal bed.

For dogs, as for humans, there is nothing like the intimacy of sleeping together to consolidate affection, from the moment that it becomes possible. I observed a retightening of our bond, I might say on a daily basis.

Dogs are naturally brought to love their masters. They are the only creatures in the world that look you in the eyes and say to you: *I love you for yourself. You can deprive me of nourishment, beat me unjustly, play a thousand dirty trucks on me, and I will love you even so. You can isolate me, leave me behind a door, and I will sit on my behind and wait. You can die, and I will find your grave, and pine away thereon.*

As a man, I adored Floriane, and I had consented to make many sacrifices for her, but without ever attained the total slavery to which I felt disposed as a dog. I had killed myself for her under the effect of a mental depression that a little philosophy might perhaps have converted into resignation, whereas my new state did not admit reflection. If St. Peter had not taken me as the subject of an experiment unique in his eternal career, I could easily have believed that metempsychosis is a divine law, that the Creator brings creatures, in a new life, close to those they loved most in their preceding life, the supreme favor being, for the most virtuous, returning as members of the canine species.

Floriane, as I said, submitted progressively to my adoration. She eventually confessed to me the same devotion that I had for her. In the morning, when we woke up, I passed from her feet to her arms. With no recall of the carnal impulses that had once united us, I floated in integral purity. She told me things; I replied with tender little growls, licking her with my pink tongue. I had become her confidant. She thought aloud for me.

"Papa," she said to me, "doesn't seem to be in a good mood. I don't know what's happening in the house . . . doubtless it's still to do with my story. Can you imagine, Zizi, that he's received the Maire, who came to ask him for a subscription for the public drinking-fountain, like a dog in a game of skittles."

She retracted that immediately: "Like a dog who isn't Zizi. You, I'd admit to my game of skittles."

Another time:

"I wonder why Louis left so quickly. Don't you think, Zizi, that it was to go back to his girl friend? Oh, when love gets hold of us . . ."

Her beautiful eyes strayed into the past. I thought she was about to arrive at our drama, and yield the exact repercussion of her heart to me. Nothing of the sort; she retreated into silence. I was always reduced to judging her in accordance with the past.

With regard to her relationship with Georges, the mystery similarly continued. Twice in a week, during breakfast, a letter with a Toulon postmark reached her. As she knew that she was being observed by her parents, she opened the letters and read them with a feigned indifference; then she slipped them into her boson.

"What is it?" Monsieur Pastel asked.

"Condolences, Papa."

"From whom?"

"From one of his friends."

"Let me have a look."

"What's the point?" She did not comply.

Her father grimaced, but did not insist. For my part, as is imaginable, I looked out for the missive, keeping close on Floriane's heels when she went up to her room to resume her reading. The same disappointment as with regard to the famous telegram, alas. She pushed me away in spite of my efforts to climb on to her knees, until she had finished the prose in question—evidently singular, since it led her to smile several times—after which she tore the letters into a thousand pieces and threw them in the toilet bucket. I gazed stupidly at the pieces, already bleached by the water, while she replied hastily on mauve paper, which she had selected in spite of the fact that white with a black border was required of her. Those few details—the case she took to destroy the correspondence, the colored paper—redeemed my memory, confirming once again her culpability.

Well, whatever people might think, my reaction to these various items of evidence was progressively attenuated. Quite sharp at the beginning, when we arrived at Les Bolois, it was eventually converted into a kind of fatalism. Yes, I could believe, to recall the terminology of the great Saint and a great comedian of similar inflection, Molière, that I was a cuckold, but I found compensation in the marks of another kind of affection that I obtained from Floriane—an anesthesia of which I can give a further proof.

Those mauve letters, in reply to those from Toulon, do you know who gave them to the postman?

It was me. Yes, me. In order not to have to get up from her chair when the mail arrived, Floriane slipped them into my teeth, saying: "Go on, Zizi, make yourself useful."

And I made myself useful by running briskly to the postman and offering him, while wagging my tail, the evidence for the prosecution.

That was where I had got to, in a week!

Let husbands and unfortunate lovers take inspiration from my example, if only to spare newspaper readers the banality of multiple conjugal murders and the hideousness of the portraits that accompany them.

The rest of the time, we were no longer apart. She took me on frequent walks around the estate. As September was freshening the lush vegetation of the park, she dressed me in a woolen coat knitted by her own hands, on which she had even embroidered a little suggestive amour. She liberated me from the gilded collar that Georges had sent to her on the same day that he promised it. Free, I gamboled madly. I yapped—that's the right word—at all the animals of nature, the horses, the cows, the goats and the pretty belated autumn butterflies, images of independence, and other dogs, my brothers, chained up in farmyards. Not because I resented being brought down to their level by St. Peter, but because my barking was the most expressive fashion of signaling to the universe my joy at being Floriane's sole companion.

It frequently happened that we stopped at the bench where, years before, we had stammered our first vows. I recognized the stone where, under the empire of emotion, not daring to raise my eyes, I had stupidly drawn my finger along a crack traced in a tree-trunk. I sniffed that crack, as if to recover therefrom the perfume of defunct amour.

"What are you doing, Zizi, always digging your little snout in there? Has some other dog been there?"

That was all she accorded to that splendid memory! One day, however, she remembered. A deep sigh certified that for me. And we didn't come back again, after that, to rest in the same place.

I retained for some time the painful impression of the motive she had attributed to my sniffing. I have to come back to it, because, although St. Peter had disguised me as a dog, he had fortunately not given me the deplorable habits that distinguish my brothers and sisters, with regard to their fashion of exchanging greetings—the cynical manner, that adjective being applicable, of going about, without the motive of perpetuating the race, incessantly sniffing the behinds of those of their fellows thy encounter.

Like Maria, Monsieur Pastel remarked on it, one day when shooting six grouse had rendered him joyful.

"Has that animal ever been ill?" he said, sardonically.

"Not that I know of, Papa," Floriane replied.

"I was wondering, because he mustn't have a sense of smell."

Someone who didn't lack a sense of smell, of course, was my comrade Castor. I'm not talking about his flair for detecting game, which was merely the millennial heredity of the time when his hungry ancestors tracked it for themselves. I'm talking about the special sense of smell of canine propriety. He made abundant use of his nostrils in that fashion. His greeting, when I sent for in Les Bolois, was of that fashion. It is probable, however, that I emanated nothing at all—thank you, St. Peter!—because he did not repeat the exercise.

Apart from that natural aspiration, Castor was a delightful companion. We liked one another, as I said, from the start. Our sympathy quickly mutated into a real amity. We understood one another in all things. People are too oblivious of the fact that animals have intellectual relationships and that they express them in a language of their own, incomprehensible to humans. From that viewpoint, the canine race is particularly well-endowed. A different pitch in barking, a raised paw, a trivial caudal agitation, a glance in one direction or another, and one is understood. At least those exchanges are clear, precise and definite. At least they spare you the floods of rhetoric that sow so many weeds elsewhere, propagating false ideas, the stuffing of skulls, and partisan spirit, such as politics entertains among the bipeds of the superior class.

Castor could say, for example, in the blink of an eye: "That Pastel, my master, is a good fellow, incapable of hurting a flea, except for the fleas he extracts from my fur. Don't bother him with noisy barking, especially in the morning, when he likes to sleep, and you'll see that he always has a sugar-lump for you."

Which was confirmed to the letter; the treat was always there, in his waistcoat pocket, ready to be offered to me when I expressed, by sitting up and begging, that I wanted it. I savored it slowly, unlike my fellows, who swallowed it in one go, the way that Spaniards eat. I should say, in passing, of that honest and chivalrous people, that their voracity always provokes my astonishment. On encountering a fat bourgeois there, alongside excessively thin people, I cannot help anticipating the cause of future social upheavals, unless the prudence of political leaders determines the equalization of bellies. I leave aside the esthetic viewpoint that makes me deplore the reign of fat in women even more. Pretty at sixteen, for the most part, they are already subject to adipose disgrace at twenty; at forty, it is immensity. All that is the result of a disordered appetite.

In her increasing tenderness, Floriane would willingly have put me on the superalimentary diet in honor beyond the Pyrenees. She had determined in collaboration with Mélanie the foodstuffs that were most agreeable to me, and went so far as to prepare them for me with her own delicate hands. In the beginning, I licked my chops, but on reflection, the concern of conserving my figure moderated me. I ended up leaving half my dishes.

My liaison with Castor delighted my father-in-law, to the point that he wanted to debaptize me in order to call me Pollux. That new denomination would have satisfied his sense of history.

"Let him do it," the spaniel advised me. "Pollux is as good as Zizi."

"I couldn't agree more."

I would have been delighted to be rid of the patronym that had been attributed to me by Georges, but Floriane stuck to Zizi, and Monsieur Pastel did not insist.

I even arrived at finding my soubriquet quite sweet, when it emerged from Floriane's mouth. She accompanied it, while nestling me against her, with ardent declarations that I had never heard in the times of my virile incarnation.

"I adore your gilded eyes, my Zizi . . . you surpass the splendors of nature . . . I'd rather have you than the radiance of a sun setting over the mountains!" Phrases that she had, I believe, fished out of my writings, and that I am embarrassed to report because, to tell the truth, they are a trifle lacking in lyricism.

One evening, before setting me at her feet, she served me up so many of them that I shed a human tear, and as I whimpered at the same time, she said: "What, you're weeping? Do dogs weep, then? It's not possible—he must have a pain somewhere. If I lost you, my Zizi, I'd go mad! Tomorrow, we'll go see the vet."

The next day, she packed her bags. Neither the insistence of her parents not the charm of the late season could retain her. She ran to the expert, for Zizi.

When we arrived at our apartment, the Aesculapius of canines was already there, waiting on the landing.

It was Georges Ferval.

VII

In civilian dress this time—a pale gray sports jacket—but supremely elegant even so, Georges Ferval manifested his joy at seeing Floriane again by repeating a hand-kiss that exceeded normal politeness. Floriane consented to it.

Then he ecstasized: "The country has done you good. You look superb."

"I could say as much for you, Georges."

"It's not for lack of worrying about you, though."

"Oh! You've been thinking about me?"

"A superfluous question. Ask the waves that I was considering while I was on watch. I heard your voice in the sound of the sea."

"Even in the tempest?"

"Even then."

"The tempest ought not to remind you of me, you know!"

"Yes, in the sense that it recalled my emotions while he was still alive."

They could not have reanimated my anger and disgust more sharply, although I had believed myself delivered from them forever, by acceptance of my fate, and by the new tenderness that Floriane heaped upon me. I could not suppress a growl of ill augury.

"Oh, there's the pooch. It's Zizi, isn't it, that we baptized him? Bonjour, Zizi. Are you still a bad boy?"

"Not at all; he behaves exquisitely toward everyone."

"I rub him up the wrong way, then."

"He'll end up tolerating you, Georges."

He was the one who opened the door. He went into my home as if it were his own. He went straight into the drawing room and liberated the windows. Then he brought into the antechamber the few items of baggage, including my niche, left on the landing.

Floriane put me down on the floor and went into her bedroom. I knew what she was going to do there. Indeed, she came back a few minutes later, powdered and lipsticked to perfection, while he, camped in front of the mirror next to the Devambez, had also prepared himself, smoothing his hair and rectifying the plats of his cravat, for a conversation in which I foresaw my definitive enlightenment.

In order not to miss anything, as much as not to hinder the movements of the seducer, if he were disposed to make any, I ignored the signal that Floriane gave me to climb up on her knees and perched on a neighboring armchair.

Here, then, is their abominable dialogue. I have not altered a single word.

Georges spoke first: "What will become of you, my poor Floriane?"

"I don't know."

"Still so young!"

"I'm over thirty, Georges."

"A thirty that one would take for twenty."

"Flatterer!"

That was all that they found to enchant one another. Their lyricism, after its initial flight, fell flat. A conductor of sailors, it is true, can dispense with being a poet. I also grasped Georges' strategy in refusing to age Floriane. Even if one is addressing a conscious and contented old frump, women are always grateful when one diminishes their age. A banal compliment, but which always hits the mark.

"Still so young, I insist," the seducer repeated, "and so lovely . . . for you can't deny it. It's astonishing that your beauty lacks adornment, that you're perpetuating your mourning. You ought not to renounce pleasure because Jacques did that stupid thing."

"Obviously."

"Coquetry is a woman's right in all circumstances."

"Not everyone is of that opinion."

"One doesn't have to take notice of what people say."

"There is, all the same, a normal delay that it's necessary to respect."

"A few months . . ."

"Let's see, Georges—since, for the moment, I have everything I need . . . thanks to you."

"I agree. But I want to see you rapidly returned to the pleasures of life, and especially out of black. It's necessary to defy prejudices, in morality as in dress . . . deep down as well as on the surface."

He hesitated over what he wanted to say; then his voice became positive again, and convincing, in order to reanimate a memory of such precision that I was to have no more doubt.

"By the way, I went past the house where we were going to meet two days after Jacques' suicide. Do you remember?"

"Perfectly."

"I saw the owner. She knows what's what, and all the more amiable because she'll touch the ten per cent. I told her that we'd go today at about five o'clock, if that suits you."

"Yes, all right."

"I also told her to put out her best sheets. She said she would and, in her contentment at our visit, promised me a cocktail."

I couldn't hear any more. This time, their dialogue, from beginning to end, confirmed their liaison and its imminent renewal. They had consented to hide it a little longer, since Floriane had, for the moment—thanks to Georges, she confessed—everything she needed, and I knew what that meant. But the light was glaring, in the confession of their access to an ignominious house, where the landlady was touching ten per cent, where the best sheets would welcome their intoxication, to which they would add spice with a cocktail swilled in my dishonor.

Oh, my bliss, my security as a little dog!

Oh, the reassuring conviction of St. Peter, my psychic guinea-pigism, my posthumous tranquility, my cosseted zizism, and the charm of Les Bolois, and the father-in-law's puns, and the confraternity of my colleague Castor—how all of that fled in a trice!

I made an effort to leap at the bandit's throat, but the blow he dealt me surpassed the resistance of my feeble carcass. A sudden paralysis blocked my entire mechanism. My eyes rolled back. I fainted, like the most cowardly of humans.

VIII

O stupor! Scarcely had I lost consciousness than the two angels were at my sides. I came round on contact with the gentle caresses they lavished upon me, accompanying them with encouraging words and parading their breath, as fresh as a spring zephyr, over my head. Then they took possession of me, all the more easily because their arrival had rendered me immaterial again. They had each seized me under an armpit, as on the previous occasion.

I soon understood the necessity of their proceeding thus, for scarcely had we quit the earth to engage in space than I felt myself progressively transforming, dilating, recovering my human form and proportions.

For the dear angels, who had never been to the cinema, where the screen can produce illusions of that sort, it must have been an original impression, that fragmented metamorphosis of a Zizi-Pollux into Giky Perdunier, his paws becoming legs, his back mutating into a torso, his tail vanishing and his muzzle flattening to take on the noble contours of a freshly-shaven face, lacking nothing but the monocle that I occasionally wedged into my orbit.

The last thing of all to reappear, on my right temple, was the hole circumscribed by bloody colts that the revolver had produced; and my fur was replaced by my indoor garments—with the result that, when I arrived in the region of the Last Refuge, while still being the same soul, I had exactly the same appearance as I had at the moment of my tragic self-suppression.

What followed was the same as on my first arrival. We cleaved through the compact clouds; we were confronted by the fictitious fortress constituted by the same opaque vapors; the drawbridge came down automatically; the row of angelic guards with flaming swords rendered us the honors; we finally reached the room of the Undoomed in the Supreme Tribunal, where the same angelic usher welcomed us.

"St. Peter is busy; you'll need to be patient for a moment," he told me, with an apologetic expression. Then he withdrew, in the company of my two transporters.

Consigned to the immense atrium, huddled on a bench, I did not regret my solitude, given the spectacle I had before my eyes, the revelation of a place superficially glimpsed, and the information that I was able to harvest there.

I had in front of me the vast corridor of rooms in which the celestial bureaucracy was at work. I was able to convince myself once again that it put more effort into regulating the final destiny of souls than the budge-tivores who occupy themselves with the fates of mortals on earth. An incessant clicking of typewriters reached my ears, discreetly adopting a harmonious cadence, which, the more I listened to it, became a symphony of the most perfect execution. Sometimes, a door opened, and one of the ravishing accountants came out, carry-ing a dossier which he took into a neighboring office.

At other times, a sound of bells rang out, similar to the angelus in our villages; its purpose was to summon a particular worker, after a certain number of chimes, to a superior on an upper floor—doubtless some ser-aph, since it is well known that the seraphim are the senior officers of the angelic hierarchy. As there was, naturally enough, no staircase leading upwards, I saw the summoned individual stand on tiptoe, leap up into the air and disappear into the vault, leaving nothing in his wake but a light blue vapor that seem dissipated: a practical short cut, which humans do not have at their disposal.

Of that formidable organization, however, I had already formed an impression during my first voyage. The outside of the palace captivated me even more. Overlooking the high enclosing walls from my elevated station, I was able to perceive the more distant regions of the unknown domain, and what I discovered there confirmed what was advertised at home.

Without even having to decipher the signposts in-dicating the directions to take once outside I saw, to begin with, straight ahead of me, displayed by a soft light emitted by things themselves, a panorama of inexpressible seductiveness, composed of magnificent palaces, nevertheless discreet in their authority, framed by restful vegetation, protective trees and cheerful lawns, where flowers bloomed on the edges of paths, until the multicolored spray of tall fountains: nothing other, in sum, than the adornment of a terrestrial city, but unreal in its harmonious beauty and limitless in its extent. That must be Paradise. It would be good to spend one's eternity there.

More confused, to my right, neutral in the gleam of space, another land appeared, not very distinct, like an unfinished earth devoid of contours, desolate in its platitude, which, from the melancholy impression I received of it, I assumed to be Limbo, the abode of newborns who died before baptism.

I quickly turned my eyes away to look at another region to my left, where the immense brazier was that I had already observed. I could double it this time, in remarking that the flames, sometimes obscured by swirls of smoke, were alimented by two distinct craters. And I had no doubt that it was a matter of Hell and Purgatory.

That distribution in eternity was, in any case, confirmed to me by the arrival in the hall, under the escort of angels armed with symbolic swords, of a hundred souls furnished with a carnal appearance, representing all races, with their different facial bone structures, their variously colored teguments and their particular costumes. They were sorted with regard to their particular judgment, divided into four distinct groups.

The first was composed of infants in swaddling-clothes, some of whom—the savages—were absolutely naked. The second, I believe I remember, comprised five or six individuals at the most, expressed by a satisfied gait that paradisal felicity had just been decreed for them. Then came the Purgatory-bound mass, resigned but nevertheless sustaining some hope. Finally, a terminal group of about ten announced their terror at falling henceforth under the rule of Satan. Contrary to the scorn in which I held my ex-fellows, the insignificance of that last group confirmed the extent to which St. Peter must allow himself to be flexibly influenced by extenuating circumstances.

Those henceforth-immortals, their fate settled, went down the steps of the Palais. Once in the courtyard, a seraph lined them up, and then, following a list, called out their names, in order to confide them one by one to the angels who transported them to their ultimate fatherland.

If we can trust in statistics, we know that a human being dies every second. So I was not surprised to see, almost immediately after those souls had drawn away, a second troop similarly divided, with only a few units at the head and the tail, while the middle categories were very numerous. I was astonished to note that the majority of the latter subjects, promised to Purgatory, had faces stigmatized by wounds, like me. Even more extraordinary was that some of them were advancing holding their heads in their hands.

"What's happened on earth, then?" I asked the angelic usher who came to fetch me.

He shrugged his shoulders pityingly. "An assassination attempt committed in Shocoslavia, against the person of the sovereign Nicolas XII, at the moment when, in front of his people, he was reviewing of a regiment of machine-gunners. His predecessor in power, ex-king Pierre IV, dethroned by him, had arranged for a bomb to be thrown at him. Clumsily set up, the device exploded in the hands of the partisan charged with the task, thus killing thirty spectators occupied in cheering frantically."

"Without the king being injured?"

"No—neither he nor anyone in his escort."

"Is the criminal the man that I see at the head of the platoon destined for Hell?"

"No, he's among those who will benefit later from celestial clemency. Look, he's the big fellow with the curly beard, a head taller than all the rest."

"Get away! And those who no longer have heads?"

"Guillotined—the victims of an immediate repression, carried out in public."

"I've just arrived from Earth. I didn't hear anything about that drama."

"Censorship prevented its divulgence. There was only mention of a skirmish."

"For what reason?"

"We don't get mixed up in international politics."

I could not get over it. I permitted myself a further comment. "That overturns all my ideas about Justice. What! That murderer's only punishment will be temporary? He'll enjoy Paradise eventually?"

"Our justice," the angel told me, "has nothing in common with the human conception. We go into the depths of consciences. Whereas Down Below, that fellow would have been sent to perdition, perhaps even tortured, we have discovered that he believed he was serving a generous cause, obedient to an ideal. That attenuates his culpability. So . . ."

"So that monstrous crime will pass without expiation?"

"Pardon me. It will be punished later, on the death of the instigator."

"Ex-king Pierre IV, you mean?"

"No, not him. Pierre IV is also a kind of visionary, not even led by ambition. The true guilty party, who will pay for everything when his time comes, is his former minister Ravitch. That one, without the excuse of working for the good of his country, filled the head of the exiled Pierre IV and, from a corner of your Boulevard Montparnasse, where he lived luxuriously on ancient prebends, arming the revolutionaries in the hope of being able to resume his former privileges, once his puppet is restored to the throne. But I can't be telling you anything new, can I? You don't have any shortage of politicians down there?"

The angelic usher informed me in his invariable gracious and tranquil tone, without a syllable of indignation. He had seen so much! He would see a great deal yet, emerging from the cattle-shed . . .

Encouraged by his impassivity, I observed: "You're decidedly magnificent in your forbearance. As little as I can plumb the depths of souls, I could not show myself so compassionate. In the troop that just fled past I only counted three destined for the eternal flames. That's really not very many."

He laughed softly. "You believe in the eternal flames, then?"

"Well, what I can see over there, to the left—that furnace—leads me to think . . ."

"Décor, Monsieur Giky! Pure décor, to strike minds. In reality, no physical torture punishes the condemned, but a moral fire, the torture of remorse . . . and believe me, the penitents suffer as much thereby as if they were afflicted in their flesh . . . the flesh that, in any case, no longer exists, since it returns, after death, to despicable matter."

"May I ask you, then, for one more item of information?"

"Go on—although St. Peter . . ."

"I'll be brief. What, then, have the three condemned to the torture of Repentance done?"

"The first, the one wearing and impermeable white garment with mother-of-pearl buttons, marinated his spouse in sulfuric acid to obtain her inheritance."

"Bravo for your justice! And the second?"

"He tortured domestic animals for the pleasure of watching their suffering."

"Your interest extends to animals, then?"

"Why not? They have souls, generally better intentioned than those of the so-called superior species. Their cruelty only derives from instinct; it's not reflective, like that of humans."

"And the woman following them, groaning?"

"Oh, don't ask me about that one," said the angel, blushing scarlet—which led me to suppose that immorality was mixed up in her story.

For the first time, my cicerone manifested a slight impatience. More firmly, he said: "But we're chatting, and St. Peter must be waiting for us. Would you care to follow me?"

As for my first appearance, we went through the labyrinth of corridors. This time, the angel introduced me without having knocked first, with the result that I fell into the midst of a conversation that I should not have interrupted, and which distracted me from the pleasure of finding my judge so sympathetic.

He had before him a well-to-do individual, freshly shaven and bald-headed, who was listening to him while plunging toward the floor a nose like a raptor's beak and penetrating eyes. With his deep voice, he was scolding him roundly.

"Know, Monsieur Zavisky, that here, you are no longer before one of the tribunals of your sphere, where your bargaining, favored by political influences that you water copiously, has so frequently saved you from handcuffs and permitted you to continue your abominable profession. Our justice is immanence itself, and consequently without appeal."

"If I may, Great Saint . . ."

"You may not. You cannot tempt my pity, nor find any justification for your ravages. I've already wasted too much time with a blackguard of your sort. I should never have had the weakness to let you appear before me. Your case was regulated in advance."

"Hell, for peccadilloes!"

"Your speculations on the Bourse, peccadilloes! All the dubious affairs into which you dragged the imbeciles who trusted you, to lead them to ruin and poverty, peccadilloes! Oh, you can't be serious! Here, we consider the thieves of savings as the worst of criminals. Savings represent effort, difficulty, privation. It's monstrous to mount assaults on them. For you, as for those who operate under the mantle of a mandate or a function, there is no pity. A notorious bandit, yes, I admit that he should be examined. There is, at least, some risk, some courage in the actions of a bandit, sometimes motivated by hunger. While you . . ."

He spat in disgust. Then, to the angels supervising the accused: "Go on, gee up! To Satan!" He threw a piece of paper after his spittle. "And pick up his form to feed the furnace."

The crook was briskly lifted up. His last protests, to declare that he had not imagined that St. Peter was so reactionary, and that he would have treated Israel better, were lost in the corridor.

And it was my turn. I expected a favorable welcome from the Saint. He recognized me immediately. A mild gaiety illuminated him.

"Oh, there you are! It's you, the metamorphosed . . . the dog, Floriane's husband . . . my experiment, in sum, my guinea-pig. Well, let's have a little chat. Wait until I light my puffer."

What! Him too, the terrestrial intoxication! I was amazed. But the odor that spread through the room at the first spiral from his pipe, although of terrestrial matter, told me that he had not yielded to the appeal of nicotine. His tobacco was incense.

"So, what do you have to say that's new? Are you reassured now about the little Floriane?"

"Less than ever, St. Peter. Your experiment only ended up convincing me even more. I witnessed a peremptory conversation just now."

"You think so?"

"Do I think so! When a gentleman comes to propose to a lady that they meet in a discreet house, kept by a landlady who offers cocktails and disposes of irreproachable bed-linen . . ."

"Sheets, the linen in question?"

"Exactly. Well, St. Peter, one would truly have to have your innocence to believe that they're going there just to twiddle their thumbs!"

I perceived at that moment that my listener was also twiddling his thumbs, but in a manifestation of amusement.

"Are you sure of having really heard what was exchanged in the course of the conversation?"

"Of course I'm sure! You've equipped me with keen enough ears, I think."

"I'm expressing myself badly. What I mean is, have you really understood?"

"Have I not conserved all my human intelligence?"

Oh, you're boasting about that!" the Saint proclaimed, joyously. He sucked at his pipe more avidly. "Jealousy," he preached, "is one of the forms of dementia when not motivated, and even when it is. The jealous man, who appropriates to his obsession the slightest words and gestures of another, is a derivative of psychiatry. Let's see, my friend, remember your sojourn in the country, with your in-laws, the Pastels. Did you suffer in your new form? Were you not happy, cosseted by Floriane?"

"I confess that at that moment, I deemed myself fulfilled."

"Ah! You see."

"Yes, although still having reasons for suspicion."

"What reasons?"

"The letters she received from Georges."

"Have you read them?"

"She hastened to destroy them, which I consider as a basis of accusation as solid as her precipitate return to Paris and the conversation I overheard."

"He won't let go!" groaned the divine instructor, surrounding himself with a cloud of incense, which his him momentarily.

When he reappeared, I saw that he was more serious. He muttered to himself: "It's enough to put you off transmutation. That attempt's enough for me. Let's send him back to his vile essence. So much the worse for him."

They were the last words pronounced by his august mouth. Already, the two conveyors were seizing me.

IX

And I found myself once again, with my human texture, in my nuptial bed. The external daylight, filtering through the large curtains of the window, permitted me to observe that Floriane was still asleep, her adorable head buried in the somber gold of her hair. Her even respiration attested that she had escaped the dream that had pursued me so relentlessly all night long. Her small warm body sent me the same calming effluvia as when

I had been a little dog in her arms. It was not possible that a sleep so tranquil, so peaceful, so chaste, could hide a troubled conscience.

And yet, that accursed telegram, the origin of my obsession, was there on the nearby table to reanimate my horrible suspicions of the previous day.

Then, no longer able to hold back, scorning the respect that we accorded to our correspondence, I took possession of the blue paper and read it from the first line to the last.

Well, St. Peter was right. I could no longer doubt the fidelity of my wife, on learning that the rendezvous with Georges was determined by the purchase of fabric for a low-cut dress for a general reception at the Théâtre de l'Athenée. In communication with the manageress of a large silk factory, Georges—the good, worthy and obliging Georges—offered to introduce my wife to the lady in question in order that she could obtain a forty per cent discount on the retail price. And I had accused Floriane of being wasteful! I had accused her of worse!

Thus was annihilated my insulting hypothesis.

Curled up on the edge of the bed, careful not to wake Floriane, I reviewed that astonishingly connected dream, of a psychological logic, undiminished by any of the incoherencies that ordinarily render dreams stupid. I rediscovered, point by point, the picturesque details, the amusing philosophy of the celestial administrator of justice, my canine neutrality cradled by Floriane. And—must I admit it?—the involuntary comparison that I established between my human condition, albeit loved by my wife, and that of the dog, adored by his mistress, leaving my uncertain as to the fate that ought to have been chosen for me.

It was Floriane who led me, even so, to remain attached to humanity. As the clock chimed eight, she opened her azure eyes wide, I closed mine in order that she would not imagine that I might have yielded to the curiosity of the telegram. Then she moved closer, putting her arms around me gently—which permitted me to pretend to wake up.

And, addressing me as *tu* for the first time, she said: "Did you sleep well? Did you have beautiful dreams?"

"More beautiful than you might suppose."

"Are you still sulking?"

I did not reply, ashamed of myself.

"Here, read it, silly," she said, crushing her breast against me in order to reach for the telegram and put it before my eyes.

I recommenced reading it with an apparent curiosity.

"You see, eh? You see that you were very silly to doubt your wife? But you'll pay me for that sheet, you know. All the more so as I'll no longer have many opportunities to put it on."

"Oh! Why is that?"

"Because my dear . . ."

I anticipated, by the sudden solemnity that was inscribed on her face, an important declaration. I did not, however, expect the confession that her lips slowly let fall, inundating me with a limitless joy—as infinite as the space through which my dream had just made me travel.

"Because," she said, slowly, "What we've been hoping for, for such a long time, has happened. I'm going to be a mother."

"My love!"

"In seven months exactly, the doctor promised me, yesterday, we're going to have a delightful little Jacques . . . unless it's a Jacqueline . . . and you'll see . . . you'll see whether I can love him and care for him, our baby . . ."

"Like a true St. Peter pooch!"

"Yes, like a gift from Paradise!" she exclaimed, without seeking any further explanation, so much had her confession transported her.

ACKNOWLEDGEMENTS

"L'Immortalité, conte philosophique" by Edmond Haraucourt was first published in the *Revue Bleue* juillet 1888; the translation was first published in the Haraucourt collection *Illusions of Immortality*, Black Coat Press, 2012.

"Quand nous aurons passé" by Frédéric Boutet appeared in *Histoires vraisemblables*, Ollendorff, 1908. The translation was first published in the Boutet collection *Claude Mercoeur's Reflection and Other Strange Stories*, Borgo Press, 2013.

"La Seconde Vie" by Charles Asselineau, was first published in the *Journal Pour Tous* 19 juillet 1847. The translation was first published in the Asselineau collection *The Double Life*, Black Coat Press, 2012.

"Une Descente aux enfers" by Judith Gautier appeared in *La Paravent de soie et d'or*, Fasquelle, 1904. The translation was first published in the Judith Gautier collection *Isoline and The Serpent-Flower*, Black Coat Press, 2013.

"Le Mort magnetisé" by Jules Janin was first published in the *Revue pittoresque* in 1845; The translation was first published in the Janin collection *The Magnetized Corpse and Other Paradoxical Tales*, Black Coat Press, 2014.

"La Survie assuré" by Paul Vibert was reprinted from an unidentified newspaper in *Pour lire en automobile, nouvelles fantastiques*, Berger-Levrault, 1891; the translation was first published in the Vibert collection *The Mysterious Fluid*, Black Coat Press, 2011.

"La Rêve de a mort" by Gaston Danville was first published in the *Mercure de France* mai 1892; the translation was first published in the Danville collection *The Anatomy of Love and Murder: Psychoanalyical Fantasies*, Borgo Press, 2013.

L'Autopsie du docteur Z*** by Édouard Rod was first published by Frinzine, Klein et Cie in 1884; the translation was first published in the anthology *The Revolt of the Machines and Other French Scientific Romances*, Black Coat Press, 2014.

"Le Clairon d'or et l'olifant d'ébène" by Catulle Mendès was reprinted in *Le Carnaval fleuri*, Charpentier 1904; the translation was first published in the Mendès collection *Don Juan in Paradise and Other Amorous Fantasies*, Black Coat Press 2019.

"Un Amour dans les étoiles" by Camille Flammarion was first published in the *Nouvelle Revue* 15 février 1896; the translation was first published in the anthology *A World Above the World and Other French Scientific Romances*, Black Coat Press, 2011.

"Minutes" by Maurice Renard was first published in *Le Matin*, 27 April 1935; the translation is original to the present volume.

"Le Fantôme dans la rose" by Lucie Delarue-Mardrus was first published in *Le Journal*, 15 octobre 1907; the translation was first published in the Delarue-Mardrus collection *The Last Siren and Other Stories*, Snuggly Books, 2020.

"En au-delà" by André Couvreur was first published in *Oeuvres Libres* 178 (1936); The translation was first published in the Couvreur collection *The Exploits of Professor Tornada, Volume 3*, Black Coat Press, 2014.

A PARTIAL LIST OF SNUGGLY BOOKS

MAY ARMAND BLANC *The Last Rendezvous*
G. ALBERT AURIER *Elsewhere and Other Stories*
CHARLES BARBARA *My Lunatic Asylum*
S. HENRY BERTHOUD *Misanthropic Tales*
LÉON BLOY *The Tarantulas' Parlor and Other Unkind Tales*
ÉLÉMIR BOURGES *The Twilight of the Gods*
ADA BUISSON *The Baron's Coffin and Other Disquieting Tales*
CYRIEL BUYSSE *The Aunts*
JAMES CHAMPAGNE *Harlem Smoke*
FÉLICIEN CHAMPSAUR *The Latin Orgy*
BRENDAN CONNELL *Metrophilias*
BRENDAN CONNELL (editor)
 The Zinzolin Book of Occult Fiction
RAFAELA CONTRERAS *The Turquoise Ring and Other Stories*
DANIEL CORRICK (editor)
 Ghosts and Robbers: An Anthology of German Gothic Fiction
ADOLFO COUVE *When I Think of My Missing Head*
QUENTIN S. CRISP *Aiaigasa*
ALADY DILKE *The Outcast Spirit and Other Stories*
ÉDOUARD DUJARDIN *Hauntings*
BERIT ELLINGSEN *Now We Can See the Moon*
ERCKMANN-CHATRIAN *A Malediction*
ALPHONSE ESQUIROS *The Enchanted Castle*
ENRIQUE GÓMEZ CARRILLO *Sentimental Stories*
DELPHI FABRICE *Flowers of Ether*
DELPHI FABRICE *The Red Spider*
BENJAMIN GASTINEAU *The Reign of Satan*
EDMOND AND JULES DE GONCOURT *Manette Salomon*
REMY DE GOURMONT *From a Faraway Land*
REMY DE GOURMONT *Morose Vignettes*
GUIDO GOZZANO *Alcina and Other Stories*
GUSTAVE GUICHES *The Modesty of Sodom*
EDWARD HERON-ALLEN *The Complete Shorter Fiction*
RHYS HUGHES *Cloud Farming in Wales*
J.-K. HUYSMANS *The Crowds of Lourdes*
J.-K. HUYSMANS *Knapsacks*
COLIN INSOLE *Valerie and Other Stories*
JUSTIN ISIS *Pleasant Tales II*